The Teenage Dirt bag years

Ross O'Carroll-Kelly

[As told to Paul Howard]

Illustrated by Alan Clarke

THE O'BRIEN PRESS
DUBLIN

First published 2003 by The O'Brien Press Ltd,
12 Terenure Road East, Rathgar, Dublin 6, Ireland.
Tel: +353 1 4923333; Fax: +353 1 4922777
E-mail: books@obrien.ie
Website: www.obrien.ie
Reprinted 2004 (twice), 2005 (twice), 2006 (twice), 2007 (twice), 2008, 2014.

Originally published in 2001 (without new material) as
Roysh Here, Roysh Now, The Teenage Dirtbag Years
by the *Sunday Tribune*.

ISBN: 978-0-86278-849-0

We would like to thank Michael McLoughlin of Penguin Ireland for agreement to use
their typographical cover concept

11 13 15 16 14 12
14 16 17 15

Editing, typesetting, layout and design: The O'Brien Press Ltd
Illustrations: Alan Clarke
Author photograph, p.2: Emma Byrne
Printed and bound by CPI Group (UK) Ltd, Croydon, CR0 4YY
The paper in this book is produced using pulp from managed forests

Other books by Paul Howard

Ross O'Carroll-Kelly, The Miseducation Years

Ross O'Carroll-Kelly, PS, I Scored The Bridesmaids

Ross O'Carroll-Kelly, The Orange Mocha-Chip Frappuccino Years

Hostage, Notorious Irish Kidnappings

The Gaffers – Roy Keane, Mick McCarthy and the team they built

The Joy – the shocking true story of life inside

Celtic Warrior

Dedication
For Karen

Acknowledgements
Thank you Mum and Dad for making laughter compulsory at all times growing up. Thank you Mark, Vincent and Richard for so many happy days. Thank you Karen – you know this guy's as much your monster as mine. Thank you Paul Wallace, Alan Kelly and Peter Walsh – hey, only we know how much of what's between these covers is fiction. Thank you Rachel, an astute and uncompromising editor who worked me like a kulak during the rewriting stage and is responsible for most of the decent storylines that I'll be claiming credit for when this book is published. Thank you Emma and Alan for making these books scream from the shelves. Thank you Michael and everyone at O'Brien Press for taking a chance on an obnoxious rich kid from the south side. Thank you Caitríona and take a raise. Thank you Ger Siggins for being generally inspiring. Thank you Maureen Gillespie and Deirdre Shearin for always being encouraging. Thank you Matt Cooper and thank you Jim Farrelly, Paddy Murray, Mark Jones and everyone at the *Sunday Tribune* for your support. And thanks to all my friends – I know who you are, and I know where you live.

Contents

Shit the bed, is it my imagination, roysh, or am I getting better looking every day? Hord to believe I've just crawled out of the sack. I stare at myself in the mirror for, like, three or four minutes. There's no doubt that face is going to break a lot of hearts this year.

I hop into the shower. Lash on some of the old Ralph Lauren shower wash that Sorcha, my ex, who's doing the DBS in Carysfort, brought me back from the States. While I'm rubbing it in, I check the old abs and pecs. The bod's in pretty good shape considering what I put it through over the summer. I wash my hair using the *Polo Sport* two-in-one daily shampoo that Sorcha bought me for my, like, birthday and shit.

I jump out. Dry myself off. Check myself out again. I run my hand over my face. Need a shave. I lash on the old *Armani Emporio* shaving gel that Sorcha gave me, I can't remember when, and give myself a really good, close shave. I lash on some of the old *Escape for Men* aftershave balm, roysh, and go back to my room.

Can't stop thinking about Nell McAndrew. No time for an old Allied Irish, though. Not this morning. I lash on the *Tommy for*

Men deodorant and hop into the old Hilfiger boxers. Only dilemma now is what to wear. My old Castlerock shirt, that goes without saying. The Blackrock goys will be wearing their shirts, so will Clongowes and the Gick. Orseholes. Have to wear your colours, though. I also go for the beige Ralph Lauren chinos, black socks and, like, Dubes.

I pull out my class schedule – 'Sports Management, 2000–2001' – and fock it in the bin. Only thing I'm gonna need this year is a map to the focking bor.

I lash on some sounds. We're talking the old Snoopmeister here. '*Gin and juice up this bitch, yaaah.*' I go back to the bathroom. Run my hand through my hair. Needs a cut. My quiff is going curly. Should have got a blade one at the sides as well. Might go later. Gel's gonna be fock-all use. It's a job for the heavy duty wax. I lash on the old Dax Wave and Groom. Check myself out again. Look-ing-good, no arguments.

'*I'm on Interstate Ten focking with this Creole.*' Go, Snoop.

I grab my mobile, the Nokia 8210 – we're talking dual band, thirty-five ringtones and 210 minutes of battery talk-time – and, like, ring Oisinn. He answers, roysh, with his mouth full. *Always* focking eating. He goes, 'Ross, my man. What's the *scéal?* Ready for your first day at college?' I go, 'Pretty much. Can't make up my mind what aftershave to wear, though.' He's there, 'So you've come to the man who speaks fluent Fragrance.' Oisinn worked in the Duty Free shop at the airport for the summer, roysh, and he has the whole focking spiel off by heart. Of course the birds go mad for it.

He swallows whatever it is he has in his mouth – probably

lard, the fat bastard – and he goes, 'The challenge, as I told Christian only a few moments ago, is to find a scent that's suited to the course you're doing. For instance, he's doing film studies. The birds on that course are going to be your Lillies, star-focker crew who still think they're going to marry Matt Damon. So, what Christian needs is something for an affirmed man who *totally* assumes his virility with the expression of a liberated, frank and provocative personality.'

I go, 'Are we talking *Body Kouros* by Yves Saint Laurent?' He goes, 'We most certainly are, my fast-learning friend.' I've heard this shit a million times before. He goes, 'We're doing sport, roysh? So ask yourself, what's going to push the girls' buttons on our course? Something that captures the fun and energy of an active life, a liberating fragrance that exudes cool. We're talking *Freedom* by Tommy Hilfiger, or *Polo Sport for Men*.' I'm like, 'See you later.'

I lash on the old *Polo Sport*, then wonder whether I've overdone it. Fock it, it's Kool and the Gang. Better skedaddle. There's ten thousand birds in UCD and I don't want to disappoint them. Couldn't live with that on my conscience. Head into the bathroom on the way downstairs to check myself out one last time. Looking great. Smelling great. Feeling great. There's gonna be a lot of broken hearts this year. And mine's not going to be one of them.

Ross O'Carroll-Kelly, you handsome focking bastard.

CHAPTER ONE
'Ross is, like, SUCH an arrogant bastard.'
Discuss.

Orlaith with an i, t and h Bracken. Fock me, haven't seen that bird since … must be three years. She played hockey for Alex. and tonsil hockey for Ireland. I was with her once or twice. She was pure quality then, but now she's an absolute cracker, roysh, we're talking Natalie Imbruglia but with bigger baps, and none of the goys in the class can, like, take their eyes off her. I catch her eye, roysh, and I mouth the word, 'Later,' to her, and I'm wondering whether she remembers that porty in her gaff when I puked my ring up all over her old dear's off-white Hampshire sofa and, like, focked off without saying anything. And she makes a L-sign with her thumb and her finger, as in 'Lo-ser', and I take it she remembers it alroysh.

Her loss. It's no skin off my nose, and anyway, roysh, she's small change compared to some of the other birds in this class. Me and Oisinn struck gold when we got on this course. This bird walks in – blonde hair, amazing bod, you'd swear it was Nicola Willoughby, we're talking perma-horn material here – and she sits roysh in front of us and storts, like, fanning her face with her hand. Then she takes off her tracksuit top, roysh, and when she turns around to put it on the back of her chair, she goes to me, 'It's hot, isn't it?' and quick as a flash, roysh, I go, 'It is from where I'm sitting,' and I'm just there hoping it didn't sound too, like, sleazy and shit, but she smiles at me, roysh, and turns back around and I'm thinking, that one's in the bag anyway.

Oisinn goes, 'We are going to have some fun working our way through this lot,' and I'm there, 'I'm hearing you, big goy. I'm hearing you.' This lecturer dude comes in, don't know who the fock he is, don't care either, and he storts, like, telling us the Jackanory, what the course is about, the lectures we have, exams and loads of other boring shite, but of course I'm not listening to a word. There's another bird up the front, roysh, wearing a baby blue airtex and a dark blue baseball cap and I wish she'd turn around because I think it's, like, Samantha what's-her-name, went to Loreto Foxrock, amazing at athletics, alroysh looking, incredible pins, kicked Sorcha's orse in an Irish debate a few years ago, even though Sorcha was in sixth year and Samantha was in, like, transition year. I had to crack on, of course, that I thought Sorcha's speech was better, but then she copped me basically trying to chat this Samantha bird up afterwards and she cracked the shits. I think she might be my first port of call because being with her would SO piss Sorcha off.

The next thing, roysh, everyone's suddenly standing up to go and the lecturer's giving it, 'Everyone enjoy Freshers' Day. And don't drink too much,' and this big roar goes up, as if to say, Yeah roysh, *as if!* Me and Oisinn head out and meet Christian and Fionn, who's blabbing away to some moonpig – a bogger by the sounds of her – about the connection between psychology and the biological and sociological sciences. Kathleen, he says her name is. Red hair, the whole lot. He goes, 'Goys, this is Kathleen,' and straight away I'm like, 'Fionn, we said this was gonna be just the lads,' and I turn around to this *thing* and go, 'Why don't you fock off back to Ballycabbage-and-potatoes, or wherever the fock you're from? You're not wanted,' and of course Fionn leaps straight to her defence, that's how desperate for his bit he is, the ugly bastard. He goes, 'I'm sorry about him, Kathleen. Somewhat lacking in the social graces is our Ross. I think a certain Swiss psychologist and contemporary of Freud would have a word for him,' and the two of them crack their holes laughing, roysh, basically trying to make me feel like a tit, which I do.

They're, like, saying their goodbyes, roysh, and I feel like I'm about to vom, so I head off towards the bor and Oisinn and Christian follow a few steps behind me. I can hear Oisinn asking Christian whether he wore *Fahrenheit* instead of *Body Kouros*, like he recommended, and Christian saying yeah, and Oisinn telling him that live florals mixed with balsamic notes are a bit 1997 and frankly he wouldn't use the stuff as paint-stripper. Then Oisinn puts his orm around him and asks what his course is like, some film shite he's doing, and Christian goes, 'I feel just like George Lucas did on his first day at USC,' and Oisinn goes, 'Should see our class. I feel just like Hugh Heffner does every time he gets up in the morning.'

I get to the bor first, order four pints of Ken. I turn around to the goys and I go, 'College life, huh? Freedom from school,' and the next thing Fionn's beside me and he's giving it, 'What the *fock* is your problem?' I'm like, 'What the fock is *my* problem? Who's the focking kipper?' He goes, 'She happens to be part of an experiment I'm conducting,' and I'm there, 'What, see can you finally lose your virginity?' He goes, 'Oh, someone bring me a corset, I think my sides have split. I'm investigating a theory actually,' and I'm like, 'This should be good,' him and his focking theories, and Christian's like, 'What is it, Fionn?' encouraging the goy. He goes, 'My theory is, redheads who come from a whole family of redheads are invariably bet-down,' and we all go, 'Agreed.' He's like, '*But* ... when you get one redhead in a family of non-redheads, she's usually a cracker.'

I go, 'Well, your friend obviously has a lot of brothers and sisters with the old peach fuzz. Now can we drop the subject? I want Freshers' Day to be a day to remember,' and Oisinn goes, 'No, no, no, my friend. Freshers' Day should be a day you're *not* able to remember,' and we all go, 'Yyyeeeaaahhh,' and high-five each other.

And then ... Fock it, I'll go into it another time.

✷✷✷

Women have peripheral vision, Emer goes, which is why they always know when a goy is, like, checking them out and why goys never know when they're actually being, like, checked out themselves. She can't remember where she read this, might have been *Red,* or *Marie Claire,* or some other shit. I'm not really listening. I'm waiting for my food to arrive and throwing the odd sly look at Sorcha, who's looking *totally* amazing, just back from Montauk, the pink Ralph Lauren shirt I bought her for her birthday showing off her, like, tan. Aoife asks her if she thinks Starbucks will ever open a place in Dublin, roysh, and Sorcha says OH! MY! GOD! she hopes they do because she SO misses their white chocolate mochas, and Aoife says she SO misses their caramel macchiatos, and they both carry on naming different types of coffee, roysh, both in American accents, which is weird because they were only in the States for, like, the summer and shit.

The food takes ages to arrive, roysh, and when the total creamer of a waitress we've been given finally brings it she forgets the focking cutlery, and Oisinn turns around to her and goes, 'I suppose a fork is out of the question?' The waitress, roysh, we're talking complete focking CHV here, she's like, 'Wha'?' and I just go, 'Are we supposed to eat this with our *focking* hands?' and she stands there, trying to give me a filthy, roysh, but then she just, like, scuttles off to the kitchen and Oisinn high-fives me, and Christian high-fives Fionn, and Emer and Aoife shake their heads, and Zoey, who's, like, second year commerce with German in UCD, SO like Mena Suvari it's unbelievable, she throws her eyes up to heaven and goes, 'Children.'

Emer knocks back a mouthful of Ballygowan and goes, 'OH! MY! GOD! I am SO going to have to get my finger out this year,' and I stort asking her about her course, we're talking morkeshing, advertising and public relations in LSB, *totally* flirting my orse off with her and watching Sorcha out of the corner of my eye going, like, ballistic.

Then, completely out of the blue, roysh, Fionn launches into this new theory he has about why public toilets are so, like, gross. He goes, 'You have to be pretty desperate for a shit to use a public toilet in the first place. And let's face it, a desperate shit is never a pretty shit,' and Zoey, roysh, she holds up her bottle of Panna and goes, '*Hello*? Some of us are trying to *eat* here.'

Erika arrives then, roysh, total babe, the spit of Denise Richards, and she throws her shopping bags onto the chair beside me and goes, 'Is it my imagination or have the shops in town storted hiring the biggest knackers in Ireland as security guards?' Emer says something about the Celtic Tiger, roysh, about them not being able to get, like, staff because of it, and Erika goes, 'I'm sorry, I will *not* be looked up and down by men with focking buckles on their shoes,' and then she orders a Diet Coke and storts texting Jenny to find out what she's doing for Hallowe'en weekend and I basically can't take my eyes off the bird, roysh, and I make a promise to myself that if I'm going to score anyone between now and Christmas, it's going to be her.

Sorcha takes off her scrunchy, slips it onto her wrist, shakes her hair free and then smoothes it back into a low ponytail again, puts it back in the scrunchy and then pulls, like, five or six strands of hair loose again. It's been two-and-a-half years, but there's no doubt the girl still has feelings for me, the focking sap. I ask her how college is going and she goes, 'Amazing. Fiona and Grace are on the same course.' I'm like, 'Cool. Are you still thinking of going into Human Resources?' playing it - *totally* Kool and the Gang, and she gives it, 'I don't know. Me and Fiona are thinking of maybe going to Australia for the year. When we're, like, finished.' She's checking me out for a reaction, roysh, but I don't say anything and she eventually goes, 'I heard you got into UCD,' and I'm like, 'Yeah, the old dear said she met you,' and she goes, 'A sports scholarship, Ross. Congrats.' I can't make out whether she's being, like, a bitch or not. I'm just there, 'Yeah, it's the Sports Management course,' and she goes, 'That's supposed to be a *really* good course. It's only, like, one day of lectures a week, or something.' She's being a bitch alroysh. I pick up my tuna melt and I'm like, 'I don't give a fock what the course is like. I'm just looking forward to getting back playing good rugby again,' which, like, so impresses her.

Erika finishes texting Jenny, roysh, takes a sip out of her Coke and, like, pulls this face. She pushes it over to me and goes, 'Taste that. That's not Diet Coke, is it?' I take a sip, roysh, but she doesn't wait for my answer, just grabs the waitress by the elbow as she's passing by and goes, 'I *asked* for a *Diet* Coke.' The waitress is basically having none of it, she's there going, 'That *is* Diet Coke.' And Erika's like, '*Hello?* I think I *know* what Diet Coke tastes like.' The bird picks it up and says she'll, like, change it, but Erika, roysh, she grabs her by the orm, looks her up and down and goes, 'If I was earning two pounds an hour, I'd probably have an attitude problem as well.' I'm like, 'Well said, Erika,' trying to make Sorcha jealous and, like, *totally* succeeding.

Zoey's talking about some goy called Jamie from second year Orts who is so like Richard Fish it's unbelievable, roysh, and Sorcha and Emer stort having this, like, debate about whether Richard Fish is actually sexy, or whether it's just because he's a bastard to women, when all of a sudden the manager comes over and tells us he wants us to leave. We're all there, 'You needn't think we're paying,' and as we're going out the door the waitress goes, 'Snobby bastards,' under her breath, roysh, and Erika gives her this, like, total filthy and goes, 'Being working class is nothing to be proud of, Dear.'

✳✳✳

It's, like, two o'clock on Sunday afternoon, roysh, and the traffic on the Stillorgan dualler is un-focking-believable, we're talking bomper to bomper here. I mean, *what* is the point of having a cor that can do seventy if forty is the fastest you're allowed to go? Mind you, roysh, get above seventy in this thing – the old dear's focking Micra – and bits stort to fall off, not that there's much danger of that happening with this bitch in front of me. She is SO trying to fock me over, roysh, driving really slowly and then, like, speeding up when she sees the traffic lights on orange, trying to make me miss the lights. I turn on the radio and flick through the presets but there's, like, fock-all on. Samantha Mumba is actually on three different stations at the same time and I'm wondering if this is, like, a world record or something, and Helen Vaughan says that 'raidworks continue to operate on the Rock Raid saithbaind between the Tara Hotel and the Punchbowl, and the Old Belgord Raid is claised to traffic immediately saith of the junction with Embankment Raid.' And three goys in a silver Peugeot 206 pass me and they all have a good scope into the cor, roysh, obviously thinking it's a bird driving it because it's, like, a bird's cor – I have to admit, I get that all the time – and when they see it's a goy they all, like, crack their shites laughing, roysh, so I just give them the finger.

✳✳✳

What the fock sociology has to do with sport I don't know, but Oisinn says it's on the course, roysh, and if it's on the course it means we probably should check it out, suss out the talent again and let the birds see what's on offer. As it turns out, roysh, my mind wasn't playing tricks on me on the first day. The talent's focking incredible, and I'm just thinking, roysh, I might actually come back to a few more of these lecture things, when all of a sudden who walks in only Aisling Hehir, as in former-Holy-Child-Killiney-head-girl Aisling, as in plays-hockey-for-Three-Rock-Rovers Aisling, as in here's-my-tits-my-orse-will-be-along-in-fifteen-minutes Aisling, and we're all there, 'Oooh, baby!'

I've never actually been with her before, roysh – despite her best efforts, it has to be said – always thought of her as a bit of a BOBFOC, the old Body Off 'Baywatch', Face Off 'Crimewatch' sort. I don't know where the fock she was last summer, roysh, but she's got the Peter Pan and she's, I don't know, done something with her hair, highlights or some shit, and she looks focking amazing, it has to be said: white Nike top, pink Juicy tracksuit top tied around her waist, Louis Vuitton gym bag over her shoulder. Everyone's eyes are, like, out on stalks when they see her and – unbelievable, roysh – don't know how I missed her on Freshers' Day, but she gives a little wave to me and Oisinn, the two of us up the back playing Jack the Lad.

Of course this doesn't go down too well with the Blackrock goys, roysh, who've been giving us, like, filthies since we got in, especially that dickhead Matthew Path who can't handle the fact that I scored his bird during the summer while he was off in

Ibiza on a post-Leaving Cert porty, roysh, getting his jollies off a load of ugly English slappers while I'm rattling his stunner of a girlfriend, Kate I think her name was. The word is he's taken her back, which to me lacks dignity, roysh, and the next time he turns around and tries to stare me out of it, I give him the L-sign.

Goes without saying, roysh, that the lecture is one big focking bore, the goy's up there blabbing on about Emile Durkheim, whoever the fock she is, and I turn to Oisinn's cousin, Kellser – he's a Mary's boy, but still sound – and I'm like, 'Are we really in the roysh lecture hall?' and he goes, 'Amazingly, yes. Can't see myself coming back, though. Hey, check out Aisling Hehir's rack.' I'm like, 'One step ahead of you, my man, one step ahead.'

Of course what happens then, roysh, but the lecturer, I don't even know what his focking name is, he totally snares Kellser and he's like, 'You up there. No, not you. Behind you. The boy with the blue shirt, white star on it.' Kellser's there, '*Me?*' and the goy's like, 'Yes, you. Would you like to come down and talk to us about dialectical materialism?' Of course Kellser goes, 'Eh, no,' and the goy's there, 'Okay, we'll cut a deal then, I'll stay down here talking to the class about Emile Durkheim and you stay up there with your mouth shut.' I turn around to Kellser and I'm like, 'Sorry, man,' and he goes, 'It's cool.'

Don't know what Oisinn's at, he's saying fock-all, just sitting there with his head down and for a minute, roysh, I think he's actually listening to the lecture, but then my mobile beeps twice and I realise he was sending me a text message and it's, like, a Limerick, roysh, and it's:

> THERE WAS A YOUNG ROCK
> BOY NAMED ROSS, WHOSE
> LIFE WAS A BIT OF A DOSS,
> UNMATCHED WAS HIS DIZZI-
> NESS, BUT HIS DAD OWNS A
> BUSINESS, AND ONE DAY HE'LL
> MAKE ROSS THE BOSS!

I'm about to send him one back, roysh, but he's, like, really good at them, the fat bastard, and I can't think of any words that rhyme with Oisinn, so I just send him back a message and it's like, **RETORD!** Pretty happy with that.

So there we are afterwards, roysh, arranged to meet Christian at the Blob, when all of a sudden this goy comes up to me – glasses, real nerdy head on him, I'm thinking, He's got to be a mate of Fionn's – and he goes, 'Didn't see you at the meeting, Ross.' I'm like, 'And what meeting is that?' He goes, 'Young Fine Gael. You joined up on Freshers' Day.' Freshers' Day, that's a story in itself. I go, 'Listen, I said and did a lot of things on Freshers' Day. If I joined whatever focking club it is you're talking about, I did it to take the piss. Now fock off,' and he calls me an intellectual pygmy or some shit, then does as he's told and focks off, and Oisinn high-fives me and tells me I'm the man.

Christian eventually comes along and he's talking to this total honey, who's apparently on his course, and he's telling her that General Carlist Rieekan was one of the best commanders the Rebel Alliance ever had and that, far from a defeat, the abandoning of the rebel base at Hoth was an inspired tactical retreat that didn't receive the recognition it deserved until he became Leia Organa's second-in-command on the New Republic Council, and the bird's nodding her head, roysh, but looking at him as though she's just walked into her bedroom and caught him trying on her best dress.

She focks off – no introductions, Christian lives in his own little world – and Fionn goes, 'What's the *scéal?* Looks like the *Fahrenheit* is working after all,' and Christian goes, 'Thanks, young Skywalker,' then he turns to me and he's like, 'What did you goys have?' I'm like, 'Sociology. It's, like, the mind and shit. I need a pint.'

We decide to hit the bor, roysh. I get the first round in and we bump into Fionn, who's doing Orts – we're talking psychology and Arabic and we're basically talking brains to burn here – and he's sitting up at the bor with these two birds who are in his class and he's telling them that, personally, he thinks Starbucks is far from the benign face of corporate imperialism that it pretends to be, that the company so beloved by liberal sophisticates for the cosy, aromatic, comfy-cushioned, *ennui*-inducing, 'Friends'-style world it has created is actually no different from McDonalds in its corporate structure and ideals, and is a major player in corporate America's plan to culturally homogenise the world. The birds are nodding their heads and telling him he is so roysh, and there's pretty much nothing I can contribute to this conversation, so I change the subject, roysh, and say I bought the new U2 album, *All That You Can't Leave Behind*, and I tell them it's *way* better than, like, their first album. One of the birds – she looks a bit like Elize du Toit except with longer hair – she looks at me funny and goes, 'Their *first* album? Which was their first, Ross?' I'm like, '*Pop*. It's way better than *Pop*,' and everyone in the group just breaks their shites laughing, roysh, including Christian, who's supposed to be my best friend, and Fionn goes, 'Anyone with information on the whereabouts of Ross O'Carroll-Kelly's brain, please contact Gardaí at Cabinteely,' and I haven't a clue what's so funny and it's only later that I remember about *Zooropa*.

✳✳✳

I get home from town at, like, four o'clock in the afternoon, roysh, and the old man's standing in the hallway, white as a sheet, and we're talking *totally* here, and he's just there, 'Ross, you're home.' Of course I'm like, 'No shit, Sherlock,' and he goes, 'Come into the kitchen and sit down. I've got some bad news.' I'm there, '*What* are you crapping on about?' and he goes, 'They're moving the Irish rugby team, Ross. They're moving them to … God, I can't even say it … the *northside*. The northside, Ross, I'm sorry.' Don't know what he's bullshitting on about, roysh, but there's a stink of whiskey off his breath and a huge whack gone out of the bottle of Jameson he got off his golfing mates for his fiftieth, the bunch of tossers. He always tries to be real palsy-walsy with me when he's locked. I'm, like, *totally* storving and I'm there, 'Where's that stupid wagon?' He's like, 'Your mother's out. She has coffee every Thursday afternoon with the girls. You know that,' and I'm like, 'What's the focking story with dinner?' but he totally ignores me, just goes, 'I've been trying to catch her on her mobile since two o'clock, but of course she's in the National Gallery, she's not going to have it on. She's a strong woman, your mother. Heaven knows I need her now …'

He pours himself another drink, roysh, sits down at the table and puts his head in his hands, so I get up, grab a pack of Kettle Chips and a handful of, like, funsize Mars bars out of the cupboard and stort moseying up to my room. Then I hear him, like, crying. *Hello?* I should have just ignored the attention-seeking bastard, but, of course, I'm too much of a nice goy for that. I'm like, 'What the *fock* is your problem?' and he goes, 'Lansdowne Road, Ross. It's over. They're building a new stadium. In … Abbotstown.' I'm like, 'Where the *fock* is Abbotstown?' Don't know why I'm actually bothering to sound interested. He's there, 'A million miles away from the Berkeley Court, that's where. Two million miles from Kiely's.' I'm like, 'So what? The Dorsh goes there, doesn't it?' He just, like, shakes his head and goes, 'Think again, Ross,' knocks back his drink, pours himself another and carries on blubbering to himself, the total sap.

There's a David Gray CD on the table, we're talking *White Ladder*, which Sorcha lent to the old dear. She is SO trying to get back with me, roysh, it's pretty much embarrassing. The old man's blabbing away again, going, 'It's all about votes, of course. Oh yes. Oh yes indeed thank you very much. Oh you should have heard that blasted Bertie Ahern on the one o'clock news, so bloody smug. A national stadium. Quote-unquote. And all to boost his popularity out in, what's this you and your pals call it … Knackeragua?'

He goes, 'Some of the guys are coming around tonight. Hennessy's four-square behind me. Going to set up a pressure group. KISS. Stands for Keep It South Side. And I am going to put myself forward as chairman. Or maybe president sounds better.' Then, next thing I know, roysh, the stupid bastard's up on his feet, practicing the speech he's planning to make tonight, going, 'Think of the northside and you immediately think of un-married mothers, council houses, coal sheds and curry sauce. You think of cannabis, lycra tracksuits and football jerseys worn as fashion garments. You think of men with little moustaches selling *An Phoblacht* outside these wretched dole offices, moth-ers and fathers in the pub from morning till night, 'Fair City', entire families existing off welfare and – sadly – the twin scourges of drugs and satellite dishes.' I'm like, 'Sit down, you're making a *total* dick of yourself,' but he just carries on, giving it, 'There are some people in this country who want our community to become a mirror of that. And that is why every white, Anglo-Saxon one of us has to stand up and treat this northside stadium nonsense for what it is: an all-out attack on our way of life. You can mark my words, this is just the thin end of the wedge. What's next? A methadone clinic in Foxrock?'

I hear the front door opening, roysh, and it's, like, the old dear, and for the first time in my life I'm happy to see the bitch. Or I am until she bursts into the kitchen and storts going, 'Charles, oh darling, I came as soon as I heard,' and the two of them stort, like, hugging each other, complete knobs the two of them, him pissed off his face on whiskey, her doped off her head on, like, cappuccino. And they both totally blank me, roysh. And we are talking TOTALLY here. She's like, 'What are you going to do, Charles?' He goes, 'We, Fionnuala. What are *we* going to do?' and she's there, 'Yes, of course. I'm with you, you know that,' and he goes, 'I'm going to fight it. Tooth and nail. Some of the chaps are coming over here tonight.' She goes, 'Oh I'm so proud of you. And because I knew you'd need cheering up, guess what I bought?' and she, like, pulls out this focking Gloria Jean's bag, roysh, and just, like, dances it up and down in front of his eyes, going, 'Colombia Narino Supreme,' and he's like, 'My favourite. I'll fill the percolator,' and she goes, '*And* I went to Thornton's,' and she pulls out this box, and I'm about to borf my ring up listening to this shit. He's got this, like, dopey focking smile on his face and he's there, 'Are they cherry almond charlottes, perchance?' and she nods and goes, 'And … walnut kirsch marzipan.'

He gets out the cups. *Two* cups. He's like, 'I've cheered right up now. I thought I was losing my mind before you came home.' Not a mention, of course, of me trying to cheer him up. He takes a filter from the packet and then stops all of a sudden and he goes, 'Why didn't I think of it before? You are *such* an inspiration, Darling,' and the old dear goes, 'I know that look … you're going to write a letter to *The Irish Times*, aren't you?' and he's like, 'You're damn right I am,' and she goes, 'I'll go get your pen.'

I'm standing at the kitchen door, roysh, still being completely ignored. The old dear brushes straight past me to go into the study and doesn't, like, say a word to me. The old man goes, 'Get my good one, Darling. The Mont Blanc.' The old dear comes back, roysh, and puts the pen and some of the good writing paper on the table. He hands her a cup of coffee and he goes, '*The Irish Times* will be behind me. Hell, I might even get in touch with Gerry Thornley,' and she's like, 'Remember what the judge said, Charles. Two miles.' He goes, 'No, no, no. That'll all be forgotten about by now … How was the gallery by the way?' and she goes, 'Oh, we went to the Westbury in the end. Change of scenery.'

And they both sit down at the table, roysh, and I just give them a total filthy and I go, 'You two are as sad as each other,' and I head up to my room and the old dear shouts after me, 'Don't go far, Ross. Dinner will be an hour. It's soba noodles with chicken and ginger.'

✳✳✳

We're in town, roysh, standing in some focking nightclub queue, so horrendufied I don't even know the name of it, and the birds are giving out yords to me and Christian, roysh, telling us to sober up big time or we're SO not going to, like, get in. Emer says that if we don't get in here we should head to Lillies, and Sophie says she was there last night and OH! MY! GOD! Jason Sherlock was there and so was Liz what's-her-name from 'Off the Rails'. Emer says she was there with Alyson with a y and *Oh My God!* she's thinking of going to Australia for the year, and Sophie goes, 'Yeah, after she, like, finishes in Mountjoy Square, Carol told me.'

Erika shoots Sophie a filthy, roysh, why I don't know, but then again Erika never needs a reason, not a proper one. She'd pretty much take offence at anything when the mood takes her.

But she's looking mighty fine, it has to be said, wearing a black Donna Karan dress that looks like it's been shrink-wrapped onto her, roysh, shows off the old melons really well.

We get up to the door, roysh, and there's no way the bouncers are going to let us in, me and Christian are SO struggling to hold it together, we're totally hanging, especially Christian who was really knocking back the sauce in SamSara, but suddenly Sophie goes, '*Oh my God!* I think I know one of the goys on the door,' and when we get up to the front of the queue she, like, flashes a smile at this big focking gorilla, roysh, and goes, 'OH! MY! GOD! Hi-how-*or*-ya?' as though they're, like, long-lost friends, and she gives him a peck on the cheek and a hug, and the goy hasn't a clue who she is, but he goes along with it, roysh, he's getting his jollies, the old sly-hand-on-the-orse routine. He goes, 'Lookin' lovely tonight, ladies,' the total focking howiya that he is.

Sophie goes, '*Oh* my God! I've put make-up on your shirt,' and she storts, like, rubbing his collar, roysh, but the goy goes, 'Don't worry about it. You can put make-up on me any time you like, love,' and all the girls laugh, roysh, all except Erika, who is SO not impressed, she's got, like, her orms folded, really pissed off at being kept waiting.

Of course the bouncer, roysh, he pushes it too far, tries to get a bit of physical contact going with the rest of the birds, and he goes to hug Erika next – I SO want to deck the focker at this stage – but of course she doesn't respond, roysh, just stands there stiff as a focking tree. And when he picks up on the vibe, roysh, he pulls away and Erika asks him what the fock he thinks he's doing, and he says he's just being friendly. He goes, 'Ine just tryin' to be your friend, love,' and she looks him up and down and goes, 'You're sexually frustrated. Why don't you get a dirty magazine, take it to the men's room and stop making a nuisance of yourself out here.'

I'm falling in love with the girl.

✱✱✱

Most of Freshers' Day is a total blur. And we're talking TOTALLY here. I remember bits, roysh, but I was basically off my tits by about four o'clock in the afternoon, so I don't know what was, like, real, and what I, like, imagined. I remember millions of people milling about the place. All these tossers standing up on stages trying to get you to, like, join stupid societies. And freebies. They gave us, like, tubes of toothpaste, roysh, and we ended up having fights with them, covering each other with the focking stuff. Blue shit. And someone else was handing out packets of johnnies. The old love zeppelins. Packets of six, yeah they're goinna last a long time, I *don't* think!

Join Fianna Fáil. Join the World Wildlife Fund. Join the Drama Society. Join the dots to reveal a good-looking goy who's only here for the beer and the birds and thinks you Society wankers should get a focking life. Big time. And we're talking TOTALLY.

Another double vodka and Red Bull. And then … Pretty much the only part I can remember after that, roysh, is chatting up these two Mounties in some focking marquee or other, don't have a clue how we all ended up there. I remember the birds coming up to us, we're talking me, Christian, Oisinn and Fionn,

and one of them, roysh, I think she's first year Social Science, she goes, 'OH! MY! GOD! did you hear about Becky?' and I'm like, 'No, what's the story?' obviously not cracking on that I don't have a focking clue who Becky is. She goes, 'OH! MY! GOD! She drank half a bottle of vodka *straight*, had to be brought home in an ambulance. Her mum is SO going to have a knicker-fit.'

I don't actually remember when these two birds focked off, roysh, but I'm sort of, like, vaguely aware that Oisinn said something totally out of order to one of them. I think he pointed at one of them and went, 'Halle Berry,' then pointed at the other and went, 'Halle Tosis,' and then the next hour is, like, a blur. I fell asleep at one stage, with my feet up on the chair opposite me, and then I woke up maybe half an hour later with all, like, spit dribbling down my chin, and this other bird, who I've never laid eyes on before, roysh, is sitting beside me, boring the ears off me about some bullshit or other. She has my mobile, roysh, and she's, like, flicking through my numbers, going, 'Keyser. Is that Dermot Keyes? *Oh* my God! I can't believe you know Dermot Keyes. I was going to bring him to my debs,' and then it's like, '*Oh* my God! You know Eanna Fallon. I kissed his best friend in Wesley when I was, like, fourteen. OH! MY! GOD! That's, like, SO embarrassing.' This goes on for quite a while, roysh, although I completely conk out again after about, like, five minutes. I don't know what the fock happens then because the next thing I know she's bawling her eyes out and asking me if I think she's fat, but all I can see is Christian across the far side of the bor and he's, like, calling me over, and he reminds me about this plan we had – didn't think we were being serious at the time, roysh – to rob this, like, ten-foot-tall inflatable Heino can from outside the student bor and hang it off the bridge over the main road.

So I just, like, get up and leave the bird there, roysh, the stupid, sappy bitch, and the next thing I know, me, Christian, Oisinn, Eanna, and I'm pretty sure Fionn as well, are trying to smuggle this, like, big fock-off can out of UCD, trying to avoid the security goys who were, like, driving around in jeeps. I remember Christian saying it was just like the time Princess Leia tried to sneak Han Solo out of Jabba's Palace dressed as the Ubese bounty hunter, Boussh, then getting totally, like, paranoid and going, 'I'm not gonna be no dancing girl in your court, you slimey Hutt,' and we have to calm the mad focker down, roysh, before we can cross the road over the bridge with the thing.

I remember hearing Fionn go, 'Is that noise what I think it is?' but I'm basically too busy trying to decide the best way to, like, attach this thing to the railings, but then, all of a sudden, roysh, I notice that the goys are gone. They've focking pegged it, I can see them in the distance and they're halfway to focking Stillorgan. Of course, in my shock, roysh, I end up letting go of the focking Heino can and it just, like, falls over the side of the bridge and lands on the road, and this black Fiat Punto has to, like, swerve to avoid it. That's when I hear the siren, and I'm instantly focking sober.

So the next thing I know is the Feds are asking me for my name, my address and my phone number. Obviously, roysh, I don't want my old pair to know that I focked this thing onto the dualler – still hoping the old man will give me the shekels to go skiing at Christmas – so I give them my name and Sorcha's address and number because I know she's actually the only one in her house at the moment, roysh, because her parents and her sister are in, like, the south of France for a couple of weeks.

I try to play it cool like Fonzie, roysh. I go, 'Is there a problem, Ossifer?' but the cop who's arrested me, roysh, he's on the radio, all delighted with himself for having lifted someone, and it's then that I stort thinking about basically pegging it, which isn't a good idea because I don't know if I can trust my legs, but I chance it anyway and I get about ten yords before the cop grabs me – must play focking bogball – and slams me up against the railings. And he's back on the radio, roysh, going, 'Assistance, assistance,' and he snaps the old bracelets on me and makes me lean over the railings, looking down onto the dualler, a mistake because I feel like I'm going to borf my ring up, and I'm made to stay like that until the van arrives and I'm thrown into the back of that.

Seems I'm not the only person who's been a naughty boy tonight either. There's this cream cracker in the back as well, roysh, who insists on trying to talk to me. He's going, 'What are you in for, Bud?' and straight away, roysh, I'm like, 'Let's get one thing focking straight: I'm *not* your *Bud*, roysh. We've both been arrested on the same night. That's all we have in common. I live in Foxrock. You live at rock bottom. I'm wearing *Polo Sport*. You're wearing the same clothes for a week. I was holding a giant, blow-up Heino can over the edge of a bridge. You were holding up someone with a syringe.' He looks at me like

I'm talking in a foreign language, which I suppose I am to him. He goes, 'I hit a bouncer a dig,' and I'm there thinking, He's not all bad then, and for two seconds I'm almost sorry for giving the creamer such a hord time.

I go, 'Please don't breathe near me. I hate the smell of turpentine,' and he smiles then, roysh – four focking teeth in his mouth – and he goes, 'You have to watch out for me, I'm a bit of a character.' I go, 'Why did you hit the bouncer?' and he's there, 'Wouldn't let me in. Said he didn't know me face. Says I, "You'll remember it de next toyim."' I go, 'I suspect it had nothing to do with not knowing your face. You were turned away because you're a skobie. You dress like a scarecrow and you smell of piss. You are one hundred percent creamer. I'm no fan of bouncers myself, but us regulars have the roysh to go to a nightclub without having to be deloused afterwards.' He's sitting there with his mouth open. With the language barrier, you could say anything to him. I go, 'You piece of vermin.'

He goes, 'D'ya tink you'll end up insoyid?' and I'm there, 'I *seriously* doubt it. I don't make a habit of being arrested, you know.' He goes, 'Don't worry, Bud, just tell the judge you're going back to do yisser Junior Cert. Dee love dat. Improving yisser self. Mustard.' I'm like, 'I *don't* think so. My old man's solicitor will get me off.' The goy goes, 'Ah, I'm on dee oul' free legal ayid meself,' and I'm there, 'No shit.'

We get to the cop shop, roysh – think it's Donnybrook – and we're brought in and this total focking bogger takes my details again, while the one who arrested me is, like, muttering under his breath with all his 'endangering the lives of road-users' bullshit, roysh, and I'm just there, 'Spare me the lecture, will you?'

So the next thing is, roysh, the copper who takes my details, he tells me to, like, turn out my pockets and hand over my belt and shoelaces and I'm like, 'Why do you need those?' and he goes, 'In case you try to hang yourself.' I'm like, *Hang myself?* Whoah, who the fock owns that Heino can? Is there something I should know here?' and he tells me I have a big mouth and it's going to get me into trouble one day and I'm like, 'Spare me.'

The reason I can afford to be so Jack the Lad about it is that I know the old man's dickhead of a mate will have me out of here in ten seconds flat. So before they stick me in the cell, roysh, I tell them I want to make a call and they give me a phone and I ring his number. He answers pretty much straight away. He's like, 'Hennessy Coghlan-O'Hara,' and I'm like, 'Hennessy, it's Ross. I've been arrested. If you tell the old man, I'll tell your wife about that time I saw you in Angels. Where are you?' and he goes, 'Outside Donnybrook Garda Station.' I'm there, 'Holy fock, that was quick. Who told you?' He goes, 'No, I've been arrested myself. It seems you can't even hold a conversation with a prostitute these days without being accused of kerb-crawling. The Gardaí have had to take stern action to stem the tide of people being civil to those less fortunate than themselves.'

The next thing the door swings open, roysh, and there he is, a cop either side of him, and he marches straight up to the counter and goes, 'Can you explain to me why the criminal justice system is squandering vital resources that could be used in the war on crime?' One of the Feds beside him goes, 'You have been charged with performing a lewd act in a public place. Do you understand the charge?' and he goes, 'I was asking the girl for directions, for heaven's sake,' and I'm like, 'Hennessy, your trousers are open,' and he looks down, pulls up his fly, fastens his belt, winks at me and goes, 'The little minx.'

I tell the Feds I am SO not sharing a cell with him, or with the goy from *The Commitments,* roysh, and they put me in one by myself and it's a bit of a hole. I lie on the hord, wooden bed and read some of the graffiti on the wall, and after a while one of the Feds comes into me and he goes, 'That number you gave us, who's there now?' I'm like, 'Sorcha. My … em … sister.'

So he goes off to ring her, roysh, obviously planning to let me out, probably needs the cell for some real criminals, but Sorcha takes her focking time getting here, we're talking *two* focking hours, and when they finally let me out of the cell, I can see why. She's, like, *totally* dressed to kill, the sad bitch, wearing the Burberry leather knee-high boots, in cognac, that her old dear bought her in New York, her long black Prada skirt, her black cashmere turtleneck sweater, we're talking the Calvin Klein one, and her sleeveless, faux sheepskin jacket by Karen Millen – as if I'm supposed to believe she always looks this well at, like, three o'clock in the morning. I'm SO glad to see her though, and I give her a hug and go to throw the old lips on her but she just, like, pulls away from me, roysh, and I'm just there going to myself, *Oh* my God, this one is in a Pauline now.

The cops decide not to charge me, roysh – happy days – but they say they'll keep the incident on file and if I'm ever arrested again, blah blah blah. They give me my shit back, but I'm still too shit-faced to put my, like, shoelaces back into my shoes, roysh, so I just stuff them into my pocket, while Sorcha spends about ten focking minutes apologising to the cops for my behaviour, totally overdoing it with the Mature Young Adult act, and we're talking *totally* here. Then she walks on out to the cor, like she's in a hurry and in no mood to take shit from me.

I see this bird arriving, roysh, dirty blonde hair, big hoopy earrings, leather jacket, denim skirt, bare legs, white stilettos – we're talking straight off the 'Jerry Springer' show, roysh – and she marches up to the desk and goes, 'Here to pick up me fella,' and I know straight away, roysh, that it's the goy who was in the back of the van with me. I just walk up to her, roysh, and I'm like, 'Your boyfriend's one hell of a goy. You're a lucky girl,' and she looks at me, roysh, real aggressive, and she goes, 'Who the fook do you tink you are?' and I'm like, 'Sorry, I've been assigned to his case. I'm his social worker,' and the stupid sap believes me, roysh, she shakes my hand – she's more sovs on her than Jimmy focking Saville – and then I turn around and go, 'I'll be in touch,' and head for the door. She shouts after me, roysh, she goes, 'He's not goin' back insoyid, is he?' and I turn back to her and I'm there, 'He's gonna get ten years. I'm sorry, there's nothing I can do,' and I can, like, hear her shrieks from outside.

Sorcha tells me to hurry up. We get into her cor, roysh, black Rav 4, we're talking amazing here, and the nagging storts straight away. She's like, 'Well, you've certainly made an impression at UCD. It was certainly a day to remember, wasn't it?' I just, like, totally blank her, which really pisses her off, but she just keeps it up, going, 'Don't worry, Ross, you'll grow out of it.'

On the other side of the road, roysh, there's, like, two or three buses turning into the bus depot in Donnybrook, and I realise that it's actually a lot earlier than I thought it was. What the *fock* was I drinking? Sorcha goes, 'By the way, that was a stupid thing you did back there. In the police station,' and I'm like, 'What?' and she goes, 'Trying to kiss me.' I'm like, 'You *love* it,' and she goes, 'You *told* them I was your sister.' I'm like, 'Incest, the game for all the family.'

Blah blah blah blah blah. She goes, 'You owe me. *Big* time.' I'm like, 'What do you mean, *owe* you?' She goes, '*Hello?* Do you think I've nothing better to do at eleven o'clock at night than drive all the way from Killiney into town to get you out of a police cell?' I'm there, 'What were you doing when the Feds called?' and she looks at me, shakes her head and goes, 'I *have* a life, you know,' which means she was doing fock-all.

I spend what seems like the next hour falling in and out of sleep, roysh, but it must only be a few minutes because when I open my eyes we're only at, like, the Stillorgan crossroads, and I realise that it's actually Sorcha's shouting that's woken me up. I keep sort of belching, roysh, and there's, like, baby sick on my chin and my jacket and Sorcha's going, 'If you borf in my cor, Ross, I am SO going to kill you.' I wipe my face on my sleeve, tell her I love her when she's angry and go to kiss her on the cheek, but she tells me that if I even think about it she'll break my orm, so I don't.

After a few minutes, roysh, completely out of the blue, she goes, 'I'm seeing someone.' She's totally dying for me to ask who, roysh, but I don't say anything and after a couple of minutes she goes, 'He's in my class. He's *actually* twenty-eight. The goys in Carysfort are SO much more mature than the goys in UCD.' She takes the roysh turn at White's Cross and she's there going, 'I am SO over you, Ross. I look back now and I'm like, *Oh my God*! what a mistake.' I don't say anything. She goes, 'I mean, is the proposition of monogamy such a Jurassic notion to you?' I'm just like, 'Okay, Joey,' and she realises that I'm not as shit-faced as she thought I was and she just goes really red and doesn't, like, say anything else for ages and I'm, like, totally laughing my orse off.

She turns up the CD then, roysh, and I hadn't even realised that she had it on. I'm just like, 'What is this shit?' and she throws her eyes up to heaven and goes, 'It's Tchaikovsky, Ross. 'Dance of the Reed Flute'. It's from *The Nutcracker*. Oh my *God*, Ross, when are you *ever* going to get with the programme?' The cover from the CD is on the dashboard, roysh, and it's like, *The Best Classical Album of the Millennium … Ever!* I turn up the sound really high, roysh, until it's blasting, and then stort, like, conducting the music, swinging my orms around the place and Sorcha goes, 'You are SUCH a dickhead.' We pull up outside my gaff and I get out of the cor and, like, stagger up to the gates of the house, and I must have left the passenger door open because I hear Sorcha getting out and, like, basically cursing me under her breath, then slamming the door shut, and the next thing I know I'm waking up and it's, like, the middle of the afternoon the next day, and I still have my Castlerock jersey and my chinos on and I'm in the total horrors. And we're talking big style.

✱✱✱

Me and Oisinn, we skip our eleven o'clock, roysh, and we're sitting in his gaff watching the telly when my mobile rings and I, like, make the mistake of answering before checking who it is, roysh, and who is it only the old man, basically checking up on me, he's like, 'Hey, Kicker, how's college?' and I'm there, 'Not a good time. I'm watching 'The Love Boat',' and I hang up on the loser.

✱✱✱

Huge row in the bor the other night, roysh. Erika was going on about the National Lottery, which she said was basically for skangers, and Claire, who basically *is* a skanger, roysh – a Dalkey wannabe who actually lives in Bray – she goes, 'But what about my mum? She buys scratch cards. That doesn't mean *I'm* a skanger.' And Erika goes, 'I'm not changing the rules to accommodate you, your mother, or anyone else in your family. Scratch cords are actually worse than doing the Lottery. Face it, Dear, you're peasant class,' and Claire storts going ballistic, roysh, screaming and shouting, telling Erika she's the biggest snob she's ever met, which Erika would actually consider a compliment, roysh, and she just smiles while Claire makes a total tit of herself in front of everyone, and eventually Sorcha takes her off to the toilet to calm her down and, like, clean up her make-up and shit, which totally pisses Erika off, roysh, I can tell, because she looks at me and goes, 'Sorry, *whose* best friend is Sorcha supposed to be again?' Then she gets up and leaves the boozer without even finishing her Bacordi Breezer.

I actually felt a bit bad for her, roysh, so the next morning, I decide to head out to her gaff in Rathgar, just to, like, tell her I thought she was in the roysh, about time someone put Claire in her place, blah blah blah, basically just trying to get in there. I check my jacket pocket to see have I any johnnies left. We all got, like, a free six-pack on our first day, roysh, off some focking Society or other, and I turned around to Christian and I'm like, 'Six? Well that's the first weekend looked after,' but that turned out to be bullshit because they're still unopened.

Anyway, roysh, I peg it out to Rathgar and her old dear opens the door – bit of a yummy mummy; with a daughter who looks like Denise Richards, of course she is – and she says Erika's not in, she's actually down with her horse, she goes, 'She spends half her life with that animal,' but I might be able to get her on her mobile if she has it switched on, which she probably doesn't because it freaks out the horse. I tell her I'll, like, head down to the stables myself to see can I catch her.

The cor pork is full of really cool cors and I'm actually embarrassed porking the old dear's Micra there, but fock it. I mooch around the place looking for her, and when I eventually see her, roysh, she's carrying this, like, bucket of I-don't-know-what, basically some type of shit she feeds the horse, and I'm straight over, playing the total gentleman, going, 'Erika, let me carry that for you,' flexing the old biceps as well, of course.

When I go to take it from her, though, she shoots me this total filthy, roysh, so I just hold my hands up and go, 'Hey, no offence.' I follow her into the stable and she puts the bucket down and goes, 'Your girlfriend has a serious attitude problem.' I ask her who she means, roysh, and she goes, 'Sorcha,' and I tell her that Sorcha isn't my girlfriend, that I'm young, free and single and I want to mingle, which she just ignores. She goes, 'I SO love her little friend, the one with the Rimmel foundation. Made such an impression in The Queen's last night, didn't she? That's what you get when you go dredging for friends in Bray.' I'm like, 'That's actually what I'm here for, Erika,' and she goes, 'What *are* you here for, Ross?' I'm about to tell her that I thought she was really badly treated last night, roysh, when all of a sudden she goes, 'Do you want to be with me? Is that why you're here?' and even though she makes it sound sort of, like, sleazy, roysh, I tell her yes and she goes, 'Okay then, let's go.'

So I basically just grab her, roysh, and stort doing, like, tongue sarnies with her, and I have to say, even though the boots and the jodhpurs are a major turn-on, she's not actually as good a kisser as I remembered from the last time I was with her two years ago. I open my eyes a couple of times, sort of, like, mid-snog, roysh, and notice that she has her eyes open the whole time, and this sort of sounds, like, weird, roysh, but it was like kissing a dead body and the only response I actually get out of her is when we fall backwards into the hay and I try to go a bit further than just snogging – can't blame a goy for chancing his orm – and she just looks over my shoulder and goes, 'Get off me. I have to feed *Orchid*.'

✳✳✳

Out this particular Friday night, roysh, and me and Christian make the mistake of hitting Boomerangs, got the old beer goggles on, of course, spot this gang of birds, roysh, obviously out on a hen's night, we're talking easy pickings here, mosey on over, give them a couple of killer lines, though I wouldn't have bothered if I'd known they were skobies. This one bird, roysh, she looks like Kelly Brook, but she talks like something off 'Fair City', and she has a laugh like a focking donkey getting taken out with an Uzi.

I go up to her, playing it cool like Huggy Bear, roysh, and I go, 'I know what you're thinking. Great body, amazing-looking, dresses well – and yet he's got something else. The X factor,' and this bird, she turns around to the bird beside her and goes, ''Cinta, have a listen to dis fella,' and I think Christian's the only one there who cops the look of, like, pure focking horror on my face. He turns around to me, roysh, and he goes, 'Jesus, Ross, these people are working class,' – can be difficult to tell these days, every slapper in town's wearing Ralph since TK Maxx opened – and I'm going, 'Play it cool, Christian. Play it nice and cool and I'll get us the fock out of here.'

She going, ''Cinta, have a listen to um,' and she turns to me and she goes, 'Go on, young fella. Say it again.' I'm not gonna be a performing seal for any skobie bird, so I just give her a different line this time, show her I'm not a one-trick pony. I'm there, 'We wouldn't be true to ourselves if we denied that there's an attraction here,' and she's off again – nah-ah-ah-ah-ah-ah-ah, hee-haw – and 'Cinta's cracking her hole as well, as are all the other birds. 'Cinta goes, 'Does de voice great, doesn't he?' and another one of the birds – focking cat – she goes, 'Ah Jaysus, he's veddy good.'

The bird who, until ten seconds ago, reminded me of Kelly Brook, she goes, 'Where are yiz from den, lads?' and I go, 'I'm from Foxrock. Upmorket area on the south side,' and they all break their shites laughing again and 'Cinta goes, 'Dee can't be serdious for foyiv minutes, can dee?' Kelly Brook Gone Wrong goes, 'Are yis gettin' dem in, lads?' We're all drinkin' Ritz, 'cept for Pamela dare who's on pints of Carlsberg and so is Anee-eh.' I go, 'Fine. We shall return presently,' and 'Cinta's going, 'Dare gas, ardent dee,' as me and Christian head off in the general direction of the bor, but take a long detour out the focking emergency exit and up the road without looking back once.

✳✳✳

I phone up Erika, roysh, on her mobile, and ask her where she is, but she doesn't answer, she just goes, 'What do you want?' so I get straight to the point. I'm there, 'Just wanted to talk to you about, you know, what happened between us,' and she goes, 'Make it quick. I'm in Nine West.' I'm like, 'Well, I just wanted to let you know that I won't say anything to Sorcha. About, you know, me and you being with each other. I know she's your best friend,' and there's this, like, silence on the other end of the line. I'm like, 'Are you still there?' and she goes, 'The line is perfect, Ross. Is that all you want to say?' and I'm like, 'Well, I just wondered whether *you* were going to say anything to her,' not that I actually give a shit one way or the other, just wanted an excuse to ring her, see if there's any chance of another bit. She goes, 'Do you think being with you is something I'd actually *brag* about?'

CHAPTER TWO
'Ross is, like – OH MY GOD! – so shallow.'
Discuss.

Me and Oisinn skip our three o'clock, roysh, and we're in his gaff watching 'Countdown' and he tells me it's my turn to go to the fridge and get the beers, so I head out to the kitchen, roysh, and, HOLY FOCK! I'm like, 'What the …' There's this, like, life-size statue of, I don't know, some dude with long hair, big fock-off wings and no mickey. I go back into Oisinn and I'm like, 'What the *fock* is that thing out there?' He goes, 'The bacon? You didn't throw it out, did you? It's only a week past its sell-by date,' and I'm like, 'I'm talking about that focking statue. Looks like the one in the paper. The one that was stolen from the Classics Museum on Freshers' Day.' Oisinn just looks at me.

I'm like, 'Are you focking *mad*? I can't believe it was you,' and he's like, '*Me*? Ross, do you remember Freshers' Day?' I'm there, 'I told you already, I was rat-orsed, pretty much the whole day is a blank.' He goes, '*You* stole it, Ross. This is *your* shit. You asked me could I mind it for you. And thanks for re-minding me, you're going to have to take it with you. My old pair are storting to ask questions.'

I've a few focking questions of my own. He goes, 'It's *Eros* apparently.' I'm like, '*Hello?* I need a little more information than that …' He's there, 'Well, Fionn said he was the son of Aphrodite. Fired magic arrows at people's hearts and made them fall in love.' He doesn't even turn away from the television when he says this. He goes, 'Actually, I thought it was Cupid did that. Consonant, Carol.' I'm like, 'You know what I mean. When did I steal it? No, why? No, how?' He goes, 'Pretending you don't remember. Cute.' There's no focking way I'm letting him pin this one on me. I'm like, 'I'm sorry, Oisinn. I didn't steal that thing. You're gonna have to prove it.' He turns around, roysh, calm as anything, and he goes, 'Ross, you were wearing the face off *Eros* in front of the UCD webcam as a dare. There was about thirty of us sitting in the computer lab watching you. I've actually got it on disk. And you mooning.'

I'm actually storting to feel faint. I sit down. I'm there, 'Is that the lot? I mean, did I do anything else that day?' He thinks for a bit and goes, 'Some ugly bird was looking for you in Finnegan's Break yesterday morning. Think you might have joined the Chess Society.' I'm there, 'I am SO never drinking again.' He goes, 'Fock me, Gyles, you're roysh, draughts does have eight letters … I'll help you carry it out to the cor.'

✳✳✳

I ask for a large latte, roysh, and the bird behind the counter, who's, like, French or some shit, she says they have no large, so I ask for a small instead and she goes, 'No small.' I'm like, 'What *have* you focking got?' and she goes, 'Only *grande*, tall and short,' and at this stage, roysh, I'm so confused I don't know what the fock to ask for, so I head back to Melissa and ask her what she wants, roysh, and she just looks me up and down and goes, 'Will you *grow* up. This is focking serious,' and for a couple of seconds I think she's talking about the coffee, roysh, but when she stands up and, like, storms out of the place, I finally cop that she's actually talking about what happened at the Traffic Light Ball. Or should I say, afterwards.

I peg it after her, but she's already across the other side of the road, up by the Central Bank, and the lights are red, but I leg it across anyway and this orsehole in a blue Nissan Almera beeps me, so I just give him the finger. I catch up with her and touch her on the shoulder, roysh, but she just, like, spins around and goes, 'Nicole was SO right about you,' and I'm going, Who the fock is Nicole? to myself, of course, and she's there, 'You are *such* an orsehole. That's what she told me, Ross. And she was right.' I'm suddenly all, like, defensive now, I'm there, 'Hey, I said I'd meet you this morning and I did,' and she goes, 'You just want to make sure I go through with it.' I'm there, 'Not true, I wanted to be here with you. This is something you shouldn't have to go through on your own.' She goes, 'You are SO full of shit. You're just thinking about what your parents would say if they found out I was …' I'm like, 'Bullshit. Anyway, you're not,' and she turns around and storts walking again, off through Temple Bar, and I, like, follow her from a safe distance.

There's a goy busking in the archway outside Abrakebabra, roysh, and it's like, 'Don't Look Back in Anger', and as we're waiting for the lights, roysh, I tell Melissa that that song has been so ruined by every busker in town playing it, but she just ignores me, as she does when I ask her why they're building a new bridge next to the Ha'penny Bridge. She just, like, shakes her head, roysh, and I am so tempted to point out that this is only, like, fifty percent my fault, that it takes two to tango, but I know it'll only make things worse if I do.

The place is next door to Pravda, and Melissa presses the button on the intercom, says she has an appointment and the next thing, roysh, there's a bird behind a desk asking her whether she's attended the clinic before, and Melissa looks her up and down and goes, 'Hordly!' Then we're sitting down in the waiting room and Melissa's filling out this, like, form and shit, which she gives to the nurse and then we just, like, sit there and wait. In total silence. I sort of look sideways at her a couple of times and I have to say, roysh, she's actually a bit better looking than I thought she was last night, a little bit like Charisma Carpenter, except with blonde hair. I only ended up with her because Christian wanted to be with her best friend, Stephanie, who actually does look a little bit like Natalie Portman, and he asked me to take a bullet for him, which, being the great mate that I am, I did. They're both, like, first year Orts.

Eventually, roysh, the doctor calls her into her office, and I'm not sure whether I'm supposed to, like, go in with her, but as I go to stand up Melissa tells me to stay outside and mind her stuff, which suits me fine. I'm sitting there, roysh, looking around and there's this bird sitting two seats down from me who I think I recognise from Annabel's, and she's a total nervous wreck, can't stop, like, fidgeting and shit.

All of a sudden, roysh, Melissa's phone storts beeping, so I grab it out of her bag and notice that she has a text message and it's from some bird called Gwen and it's like, **OMG**, which I presume means Oh My God, **RACHEL KISSED ROSS**, which I'm guessing is, like, a reference to 'Friends'. Two sad bitches, and we're talking TOTALLY here. I flick through her numbers, roysh, and notice that she knows four or five chicks I've been with before. I still don't have a clue who this Nicole one is, and I think about writing down her number, roysh, but in the end I don't bother. I lash her phone back in her bag and stort flicking through a copy of *Now!* that the bird two seats down has just put back on the table. Says you can achieve the Liz Hurley look by using this gel, lactic acid or some shit, to increase the flow of blood to the lips, making them look fuller.

About ten minutes later, roysh, Melissa comes out and it's all, like, thank-you this and thank-you that to the doctor, but her face changes when she sees me and she just, like, heads straight for the door and I follow her down the stairs. We walk back towards Grafton Street and even though I have no real interest in seeing her again, I ask her what she's doing later and she goes, 'Leaning over the toilet and getting sick, I would imagine.' I ask her what she's bullshitting on about and she goes, 'Do you have *any* idea what I've just taken?' and I go, 'The morning-after pill,' and she just shakes her head and tells me I haven't got a clue.

She says she's going down for the Dorsh, roysh, and I tell her
I'm going to get the 46A. And I don't know why, maybe because
I feel sorry for her, I ask her whether I'll see her in college
tomorrow and she tells me not to get my hopes up, that she's
seeing someone.

***

The old man comes into my room and he's there, 'Ross, is there
any reason why there's a Greek statue in the laundry room?' I
just give him a filthy and go, 'You have SUCH a focking attitude
problem.'

***

I ring Sorcha, roysh, and tell her that the Castlerock debs is
coming up at the end of November and, well, would it be
alroysh if I called out to see her tonight because there's, like,
something I really want to ask her. She's there, 'Of course. Make
it after eight. Mum and Dad will be at the sailing club annual
dinner.'

So after half-eight, roysh, I mosey on out to Killiney and
Sorcha, roysh, she's made the effort, there's no doubt about
that, she opens the door and she's wearing her black halterneck
from Pia Bang, her black Karen Millen trousers and the black
Prada boots I bought her for her birthday last year, and half a
focking bottle of *Issey Miyake*.

She air-kisses me and asks me whether I want, like, marsh-
mallows in my hot chocolate. I'm like, 'Cool, yeah,' and I follow
her into the kitchen and we sit at the counter, roysh, sipping hot

chocolate and making small talk and she's like a child she's so excited.

Eventually, I go, 'Sorcha … em … as you know, the debs is coming up. And it's weird, but I'm … em … a bit nervous asking you this.' Her face is all lit up. She's like, 'Go on, it's okay.' I'm like, 'Well, we've known each other since … forever, haven't we? You know you're very special to me. How's that goy you're going out with, by the way, the twenty-eight-year-old?' She's like, 'Cillian? I have to be honest with you, it's not really serious. We're only really, like, *seeing* each other.' I'm like, 'Good, good. Anyway, Sorcha, as you know, there's no one in the world who I value more than you. Which is why I wanted to ask you, with the debs coming up in two weeks, if you'd mind if I asked Erika to go with me.'

She's like, 'What?' and I go, 'Erika.' She's there, 'Erika? Erika as in my best friend Erika?' and I'm like, 'Have you got a problem with that?' She's, like, staring into space, trying to get her head around this, but of course she doesn't want to let herself down. She goes, 'No, I've no, em, problem with it. Ask her if you want.' I'm like, 'I will. I'm glad you're cool about it.'

She goes, 'Actually, I was hoping you weren't going to ask me. I know I said me and Cillian were only seeing each other, but I think he wants to be a bit more serious about things.'

Pathetic. I know I could have her now if I wanted her.

I finish my hot chocolate and get up to go. I'm there, 'I like that music, by the way,' and she goes, 'It's Bizet. It's from *Carmen*,' and she's trying her best not to cry, but I can see the tears in her eyes.

✳✳✳

JP sends me a text message, roysh, and it's like:

> **SCORED A JUDGE'S DAUGHTER LAST NIGHT! AFFLUENCE!**

✳✳✳

I'm in the bor, roysh, shooting some pool with Christian, two o'clock in the day and the two of us gee-eyed. Christian was locked when I met him at ten o'clock this morning, totally paranoid as well, keeps telling me that the UCD water tower is the secret headquarters of the Prophets of the Dark Side and I ask him who the fock they are – why I encourage the goy I don't know – and he tells me they're essentially a band of imperial operatives posing as mystics who are strong in the Dark Side of the Force, and whose real function is espionage. I go – quick thinking, this – 'They're probably listening to us now. Let's be careful what we say,' and he nods and goes, 'Well, they have a vast network of spies as well.' The goy is losing it.

Anyway, there we are playing pool, roysh, and this total twat comes up to the table – long black coat, black hair in a ponytail, looks like the goy out of the comic shop in 'The Simpsons'. So Christian, roysh, he holds his cue like a sword and he goes, 'Supreme Prophet Kadann sent you, didn't he?' and the goy goes, 'Hey, *The Lost City of the Jedi*. What a book, dude,' but Christian looks at him sort of, like, suspiciously and goes, 'Be careful. I think this one's a changeling.'

The goy goes, 'I'm actually here to see you, Ross.' I'm like, 'What the fock could we possibly have to talk about?' and the goy goes, 'The We Are Not Alone Society. I spoke to you on Freshers' Day.' Not another one. I go, 'Look, I was locked. It didn't mean anything. Now get over it.'

Then I tell him to fock off.

***

I send Erika a text message, roysh, and it's like, **w%d u llk 2go2 my debs?** and straight away I get one back and it's like, **GAL**, which I presume stands for Get A Life, because that's what she always says. She actually says it to everyone. It's like, '*Get* a life!'

***

Oisinn grabs me by the lapel, roysh, and smells my neck and goes, '*Bvlgari pour homme*. Notes of perfumed darjeeling with citrus and aquatic notes. Classic … and yet modern.' I straighten his bow-tie and I go, 'Oisinn, my man, looking good. Look-ing-good.' He goes, 'Yeah, I was quite surprised myself to discover that Hugo Boss does tuxes for goys of my generous build. So some of the credit for what you see here before you must go to Mr HB Esquire.' Then he turns around to the bird beside me and goes, 'And who, pray tell, is this little … beauty?'

The little beauty happens to be Elspeth Hadaway, who's, like, third year Orts in UCD, pretty decent-looking, a little bit like Catherine McCord, except in the old body department. It's a bit of a long story really. Erika knocking me back came as a bit of a shock, roysh, and didn't leave me much time to find an alternative – forty-eight hours to be precise. Then JP tells me about this bird he knows, plays tennis with his sister and was going out with this Trinity wanker – I knew him when he was in Terenure, a total dickhead – who, it turns out, did the dirt on her when she was in Germany for a year on Erasmus.

JP goes, 'We're talking about a mutual convenience of wants here, Ross. She wants the word to go back to this tosser that she's seeing someone else. And you want someone to go to the debs with so you don't look like a sad bastard.' I'm like, 'Thanks, JP.' He goes, 'Cheer up, it's a win-win situation. Let's throw this idea out of the 'plane, see does its parachute open.'

So I meet her the night before the debs, roysh, we're talking Eddie Rockets in Stillorgan. She pretty much insisted on inspecting the merchandise beforehand and, not being big-headed or anything, I think I can say she wasn't disappointed. And I have to say, roysh, I thought she was alroysh as well, no complaints, until she switched on the focking waterworks and storted telling me I'd never guess who it was her *so-called* boyfriend did the dirt on her with, we're talking Shauna, the girl who is *supposed* to be her best friend. I'm just there going, 'Bummer,' but on and on it goes, she's giving it, 'This is the girl who I actually helped through her break-up with Tadgh.' The girl's pretty much hysterical at this stage, roysh, and we're beginning to attract a bit of an audience, so I just go, 'Look, have you got a focking dress?' and she's like, 'I'm going to wear the one I wore to the Orts Ball two years ago. And I am going to look SO amazing. I'm going to–' I just go, 'Fine. Meet me at eight in the bor in the Berkeley Court.' That's where the gig was on. I'm there,

'And get all that focking crying out of your system tonight. Don't want you making a tit out of me,' then I drop a tenner on the table, which should cover my buffalo wings, chilli-cheese fries and vanilla malt, and I get the fock out of there.

Twenty-four hours later, of course, I'm regretting being such a dick to her – and leaving her to get the bus home – because she looks focking amazing in this, like, pink satin dress that she says is a Donna Karan original, and all the goys, roysh, their eyes are out on stalks when they see her. This bird lights up the room.

Oisinn's bird lights up a John Player. The goy has surpassed himself this time. We're talking Jo Brand with orange hair and a face full of double-u double-u dots. She's wearing a purple dress she must have borrowed from Fossett's circus. She is a - *total* mutt, which seems to make Oisinn very proud. I introduce him to Elspeth and he introduces me to, Julia I think her name was, didn't get a chance to check her collar. He's like, 'Isn't she pretty?' and then, roysh, in front of her face he goes, 'Pretty *ugly*,' and Julia sort of, like, slaps him as if to say, You're terrible, Oisinn, like she thinks the goy's joking.

Fionn has brought Eilish Hunter, this total lasher from his class who looks a bit like Faye Tozer and who, for some bizarre reason, actually has the big-time hots for the boring, drippy-looking geek. And he's SO focking smug about it. He's giving it, 'Lots of girls have a thing about glasses, Ross. Especially since *Jerry Maguire* came out. They think if we have kids, they'll turn out like the kid in that film.' I'm like, 'Please. I'm gonna vom my lemon sorbet back up in a minute.'

Then, roysh, just to, like, rub it in, he goes, 'Heard yours was an *arranged* date,' and he tries to make it sound really sleazy. I look at Elspeth and she's chatting away to Oisinn, no way she can hear me, then I turn around to Fionn and I'm like, 'I think she's fallen for me. Big time,' which is total bullshit because she's been stressing the whole 'We're just friends' bit all night, but I'm not letting him get one over on me. Fionn goes, 'Catching a girl on the rebound can be fraught with problems, because you never know what angle they're coming back at you from,' as if I need advice from *him*. Then he turns to Eilish and they stort talking about some, I don't know, stupid intellectual thing.

I look over and I cop Aileen Hannah-Lynch, this bird I used to know – in the biblical sense – and she's getting up to leave with Andrew Beirne, and it looks like they're about to get to know each other in the biblical sense too, roysh, because Fionn says they've got a room booked and I'm there thinking, We haven't even had the main course yet. Jammy bastard.

The night drags. I'm on a shit buzz. Me and Elspeth have hordly said two words to each other, roysh, and I can hear Oisinn giving it the whole 'bouquet of floral, amber and powdered notes' bullshit, and he's got Elspeth and the hound he brought hanging on his every word.

I end up horsing down the Bailey's ice cream and focking off to another table to talk to Woulfie, Ed and Barser, three goys who were on the S with me, brains to burn the three of them, they're doing politics or some shit in Trinity, but they still like their rugby. So we're basically there shooting the breeze, roysh, when all of a sudden this bird comes over, Lia – nice boat-race, great rack – and she goes, 'Ross, have you seen Christian? Carol is, like, SO worried about him.'

I'd totally forgotten about Christian. He was in the bor earlier but I sort of, like, slipped away from him when he storted telling me that Tibanna gas is the best hyperdrive coolant there is and no one can blame Han for heading for Bespin like he did. You've SO got to be in the mood to listen to Christian's shit, and I wasn't, so I left him with Carol, who JP reckons looks like Susan Ward, though I don't see it myself.

I go off looking for the dude and, considering how shit-faced he was when I last saw him, roysh, my first port of call is the jacks. And he's there. He's standing at the sink, roysh, with his face pressed up against the mirror. I call his name, but he doesn't answer. I go, 'Christian,' again. Still nothing. I pull his head away from the mirror and I see that he's crying. He's bawling his eyes out. I go, 'Christian, what's the focking story, my man?' He looks at me, roysh, like he's trying to focus on me and he goes, 'I can't tell you, Ross.' I'm there, 'Too focking roysh you can. I'm your, like, best friend,' but he just bursts into tears again.

The dude is focked. I decide to take him back to my gaff, roysh, just to sleep it off. I'm having a mare of a night anyway, so it doesn't bother me to fock off so early. I manage to walk Christian out as far as, like, reception, plonk him in a big orm-chair, then ask the bird at reception to call us a Jo. There's, like, couples slipping upstairs and couples slipping outside, basically all doing the debs thing. Elaine – don't know her second name, I was with her once, second year Orts UCD – she's bet into some bloke, can't see his face, think it might be Kellyer, this tosser who was on the Castlerock second team and had big ideas about taking my place on the S.

Weird as it sounds, roysh, I actually feel a little bit bad about focking off on Elspeth without saying anything. But then all of a sudden, roysh, I can't believe what I'm seeing. Woulfie, the focking sly old dog, he's making a move on her and we're talking big time. Trying to bag off with *my* bird. They're behind this, like, pillar in the lobby, roysh, I can't see them but I can hear them, and Woulfie's asking her does she want to go for, like, a walk, we're talking along the canal.

Woulfie goes, 'We can look at the swans,' and Elspeth's like, '*Oh* my God! I so love swans,' the slapper, and Woulfie's like, 'They represent hope for humanity, don't you think. They symbolise how everyone can grow into a beautiful creature and have a meaningful life.' He's a slick mick, I'll give him that. She pulls away and looks at him like he's focking mad or something and she's there, 'Everyone?' And he goes, 'Well, everyone with money.' She's there, '*Oh my God!* I so want to be with you.'

And even though I want to go over and deck Woulfie at that particular moment, even though I so want to deck the focker, I can't. I just have to admit, the goy's got class. The bird at reception goes, 'Taxi for O'Carroll,' and as I'm helping Christian up, I go, 'It's actually O'Carroll-*Kelly*.'

✳✳✳

I bell JP on his mobile. Feel a bit sorry for the dude, he must be feeling a bit left out of things lately. I mean, me and the rest of the goys, we're all in college, roysh, on the beer everyday and basically screwing our way through every chick on campus, while he's stuck doing an MDB – Managing Daddy's Business – namely Hook, Lyon and Sinker Estate Agents. He's been left out of the loop a bit, so I give him a ring, roysh, and he's telling me he's just got four hundred thousand sheets for a gaff in Sandymount that's no bigger than a focking coalshed. I'm telling him all about the Traffic Light Ball, roysh, about me wearing a red spot instead of a green one – we're talking red as in No Go – and ending up scoring seven times, or eight if you count that bogger from Ag. Science, which I don't, and how it all goes to prove the theory that what birds really want is what they can't, like, have.

Then I mention to him that I've got my driving test the next day, roysh, and how I'm pretty much gicking it because I've, like, sat the thing more times than I've sat the Leaving Cert at this stage and, well, let's just say the last examiner told me that if there was a Certificate for *In*competence, I'd walk it. Of course, I never copped that he was taking the piss until a few days later.

JP tells me he aced his and he suggests we have a quick mind-meld, which, to those of us without a degree in Bullshit, means we should meet up, put our heads together, see can we come up with some way for me to pass this focking thing once and for all.

We meet for a coffee in Donnybrook. I tell the bird who's cleaning off the tables that I want an ordinary cup of coffee and she tells me I'll have to go up and order from one of the *barristas*, and I'm like, 'The what?' JP's there, 'I'll go. I speak reasonably good Coffee. A Long Black is what you're after,' and he comes back a few minutes later with two cups of ordinary coffee.

Anyway, roysh, to cut a long story short, fair focks to him, the dude has already come up with a plan. He asks me what test centre I'm doing it in, and I tell him Rathgar, and he tells me he knows where he can get his hands on a JCB. I'm there, 'What the *fock* has that got to do with the price of cabbage?' and he's like, 'The second you come out of the test centre, I'll pull out in front of you and drive at, like, fifteen miles an hour. You'll end up doing your whole test in, like, second gear.' I'm there, 'But he'll just get me to turn off somewhere to get away from you.' He goes, 'Soon as I see you indicate, then I'll turn that way too. Trust me, Ross, it'll work.'

I'm there, 'Well, I suppose it won't cost anything to try,' and then I cop the big shit-eating grin on JP's face and I go, 'How much?' He blows on his coffee, takes a mouthful and goes, 'Weighted with overheads this job, Ross. Got to pay the site foreman to turn a blind eye while the JCB goes walkies. There's my time. Danger money.' I'm like, '*Danger money?* You said fifteen miles an hour,' and he's there, 'Of course, you don't have to take the idea offline if you don't want to,' and he gets up to go and I'm like, 'Okay, okay. How much?' He goes, 'Five hundred bills,' and I go, 'Okay, five hundred bills it is.'

So the next day, roysh, I'm pulling out of the test centre and the examiner – no crack out of him *what*soever – tells me to pull out roysh onto the Orwell Road. So there I am, in first gear, nosing my way out the gate, and there's JP porked opposite the entrance, and I'm thinking the focker might have dressed down for the day because basically no one digs the roads in a two-thousand-lid Armani suit, Celtic Tiger or no Celtic Tiger, and I'm storting to think we're never going to get away with this.

JP sees me indicating roysh, roysh, and pulls out into the middle of the road and I slip in behind him and we're doing, like, ten miles an hour all the way up Orwell Road. Before we hit the lights, the goy tells me to hang a left, roysh, so I indicate left and in front of me, sure as houses, JP swings the big beast left onto Zion Road. The examiner tells me to hang a quick roysh onto Victoria Road, not leaving me much time to indicate, but JP slams on the brakes in front of me, makes the turn and I crawl over the speed bumps behind him in, like, first gear. Ten minutes into the test and so far, so good.

Then we hit what I think is a problem, roysh. The examiner goes, 'I want you to pull in just beyond this left junction here and show me your reversing around corners,' and I'm basically kicking myself for not copping this before. We're going to pull in, JP's going to carry on driving and this dude's going to find out that I can't drive for shit.

Probably should have had a little more faith in JP. He takes the left turn and I continue on and pork, then turn around in my seat, lash the gears into reverse and stort moving backwards slowly. The next thing, roysh, JP pulls up roysh at the corner I'm supposed to be backing around, blocking me off, and he hops down out of the JCB and pretends to be taking a big interest in the grass verge. He's got his Hugo Boss shoes on as well. I'm like, 'Must be a lot of money in pipe-laying these days,' trying to strike up a bit of banter with the dude in the cor, but he's having none of it, he has his eyes closed and he's, like, shaking his head and he tells me to turn around and go back down Victoria Road.

JP sees me indicating to pull out and he's back at the levers in, like, two seconds flat and he pulls out in front of me again, and we're heading back the way we came, going over the ramps so slow that if we went any slower we'd stop. Bottom of Victoria Road we hang a left back onto Zion Road and then a roysh at the lights onto Orwell Road.

The tester goy's like, 'Proceed to the test centre.' We've only been out, like, fifteen minutes. I'm there, 'You don't want to see my hill-stort?' and he goes, 'No, I've seen enough to make my determination,' and in my mind I'm going, YES! and I think about flashing my lights at JP, just to tell him, 'Piece of piss,' but in the end I don't chance it.

I hang a left into the test centre, pull into a space and the goy tells me to come inside, and I suppose it's just, like, procedure. I follow him in and he tells me to sit down on the opposite side of this table, roysh, then he sits down himself and goes, 'You've failed your test.' I punch the air. I'm like, 'TOUCHDOWN! YESSSS!' and I'm already planning to hire a big fock-off Porsche, head out to Erika's and impress the knickers off her. And we're talking *literally* here. The goy's like, 'You obviously misheard me. You *failed*.'

I'm there, 'Failed?' How *focking* embarrassing. I'm like, 'How could I have failed. I never got out of second gear.' He goes, 'Well, let's start with the questions I asked you.' I'm like, 'Go on, let's hear it, this'll be good.' He goes, 'When I asked you an occasion on which you might turn on your full lights ...' and I'm like, 'Go on,' and he's there, 'You said, "When some stupid bitch won't pull over when you're trying to overtake".' He's basically one of these nit-pickers. Then he goes, 'What was the first thing you did when you got into the car?' and I'm like, 'Stort the engine,' and he goes, 'No, you turned on the radio.' Of course I'm like, '*Hello?* There's a law against driving with the radio on now, is there?' and he goes, 'You changed a CD while you were driving.' Trust me to get one of those fockers who's trying to trip you up. Then he goes, 'And you didn't look in your mirrors at all.' I'm like, 'That's bullshit,' and he's there going, 'Sorry, you did. Once. To check your baseball cap was on straight.'

I stand up, roysh, and I'm like, 'You're going to be hearing from my old man's solicitor. Have you ever heard of Hennessy Coghlan-O'Hara?' He thinks for a few seconds and goes, 'Yes, matter of fact I have. I read about him in *The Irish Times* this morning. The Law Society are considering striking him off.' This focker's got an answer for everything. I'm like, 'I'm obviously wasting my time here,' and I go to leave, roysh, and just as I reach the door, he goes, 'He's a friend of yours, isn't he?' I stop and without looking at him I go, 'Who?' He's like, 'The guy in the JCB.' I'm there, 'You can't prove that,' and he goes, 'It's just that it's the fourth time it's happened in the past six weeks. Quite a little business he's got going obviously. You should tell him to be a little less conspicuous, though, change his routine. Maybe try a steamroller next time.'

JP dies.

✳✳✳

Been seeing this girl for about three weeks, roysh, Georgia's her name, you probably know her to see, she was one of the weather girls on, like, Network Two, a little bit like Laetitia Casta, but thick as a focking brick, and we're talking TOTALLY here. We're in Annabel's one night, roysh, and we're sitting with Wally and Walshy, these two goys I know from Castlerock, doing anthropology or some shit, total focking brainboxes, not really into rugby, but, like, sound anyway. So we're there and the Nice Treaty comes up in conversation, roysh, and I have to say I know fock-all about Northern Ireland, but I do know to keep my mouth shut in case I, like, embarrass myself. Georgia, of course, doesn't. She goes, 'OH MY GOD, I am SO sick of all these, like, referendums and stuff. I don't know why they can't just rip up the Constitution and just have one article that says, like, you know, *Whatever.*' And the goys, roysh, fair play to them, they just stort, like, nodding their heads as though she's made an amazing point, but I can tell, roysh, they were looking at her going, 'What the *fock* is Ross going out with?'

I'd already storted to ask myself the same question – Oisinn and Fionn, roysh, they call her Clueless – and I'm seriously thinking about giving her the flick this particular night in Annabel's, having done the dirt on her three days ago with Heidi, this sixth-year Mountie who's so like Yasmine Bleeth they could be twins. Anyway, roysh, being the nice goy that I am, I don't actually have the heart to give Georgia the flick tonight because, as it turns out, RTÉ have done exactly that that same day. Why, I don't know, I was pretty shit-faced when she explained it to me and I really couldn't have been orsed listening, even though she was, like, bawling her eyes out.

Of course, coming up to the end of the night, roysh, when it's clear I'm not going to get my rock and roll elsewhere, I'm pretending to be all concerned, giving her hugs and kisses and shit and giving it, 'They must be mad, letting you go,' – she probably stuck a focking rain cloud on the map upside down or something – 'they'll regret that one day. You'll be the star they let slip through their fingers.' And she goes, '*Hello?* I have a degree in communications from ATIM, Ross,' – Any Thick Idiot with Money, we call it – 'I'm *hordly* likely to walk into another job.' I'm like, 'With your looks?' Of course this does nothing to cheer her up. She gives me this total filthy and goes, 'You think I'm an airhead, don't you? Good-looking with nothing between my ears.' And the tears stort again.

I stort going, 'Of course I don't,' but I'm struggling to keep a straight face, roysh, because I can hear all the goys – we're talking Christian and JP – and they're *totally* ripping the piss, giving it, 'Tomorrow will be a clidey day,' and 'There'll be scashered shars throughout the country,' basically taking off her accent, roysh, and I'm caught between wanting to look all, like, sympathetic to make sure I get my bit later on, while at the same time playing Jack the Lad in front of the goys, letting them know I'm actually ripping the piss out of her myself. It's a focking tightrope, but I manage not to burst out laughing in her face and all of a sudden, roysh, a couple of her mates arrive over – birds she knows from Loreto on the Green, JP was with one of them once – and they take her off to the toilets.

Oisinn comes over and high-fives me, roysh, and asks whether I heard about Fionn, and I say no, and he tells me he's copped off with *Georgio Sensi*, which could be a bird's name, though I doubt it, and I reckon he's talking about Olwyn Richards, who Fionn was chatting up at the bor at the stort of the night, the jammy, four-eyed focker.

Oisinn's off his tits. He's there, 'Where's the weather girl?' I'm like, 'Toilets,' and he goes, 'What was all that crying about? Did she find out about …' I'm like, 'No, no, RTÉ gave her the old heave-ho.' He nods sort of, like, thoughtfully, roysh, even though he hasn't really got a clue what I said, the music's so loud, and he goes, 'Bummer,' and I'm there, 'Total.'

'Shackles' comes on, roysh, and JP's giving it loads out on the dancefloor and he gives me the old thumbs-up, roysh, and I do it back – focker still hasn't given me my five hundred bills back – and Christian's chatting up some bird I know to see from the M1 and he's telling her that he senses a strange disturbance in the Force, which is his usual chat-up line, roysh, and she's sort of, like, leaning away from him, as though he's completely off his rocker, which he actually is. I'm worried about the goy, though, the way he's been tanning the beer lately.

The next thing I know, Georgia's back from the toilets and she's, like, tied her cardigan around her waist, roysh, and she's wearing this halterneck top, which is pretty revealing and it's only when she goes, 'Do you want to stay in Amy's house with me? Her parents are in Bologna,' that I realise she's a lot more pissed than I actually thought and I tell her I'll basically go and get my jacket. Probably a bit of a shitty thing to do actually, giving her an old rattle tonight, then the Spanish archer tomorrow, but as the goys always say, you don't put three weeks of spadework into a job and then give up when the treasure's in sight.

I knock back the rest of my pint, roysh, and I look up and – FOCK! am I cursed, or something? – you will not believe who's suddenly standing there in front of me. We're talking Heidi, the bird I was with three nights ago, the Yasmine Bleeth ringer, who may have got the impression, from some of the things I said, that me and her were an item now. I'm just there going, How the *fock* do I get out of this one?

Heidi looks at me and goes, 'Hi, Ross,' and Georgia, roysh, sensing another bird moving in on her patch, she sits beside me on the couch, or sort of, like, flops down, she's that off her tits, and she links my orm and Heidi – who I have to say is actually looking really well – she goes, 'Oh, I see you've moved on, Ross.'

I'm fairly well-on myself at this stage and I can hordly string a sentence together, it has to be said. I go, 'That's roysh, Heidi. Onwards and upwards,' which I'm kicking myself for saying because it's her I'd rather be with tonight. Heidi, roysh, she looks Georgia up and down and she goes, 'I'd *hordly* call that upwards.' And Georgia, roysh, she's having none of it, she turns around to me and she goes, 'Sorry, who is this … *girl?*' Heidi, roysh, who's, like, well able for her, fair focks to her, she goes, 'I'm Heidi. And I know who you are.' Georgia goes, 'Oh, I recognise you now. What school was it you went to, Mount Anything?' And Heidi's like, 'Better than Collars-Up, Knickers-Down.'

I have to say, roysh, it's fascinating to watch. One says something really bitchy and just as you're thinking there's no coming back from that, the other says something even better. Georgia goes, 'You're in Emma's class, my *little* sister,' trying to, like, put her down, making out she's only a kid or something, but Heidi's there, 'Your sister is a knob, just like you.' Georgia stands up, roysh, and she goes, 'My sister is *not* a focking knob,' and Heidi laughs, roysh, shakes her head and goes, '*Oh* my God, she does supervised study, like, every night.'

At this stage, roysh, it looks like it might get ugly, so just, like, to defuse the tension, if that's the roysh word, I decide to go and get another pint in, maybe find the lads, but Heidi all of a sudden goes, 'Ross obviously hasn't told you about us, has he?' Oh fock. Georgia's like, 'I'm not interested in whatever mistakes Ross might have made in the distant past.' And Heidi goes, 'Distant past? Try Wednesday night.'

So Georgia's just sitting there, roysh, with her mouth open, like a fish, and she's storting to, like, hyperventilate, she can't get any words out, so she just picks up a bottle of Coors Light and, like, dumps the whole lot over my focking head, then runs out of the place bawling her eyes out. Heidi tells me I'm pathetic and focks off as well.

One of Georgia's mates, roysh – not the one JP was with, the other one, I think she's doing Tourism Management and Morkeshing in LSB – she comes over and tells me I'm an orsehole and, in my defence, I'm there, 'I wasn't going out with Georgia, you know. We were only seeing each other.'

I sit there for a few minutes, completely focking soaked, just knowing that my new light blue Ralph is going to reek of beer now, and I'm sort of thinking about maybe heading to the jacks to stick it under the drier and then going off to look for Heidi, but I'm so off my face at this stage I really couldn't be orsed.

I can't actually remember how long I'm sitting there when all of a sudden JP comes over, roysh, and sits down next to me and he goes, 'What the fock happened?' I'm like, 'Georgia found out about Heidi. You owe me five hundred bills, by the way.'

He goes, 'It's coming, my man. You were going to give Georgia the flick anyway, weren't you?' I'm like, 'Yeah, *totally*,' and he smiles and goes, 'Well then, every clide has a silver lining,' and I have to laugh.

✳✳✳

I skip my three o'clock, head out to Oisinn's gaff and I find him sitting at the kitchen table with a scissors, a Pritt Stick and a stack of newspapers. I'm there, 'I didn't know we'd homework,' and he goes, 'Not homework. I've come up with a plan for the statue. Look at *this*.'

We've Got eros
A grand in the bin
next tO the bLOb
AT NOOn On
FRIDay
Or youLl nevVer
sEe him agAin
No Feds

I go, 'Like it, Oisinn,' and he winks at me. I'm like, 'Is it gonna work?' He goes, 'You are looking at a criminal mastermind.' I'm there, 'Glad to hear it. I could do with the shekels. The debs cleaned me out.'

***

I get this text from Georgia, roysh, and it's like:

> WE REGRET TO INFORM
> CUSTOMERS THAT THE
> EIRCELL NETWORK HAS GONE
> DOWN. HOWEVER THIS WILL
> NOT AFFECT YOU AS NOT
> EVEN A NETWORK WOULD GO
> DOWN ON YOU!

What a total bunny-boiler. I'm just, like, you know, 'Get over it, girl.'

CHAPTER THREE
'Ross is, like, SUCH an orsehole to women.'
Discuss.

When Christian asked me to go with him to the premiere of that focking *Bridget Jones' Diary*, roysh, he never told me it was in the Savoy, we're talking on the focking *northside* here. Pork the cor in my usual spot in Stephen's Green, and as we're, like, walking down Grafton Street, I'm suddenly thinking, Hang on, what cinemas are on the southside?

Of course my worst fears are confirmed, roysh, when we cross over onto Westmoreland Street – that sort of, like, no man's land between *us* and *them* – and I realise the crazy bastard is actually thinking of bringing me the other side of the Liffey.

I stop, roysh, just before we cross over the bridge, we're talking O'Connell Bridge, and I go, 'You are *not* focking serious, I hope.' He's like, 'Don't centre on your anxieties,' and I'm there, 'Quit it with that Obi Wan bullshit, will you? Do you know what they do to people like us over there? These people aren't walking uproysh that long.' He just laughs and carries on walking and, well, the goy's my best friend, roysh, can't let him do this on his own, so I follow him across the bridge and I go, 'This is suicide.'

There's a goy selling newspapers who shouts something in Northside, which I don't understand, though I think I caught the word 'Hedild' in there somewhere. The whole focking street is just, like, burger bors, with all these peasants in them getting their dinner. We cross over onto this traffic island, and this goy – twenty-quid jeans and hundred-quid runners, the usual skobie uniform, and a big red inbreeder's face to go with it – he bumps me with his shoulder as he's passing me, we're talking on purpose here. I mean, there's two of us, roysh, and one of him, but he doesn't give a fock. I turn around, roysh, and he's come back towards me, going, 'Have you got a bleedin' problem?' I'm there, 'You just bumped into me. Did your old dear not teach you how to say sorry, or was she too busy on the game?' He looks totally, like, stunned by this, doesn't know what to say, roysh, he's obviously so used to people going, 'Oooh, no, I haven't got a problem,' and he just manages to get out the words, 'Are ye wantin' yisser go?' when all of a sudden, roysh, Christian hits him a box that comes from, I don't know, the next focking postal code – BANG! – and the goy's laid out flat on his back. I stand over him and go, 'See what you get when you fock with the Rock, you piece of vermin. You'll be selling your cigarette lighters tomorrow in a neck-brace.'

We head on, roysh, manage to get to the Savoy without any further incidents. Christian hands me my ticket outside and we head in and meet a few of his friends from his film course in the lobby, roysh – two blokes who are both complete dickheads and four birds, three of them are bet-down, the other I'd file under 'Ugly But Rideable'. Anyway, roysh, they're wanking on about how Hugh Grant has been typecast as the slightly repressed, upper-class, English fop and how this new role has opened up a whole new anti-hero persona that will allow him to explore his range as an actor. I just go, 'Yeah, roysh,' and head off for a wander, see if there's any scenario about the place.

So there I am, roysh, scoping this bird who looks a bit like Winona Ryder – or I Wanna Ryder, as I call her – when all of a sudden, roysh, there's all these flashbulbs going off outside and who walks in? We're talking Renée *focking* Zellwegger, and she looks incredible. I decide there and then, roysh, that I'm going to try to be with her, so I join this queue of all these film-industry tossers waiting to talk to her. About ten minutes later, roysh, I'm in front of her and I'm giving it, 'Hey,' and she's there, 'Hello,' and I'm like, 'You having a good night?' and just as she's about to answer, roysh – and I'm *really* pleased with this – I go, 'Shut up. Just shut up. You had me at Hello,' and she cracks her shite laughing, and I'm in, I am SO in.

She goes, 'It's great to see you again. How was Paris? Did you go to that restaurant I told you about?' and it's pretty obvious, roysh, that she thinks I'm someone else, and that's alroysh by me because she's focking quality and I'm there telling the old pant python to behave himself. I'm like, 'The restaurant? Yeah, it was Kool and the Gang,' and suddenly, roysh, everyone's going in to watch the film and Renée Zellwegger links my orm – links MY focking orm – and we're heading into the VIP area when this bouncer, the biggest creamer you've ever seen, stops me and asks me where my pass is. He goes, 'Where's yisser pass?' I'm there, 'It's alroysh, I'm with Renée Zellwegger,' and he's just like, 'No one gets in wirourra pass.' Stick a skobie in a monkey suit and give him a walkie-talkie and he thinks he's the focking Terminator.

Probably took the wrong tack with him, roysh, when I went, 'It'll be back to the dole queue and stealing fireplaces from building sites for you when Renée Zellwegger's people find out you've dissed her date for the night.' He goes, 'Couldn't give a bollicks,' and, of course, Renée Zellwegger's off talking to some other bloke now, this tit with a ponytail and, seeing the head-lines 'Renée Zellwegger's New Mystery Man' slipping away, I make the mistake of going to step over the rope into the VIP section, roysh.

Next thing I feel this orm around my neck and my feet are, like, off the ground, and I can see Christian and his orsehole film mates staring in, like, horror as the skobie in the tux carries me out of the cinema and basically throws me out onto the street, in the middle of Knackeragua. He's there, 'You were warned,' and I just, like, dust the old chinos down and go, 'Your orse is SO fired.'

✱✱✱

To whom it may concern,

Many thanks for your recent ransom note. Please accept my apologies for the delay in replying. My secretary is away on maternity leave at the moment and I'm not very well organised. Your letter got mixed up in a stack of essays I was correcting and I've only this minute laid my hands on it again.

As to your request for £1,000, unfortunately the department doesn't have sufficient finance to undertake this kind of project at this time. We will keep your letter on file and, in the event of a budget being set aside for meeting extortion and blackmail demands, we will endeavour to contact you.

Can you please pass on the best wishes of everyone in the Classics Department to *Eros*. We all miss him.

Best wishes,

Francis Hird,
Classics Department, UCD

*** *

Emer's parents' house is worth over a million, roysh, or so she tells us, but Sophie says that that's nothing because there's council houses, *actual* council houses, in Sallynoggin, we're talking Sally-*focking*-noggin here, which are going for two hundred grand. All of the girls go, 'OH! MY! GOD!' and all of the goys go, 'Crazy shit,' except me because I'm only sort of, like, half-listening. Erika is sitting opposite me, roysh, and she's looking pretty amazing I have to say, with that, like, permanent scowl on her face, that's what Fionn calls it – a permanent scowl.

Sent her a text message the other night and it was like, **U R my fantaC. C U l8r**, but she didn't answer it, don't know if she even got it, and now I'm trying to, like, catch her eye, roysh, maybe wink at her across the table, or blow her a kiss, something stupid just to say, you know, 'Me and you. Our little secret,' whatever, but she's totally ignoring the fact that I'm there.

When she finally does look at me, roysh, she goes – at the top of her voice, we're talking – she goes, 'Ross, why are you staring at me?' and I can feel myself go red and Sorcha, roysh, she stares at me and goes, 'How was the debs, by the way,' and it's obvious Erika's told her about knocking me back.

All the goys are cracking their holes laughing, roysh, and I'm so morto I don't know where to put myself, but Sophie rescues me by changing the subject. She goes, 'It's a pity you can't buy, like, a glass of boiled water in a pub,' and Emer's there, 'Oh my God, that reminds me, how many points is a muffin?' and Sophie's like, 'Five-and-a-half.' And Emer's there, 'There's no way that muffin was five-and-a-half,' and Sophie goes, 'Emer, it was an American-style muffin and an American-style muffin is five-and-a-half points. I told you you shouldn't have had it, so don't take it out on me,' and Emer just gives her daggers.

Fionn turns around to me, roysh, and he goes, 'Girls are obsessed with points, aren't they? When we were doing the Leaving, it was getting as many as possible. Now it's eating as few as possible,' which is way too deep for me.

Christian is, like, really quiet, roysh and I ask him if he's alroysh and he says he's cool, but he's tanning the Ken, knocking back two pints for every one I'm drinking.

The girls stort talking about some bird called Rachael who was in Loreto Foxrock and has put on SO much weight since she went on the Pill, and then they're talking about this big night out they have planned, they're going to see Vonda Sheppard, a girls' night out, even though Sophie thinks her latest album SO isn't as good as her last one. And Sorcha says she wouldn't know because she's been listening to mostly classical music lately, especially Elgar's 'Third Movement from Cello Concerto in E Minor Op 85'. Emer goes, 'Oh my God, have you got *The Best Classical Album of the Millennium ... Ever?*' and Sorcha, roysh, real defensive, she goes, 'Yeah, but I've got, like, loads of other classical albums as well as that.' And Fionn goes, 'You've probably got *The Best Classical Album of the Millennium ... Ever Two, Three, Four* and *Five*, have you?' and I high-five him, even though, to be honest, roysh, I don't really get the joke.

Sophie says she *loves* Pachelbel's 'Canon', and Sorcha says she *loves* Rachmaninov's 'Variation 18 from Rhapsody on a Theme by Paganini', roysh, and this pretty much goes on until

Fionn asks whether or not we're going to The Vatican, and that's when we all grab our jackets and stort heading up towards, like, Harcourt Street.

We're pretty much halfway there, roysh, and me and Fionn are walking ahead of everyone, basically talking rugby – Ireland's chances in next year's Six Nations, whether I could be as good as Brian O'Driscoll if I got my finger out, all that – when all of a sudden, roysh, Sorcha shouts up to me, 'Ross, where's Christian?' and I turn back and I go, 'I presumed he was with you goys.' She's there, 'No, he was behind us.'

I tell them all to walk on up, roysh, and I head back towards Grafton Street and I find him outside Planet Hollywood, arguing with the bouncers. They've got, like, whatever they're focking called, C3PO and R2D2, in the window, roysh, and Christian, who's off his face, he wants to go in and touch the two robots, to see if they're, like, the real ones, the ones they used in the movie, which Christian reckons they're not, but the bouncers – you can't blame them – they're having none of it, they're trying to move him along, and all of a sudden he storts going ballistic at them, giving it, 'YOU DON'T OWN THEM! THEY BELONG TO THE PEOPLE!'

I grab him, roysh, and sort of, like, drag him up the street, but we only get, like, ten steps up the road when all of a sudden he stops and storts crying his eyes out, and I keep asking him what's wrong, roysh, but he's too upset to talk and he just grabs me and hugs me there on the street and I'm sort of, like, you know, looking around to see who's, like, watching, not wanting people to think I'm a steamer, obviously.

I'm like, 'What's wrong, Christian?' and he squeezes me horder, roysh, and I can hordly breathe at this stage, and I'm like, 'What is it?' and he goes, 'My parents are getting divorced,' and I can't think of anything to say to the dude, even though he's been my best friend since we were, like, four, and I just end up going, 'That's heavy shit, man.' He's lost it, he's bawling like a baby, going, 'I don't want them to break up. I don't want them to break up,' and I'm there still hugging him, going, 'This is SUCH heavy shit.'

✷✷✷

When we were kids, roysh, Christian's old pair brought the two of us to Lansdowne Road to see Ireland play. It was, like, a Five Nations' match, roysh, against, like, Scotland, and though I remember pretty much nothing about the game, roysh, I know we lost by, like, three points, or maybe it was six, but we lost anyway. Christian said Ireland were crap and his old man said they were far from crap, that if they had in their legs what they had in their hearts then they'd win the Grand Slam every time.

We waited in our seats until about ten minutes after the final whistle, roysh, then we headed around the back of the West Stand and Christian's old man decided we were going to, like, wait in the cor pork and cheer every Irish player onto the bus, to let them know that their courage was appreciated by at least some of the fans.

Me and Christian both had programmes, roysh, and his old man gave us a pen each to get the autographs of the players as they came out. I'm pretty sure it was raining and Christian's old dear put up her umbrella and, like, pulled the two of us under it. And what I remember about that is the smell of her perfume.

After about an hour, roysh, the players storted to come out in twos and threes and, like, make their way to the bus, but I didn't really recognise that many of them, except Brendan Mullin and Donal Lenihan and maybe Willie Anderson. Got loads of autographs, though. Brendan Mullin asked me my name and then he signed it, 'To Ross, best wishes, Brendan Mullin,' which I remember Christian's old man telling me he didn't have to do. He goes, 'A great ambassador for his sport and his country. Didn't have to do that, you know.'

Then Brian Smith came out, roysh, and pretty much everyone there wanted to get his autograph because he was, like, a major stor at the time, so there was all this, like, pushing and shoving to get at him, roysh, and I ended up falling over in this puddle and I was, like, soaking wet and my knee was all, like, grazed and shit. I was, like, bawling my eyes out, more out of embarrassment than anything else, roysh, and Christian's old dear helped me up and told this man who just happened to be standing beside me when I fell that he ought to be ashamed of himself, carrying on like that, and the goy told her he didn't push me, that I fell, and Christian's old dear just looked at him and shook her head.

I remember she rolled up my trouser leg and she took, like, a piece of tissue out of her pocket and used it to clean the blood off my knee. Then she used another piece to wipe my eyes and she, like, gave me a hug and Christian's old man asked us how we'd like a Coke and a packet of crisps, and we went to the Berkeley Court, or maybe it was Jury's, it was one or the other, and that's what we had, Coke and crisps. And me and Christian, roysh, we were, like, flicking through our programmes, looking at all the autographs we'd got, trying to make out who they all were, and I had this, like, squiggle that Christian didn't have and his old man asked to see it, roysh, and he told me it wasn't an Irish player at all, it was actually Gavin Hastings, and he told me I was a lucky man to get the great Gavin Hastings' autograph.

✖✖✖

Sophie rings me, roysh, to tell me that she's going to be late – said I'd go Christmas shopping with her – but there's a signal failure on the Dorsh *again* and – OH! MY! GOD! – it's taken her an hour to get from Glenageary to, like, Booterstown. She goes, 'The Dorsh is a jake, Ross. A complete jake.'

✖✖✖

It's the last day of term, breaking up for Chrimbo today, roysh, and I've got a letter from the head of the course informing me – 'we'd like to inform you' – that I've attended a grand total of ten lectures this term, which is news to me, I didn't think it was as many as that, roysh, but it's not a letter of congratulations. It's like, blah blah blah, doubts about your commitment to the course, bullshit bullshit bullshit, academic dimension to the course must be taken seriously, wank wank wank, monitoring your attendance over coming months. I go to Oisinn, 'Spoke too soon about freedom. School wasn't this focking bad,' and he's like, 'Come on, Ross, cheer up. We're out of here for *four* weeks.'

And you can tell it's the last day of term, roysh, because all the boggers are walking around with, like, rucksacks full of dirty washing, bringing them home to their old dears to wash over the holidays. I see Fionn saying his goodbyes to Kathleen with the peach fuzz. There's more to that than him sussing out a theory. He likes the bird. They're well-suited if you ask me, one's as focking ugly as the other.

She's wearing a Galway bogball jersey, roysh, and it turns out she's from a place called Gort, which I think we passed through on the way down to, like, Ennis two New Years' Eves ago, one of those shithole towns where old men with red hair stand outside the local supermorket on a Sunday afternoon with their mouths open and 'the wireless' up to their ears, going, 'You can never write off Cork,' to passersby. In fact, the red hair's storting to make a bit more sense now. Fionn kisses her goodbye, a big slopping wet one, on the lips, and when he comes over to me and Oisinn, I go, 'You'll need a shot of Ivomec after that,' which I'm pretty happy with because for once, Fionn has no focking answer.

We hit the bor and get off our faces.

✱✱✱

donT fOck About
˄ graNd Oi Well
seND It back to
You in PiECeS

***

It's the day before Christmas Eve, roysh, and we're all having drinks in The Bailey, middle of the afternoon, and Sorcha hands Aoife a present, roysh, and Aoife goes, '*Oh my God!* I haven't got yours with me. I was going to wait until tomorrow night,' and Sorcha says it doesn't matter and Aoife opens the present and it's, like, a 'Friends' video. Aoife's face lights up and Sorcha goes, 'I hope you haven't already got that one,' and then Aoife's face drops, roysh, and she's like, 'Oh shit, I do,' and Sorcha's like, 'I don't believe it. I asked your mom to check whether you had Series 5, Episodes 17-20, 'The One Where Rachel Smokes', and she said you didn't.' Aoife goes, 'She is SUCH a stupid bitch, my mother. It's Series *3*, Episodes 17-20 that I don't have.' Emer, who's, like, first year Morkeshing, Advertising and Public Relations in LSB, she goes, 'Which one is that?' and Aoife's there, "The One With The Princess Leia Fantasy'.' Emer says that is SUCH a good episode, and Sorcha says it's okay because she kept the receipt, just in case.

Emer says there were three refugees outside her old dear's coffee shop all day yesterday, wrecking everyone's heads with their music, those bloody accordions, and Erika says she read somewhere that they're making up to a thousand bills a day – we're talking *each* – from begging and busking, and Emer goes, 'If you could call it busking.' I don't know why, roysh, but I turn around and I go, 'Why don't you lay off the Romanians,' and everyone at the table turns to me, roysh, and looks at me like I'm totally off my focking rocker, and I probably am because *I* can't believe I said it myself. Erika goes, 'Sorry, Ross, *where* is this coming from?' I'm like, 'I don't know. I mean, it's Christmas. Could we not be, like, a bit more, I don't know … caring?'

Erika goes, 'Caring? *Caring*? *Hello*? This *is* Ross O'Carroll-Kelly I'm talking to, isn't it? Most selfish bastard who ever lived.' I'm there, 'I'm not selfish.' And Erika goes, 'Aoife, tell Ross what Bronwyn told us. You remember Bronwyn, Ross? You were with her at the Loreto on the Green pre-debs.' Fock! I know what's coming next. Aoife's cracking her hole laughing, roysh, and she goes, 'According to her, Ross, you bought a packet of condoms. Ribbed, extra-sensitive, for *her* pleasure. Well, according to her, you tried to put one on … inside out.'

I'm there, 'That was a focking accident and she knows it,' but everyone's, like, cracking their shites laughing and I go, 'Look, all I'm saying is, you know, these refugees, they've lost their, like, homes and shit. I mean, how would you like it if you were suddenly dropped in the middle of, I don't know … Budapest,' and Erika goes, 'The capital of Romania, Ross, is Bucharest. And they have Prada there. And Amanda Wakeley.'

***

Christmas in my gaff is a complete mare, and we're talking total here. I wake up in the morning, roysh, about eleven o'clock, feeling pretty shabby I have to say, a feed of pints the night before, hanging big style, and I can hear the old pair downstairs all-focking-over each other, we're talking *total* borf-fest here. It's all, like, squealing and, 'Oooh, it's just what I wanted,' roysh, and I go downstairs to tell the two of them to keep it down, my head hurts. Turns out, roysh, the old dear bought the old man a Callaway ERC2 driver and he bought her, like, jewellery, a shitload of Lladro and a mid-week break at the Powerscourt Springs and they're, like, hugging and kissing each other, roysh, and it's all, 'Happy Christmas, Darling,' and I'm finding it pretty hord to keep this toast down.

They've got me a cor, roysh, a Golf GTI, black, *total* babe magnet, or should I say they're *going* to get me one. I told them to wait until the New Year, roysh, to, like, get the new reg. So anyway, roysh, the old dear hands me this present and she's like, 'Oh, we wanted you to have something to open on the day,' and I'm like, 'What am I supposed to say, yippee-hoo?' but I open it, roysh, just to keep them happy and it's a phone, a *so-called* phone, a Motorola T2288, we're talking a crappy eleven ringtones, we're talking no vibration alert, we're talking only 210 minutes of battery talk-time. I'm like, 'Sorry, what is *this* supposed to be?' and the old man goes, 'It's a mobile phone, Kicker,' and I'm like, 'You are taking the *total* piss here. It's not even focking WAP-enabled,' and I fock it across the table and go upstairs to, like, get dressed. As I'm going up the stairs, I can hear the old dear asking the old man what WAP-enabled means, roysh, and then she says she's so sorry and she feels she's ruined Christmas and then she storts, like, bawling her eyes out, the attention-seeking bitch.

About, like, ten minutes later, roysh, the old man shouts up the stairs to me and he goes, 'Don't be too long, Ross. We're going to go to twelve Mass. As a family,' and I'm like, 'Get real, will you? You retord,' but I end up going anyway, roysh, anything for an easy life, and it's the usual crack, Holy Mary, Mother of God, blah blah blah, and I end up sitting there for the whole thing, texting Christian, Oisinn and everyone else I know to give them, like, my new number and tell them I might see them l8er.

Sophie actually phones me back straight away to say thanks for the Burberry scorf, which I bought her pretty much to piss off Sorcha, who was basically dropping hints to me that she wanted one herself. So Sophie rings, roysh, and I have totally forgotten that the ringtone is switched to, like, 'Auld Lang Syne', and when it goes off this old focking biddy sitting in front of me, she turns around and gives me a total filthy, we're talking daggers here, and I'm like, 'Hang on a sec, Sophie,' and I go, 'Turn the fock around,' and she does as she's told.

And *Oh my God*, roysh, you should have *seen* the state of my old dear, we're talking dressed to focking kill here, and it's, like, guess who spent a grand in Pia Bang yesterday? When she comes back from Communion, roysh, I hear her go to the old man, 'Ann Marie is wearing the same coat she wore last year,' and the old man goes, 'OH! MY! GOD!' out of the corner of his mouth.

Dinner is, like, majorly painful. Dermot and Anita, these dick-head friends of the old pair, roysh, they're invited around and, of course, the whole conversation is dominated by this new campaign they've storted, which is, like, Move Funderland to the Northside. I mean, we don't live anywhere near the focking RDS, roysh, but Anita lives on Sandymount Avenue and, of course, the old dear can't resist it, keeps saying that Anita was so helpful with the Foxrock Against Total Skangers Anti-Halting Site campaign, roysh, that she simply *had* to get involved. What a sap.

She's there going, 'I don't know how you cope, Anita. I really don't,' and Anita's there going, 'We've put up with it for twenty years, Fionnuala. Gangs of what can only be described as gurriers walking by, carrying giant elephants, urinating in our gardens, off to get the Dorsh to – what's this it's called? – Kilbarrack, and God knows wherever else.'

She's going, 'Now don't get me wrong, Charles. We're not anti-Funderland *per se*, are we Dermot? But somewhere like, I don't know, Ballymun, would be a far more appropriate place for it, surely.' The old dear goes, 'Now don't get upset, Anita.

Charles will print out those posters for you tomorrow. Have another drink.'

And Anita, roysh, you can see she's storting to get emotional, already half-pissed on Baileys and mulled wine, and she's going, 'I'm going to picket the RDS, Fionnuala. On my own if I have to. I'm going to flipping well do it.'

This goes on for ages and I basically can't take it anymore, roysh, and I end up going, 'Is this a family dinner or a focking campaign meeting?' and everything goes silent. The old man goes, 'Well, what would *you* like to talk about, Ross?' and I don't know what to say, roysh, so I just end up telling them what a bunch of tossers they look in their paper hats and the old man goes, 'Ross, if you can't keep a civil tongue in your head, I suggest you leave the table,' and I'm like, 'With focking pleasure,' and I grab three cans out of the fridge and head into the sitting room to watch the Bond movie.

So I'm sitting there, roysh, and it's, like, *Octopussy*, and I'm knocking back the beers, milling into the old Quality Street, and my phone rings and it's, like, Fionn, and I'm just like, 'Yo, Fionn, Happy Christmas, my man. Speak to me.' He goes, 'Having a great day here with the family,' – focking weirdo – he's like 'Greetings and felicitations to you and yours.' I'm there, 'What time did you leave the M1 last night?' and he goes, 'It was late. Hey, you won't *believe* who I ended up being with last night.' I'm like, 'Who?' and he goes, 'Esme.' This is the only reason he's ringing me.

I'm just there, 'Who's Esme?' knowing full well who she is, roysh, and he goes, 'Esme. *Hello?* Second year business in Portobello? Looks like Elize Dushku, or so you said.' I tried to be with her two weeks ago in Annabel's, totally crashed and burned, and we're talking TOTALLY. I go, 'I never said she looked like Elize Dushku,' and Fionn's like, 'I *know* you tried to get in there, Ross. No hord feelings. Turns out she goes for goys with glasses. Thinks they're a sign of intelligence.' I'm there, 'What an airhead ... I never said she looks like Elize Dushku,' and Fionn laughs and goes, 'Anyone with any information on the whereabouts of Ross O'Carroll-Kelly's dignity, please contact Gardaí in Dún Laoghaire.'

He goes, 'Christian ended up with this bird from Iceland.' I'm like, 'As in the country?' and he goes, 'No, as in the supermorket. Of course the focking country. What's wrong with you today?' I'm there, 'Sorry, man. Distracted.' He's like, 'Does this have anything to do with Sorcha? I saw her at Mass this morning. Wasn't a happy camper. Asked her whether she'd been talking to you and she practically storted crying.' I'm like, 'Starring role in a period costume drama?' and he goes, 'Maybe. I wondered if she found out about you and Erika.' I'm like, 'Erika. Now you're getting to it. Can't stop thinking about her, Fionn. Fock, don't know why I'm spilling my guts like this, sounds a bit gay, I know.'

Fionn goes, 'Take my advice, Ross. Do *not* go there.' I'm like, 'JP reckons she's saving herself for Ben Affleck,' and he goes, 'It's not that, Ross. She's into horses.' I'm there, 'And your point is?' and he's like, 'Take it from someone who's pissing his way through first year psychology. I know what I'm talking about. No girl who's into horses can ever truly love a goy.' I'm like, 'Is that because of the size of their–' and he goes, 'Ross, try to forget about your schlong for one minute, will you? Now think about all the girls we know who have horses. Alyson Berry. Amy Holden. Caoimhe Kelly.' I'm there, 'I thought you told me to stop thinking about my schlong,' but he ignores me and goes, 'Medb Long. Becky Cooper. Maggie Merriman. What have they all got in common?' I'm like, 'I've been with them all,' and he goes, 'Apart from that?' I'm like, 'Em, they've all got horses.' He goes, 'And they're focking wenches. Stuck-up. Moody. Selfish. Cold. Stubborn. Whatever. The very qualities you associate with horses. I'll make this simple for you. Horses aren't nice animals. They're not loyal. They're not friendly. And they don't need human love. They want apples and carrots and if you don't bring them, they go into a sulk.'

I'm like, 'I'm missing *Octopussy* here, Fionn.' He goes, 'Girls like Erika, they've been trying their whole lives to relate to these animals, to get love from them, but they can't. Erika knows that however much she feeds that animal, brushes him, cleans him, he's never going to feel the same way about her as she does about him. The first love of her life was unrequited. And that's focked her up. Goes for all girls whose daddys buy them horses when they're kids.'

I'm there, 'I've got to go. Bell you later.'

The next thing I hear when I get off the phone, roysh, is the old dear coming into the room, with a bottle of Sheridans in one hand and a big heart-shaped box of, like, Butler's chocolates in the other. I'm like, 'What do you want?' and she goes, 'Three o'clock, Ross. The Queen's speech,' and I'm there, 'If you think you're coming in here to watch that bullshit, you can think again.' She goes, 'It's only ten minutes long,' and I'm there, '*Hello?* There are six other televisions in this house. Watch one of them, you stupid wagon,' and she focks off.

I sit around for another, like, ten or fifteen minutes, just thinking about Erika, roysh, and about what Fionn said and whether I only really want her because she's the only girl in the world I can't have roysh now. I decide to give her a call. The best way to play it, I decide, is Kool and the Gang, so I phone her up, roysh, and I'm like, 'Hey babe, how the hell are ya?' She goes, 'Who is this?' sounding like she's pretty pissed off about something, which is pretty much the way she sounds all of the time. I'm like, 'It's Ross. Just wondering how your Christmas is going.'

She goes, 'Look, I'm going to save you a lot of heartache and save myself a major headache by telling you, *again*, that I have no interest in you.' I'm there, 'Hey babe, why so hostile?' and she goes, 'I'm only stretching this conversation beyond one sentence because I want you to get this into your head once and for all.' I'm there, 'Well, you seemed pretty interested a few weeks ago. The stables, remember?' She goes, '*Get* a life, will you. If you must know, I did that because I was pissed off with Sorcha.'

I'm like, 'Sorcha?' and she's there, 'Sorcha. You know, as in your girlfriend? *"All this subtext is making me tired".*' I have to say, she does the voice really well. I'm like, 'Look, why don't I call over to your gaff?' and she, like, breaks her shite laughing, roysh, and goes, 'You really think that under this hord outer shell there's a vulnerable, sensitive little girl who's going to melt into your orms when she hears all your bullshit lines, don't you?'

Not trying to be big-headed or anything, but I go, 'You did in the past,' and she's like, 'We were at school then. I was sixteen. That was back in the days when you *were* someone,' and I'm like, 'Meaning?' She goes, 'You were on the senior rugby team, Ross. Being with you was, like, a status thing. Who are you now? You're doing Sports Management, for fock's sake. You're not even playing for UCD.'

Below the belt. I go, 'Yeah, I've been mostly chilling this year. I mean, I SO have to get my finger out, I know that. The goy who has my place on the team, Matthew Path, he's shite. He's a focking Blackrock boy, for fock's sake. I could easily take his place. If I do, would you be interested then?'

She tells me I'm basically making a fool of myself, roysh, then says she has neither the energy nor the interest to continue the conversation further and she hangs up.

I think about calling her back, roysh, but she's left me a bit shell-shocked, to be honest. She's roysh. My name used to mean something. Every girl wanted to say she'd been with Ross O'Carroll-Kelly. Time has moved on, I guess.

In the kitchen, the old dear has put on her new Charlotte focking Church album and the old man gives one of his big false laughs to some obviously unfunny thing that, like, Dermot has said. I go into the study and grab the tape of the senior cup final, fast-forward it to my winning try and spend the next, like, twenty minutes watching it and then rewinding it and watching it over and over again. Rewind and play. Rewind and play. Then my interview with Ryle Nugent. 'That's a good question, Ryle. I can't take all the credit for this victory, though. Some of it has to go to the goys.'

And in the background, roysh, you can see all these blue jumpers. Mounties. We're talking hundreds of them. And I think I can even make out Erika – her hair was shorter then, still a dead-ringer for Denise Richards though – and she's hanging on my every word. I think I might have even been with her that night …

I put the lid back on the Quality Street, knock back the last of the cans and make my New Year's resolutions. Get fit. Get on the UCD team. Get Erika.

Then I go into the kitchen and tell the old man to keep the fake focking laughter down.

✱✱✱

I call out to Sorcha's gaff on Stephen's Day, roysh, and it's the usual crack from her old dear, who SO wants me to get back with her daughter it's not funny. She's all over me, we're talking TOTALLY here. It's all hugs and kisses and I'm just there going, Guess who got a bottle of Chanel No 5 for Christmas? The gaff is full, of course. The Lalors always have, like, half the focking world around to eat the Christmas leftovers, and when the old dear's finished air-kissing and squeezing the shit out of me, she leads me around the house, introducing me to aunts and uncles and neighbours and clients of the old man and a few ladies-who-lunch types who, I presume, spend a lot of money in that boutique she has in the Merrion Shopping Centre. Sometimes she goes, 'This is Ross O'Carroll-Kelly, Sorcha's friend. He was on the Castlerock team that won the cup,' and other times it's, 'This is Ross, Charles O'Carroll-Kelly's son, very good friends with Sorcha.' Then she offers me, in the following order: a slice of banoffi, a glass of mulled wine, a turkey-and-stuffing toasted sandwich, a piece of plum-pudding, a can of lager, some Baileys and a home-made mince pie, and I say no to all of them and then there's pretty much nothing else to say, roysh, and we're both standing there like a couple of spare pricks, so she just tells me that Sorcha's in her room and to go on up to her.

She's lying on her bed, roysh, wearing her black Armani jeans and a white airtex with the collar up, and she's, like, flicking through the channels on the telly. She doesn't even acknowledge me and I just sort of, like, hang around in the doorway and I ask her whether she's pissed off with me about something and she goes, 'Why would I give a shit what you do with your life?'

Her room has actually been decorated, pretty recently I'd say, and I basically tell her that it's changed a good bit and she looks at me for the first time and goes, 'It *has* changed, Ross. The last time you were in here, you were with my little sister,' and I turn around and stort, like, heading downstairs, but she calls me back and says she's sorry and then she, like, gives me a hug and wishes me a Merry Christmas. She goes, 'I don't know why I insist on reliving, in excruciating detail, one of the most painful experiences of our lives. Maybe it's my perversely self-deprecating way of moving on. Or maybe I'm still trying to punish you.'

I sit down on the bed and she lies down with her head on my lap and asks me to, like, pet her face, which is something I used to always do when we were, like, going out together, and I can't work out whether she actually wants to be with me, or whether it's just, like, a prick-tease, but I do it anyway.

I ask her why she's not downstairs at the porty and she goes, 'Because I'm tired of my mother's projection fantasies,' and I don't have a focking clue what she's talking about, so I just go, 'Bummer.'

She says that the millennium turned out to be one complete bummer and that Cillian was the only decent thing that happened to her in the year 2000, and I'm like, 'Is this the twenty-eight-year-old?' and she nods and goes, 'I should say that Cillian and *you* were the only decent things that happened this year,' and all of a sudden, roysh, I'm pretty certain that I'm going to end up, like, getting my bit here and I stop petting her face and go, 'What do you mean, *I* was one of the decent things that happened?' She goes, 'Well, not so much *you*, Ross, as *us*.

After years of gratuitous self-examination, we've finally got past that whole relationship checkmate thing.'

Your guess is as good as mine, but I get the impression, roysh, she's trying to get across the point that she's not actually interested in me anymore, which is total bullshit because I notice she has *The Very Best of Ennio Morricone*, the CD I bought her for her birthday last year, on her bedside locker – I say *bought*, I actually robbed it off the old man – and I'm pretty sure that before I arrived she was listening to 'Gabriel's Homo', or whatever it's called, wondering whether I was going to call up.

But she's obviously playing hord-to-get, roysh, so I sort of, like, change tack and go, 'I was talking to Erika earlier,' but instead of getting jealous she goes, 'She's making a fool out of you, Ross,' and I'm like, 'Spare me.' She goes, 'Nothing that girl does bothers me anymore. You know what she said in the bor the other night? She said that wheelie bins are working class. I'd hate to see you get hurt, Ross. She's an orsehole. I should know, she's one of my best friends.'

We lie there on her bed for a couple of hours. We watch 'The Royle Family'. Eventually I tell her that I've got to go and she tells me she's SO happy I called up, that Christmas wouldn't be the same without seeing me and that she's glad we're over 'that whole relationship trauma'. I tell her I'm going back playing rugby and she tells me it's not going to change the way she feels about us. She goes, 'Me and Cillian are too strong.'

She takes off her scrunchy, slips it onto her wrist, shakes her hair free and then smoothes it back into a low ponytail again, puts it back in the scrunchy and then pulls five or six, like, strands of hair loose.

As I'm leaving, roysh, she asks me how Christian is. I go, 'Not good. You heard he was done for drunk-and-disorderly last weekend?' Sorcha's like, 'I can't *believe* his parents are splitting up. Trevor and Andrea? OH! MY! GOD! It's, like, SUCH a shock.'

I go, 'I know,' but I can't look at her when I say it. She gives me a hug and says that Christian's SO lucky to have a best friend like me and she knows that I'll be there for him. I go, 'I don't know what to say to the goy,' and she goes, 'Just be yourself and be there for him.'

CHAPTER FOUR
'Ross, like, so loves himself it's not funny.'
Discuss.

Hazel is this bird I met in the M1, roysh, a Montessori teacher and a total lasher, we're talking SO like Rachael Leigh Cook it's just not funny. There I was, roysh, sitting up at the bor with Christian and Fionn, just talking about, like, rugby and shit, when her and a couple of her friends – recognised one of them from The Palace, Orna I think her name is, second year Law in Portobello – they come up and they're, like, ordering drinks, roysh, and this Orna one picks up Fionn's mobile phone and, the usual, storts, like, scrolling down through his phonebook, going, 'Keavo? OH! MY! GOD! is that Alan Keaveney?'

I turn around to Hazel, who's paying for, like, two vodka and Red Bulls and a Smirnoff Ice, roysh, and stort chatting away to her, working the old charm on her. I ask her what Montessori actually is, roysh, but of course I'm too busy thinking of my next killer line to listen properly to what she's saying, though from what I can make out it's pretty much the same as, like, a normal nursery school, except that instead of giving the kids, like, paint and jigsaws and shit, they teach them focking Japanese and how to play the violin.

Of course, I'm there cracking on to be really interested. End of the night, roysh, Christian's focked off home, because his old man moved out of the house today and he wants to make sure his old dear is alroysh, I mean, I offered to go with him, but he said he wanted to be on his own, and it's just me, Fionn, Orna and Hazel left. Orna is completely off her tits, roysh, and she keeps telling us she has to have an essay in for Tort tomorrow and she hasn't done a tap on it and that the Law course in LSB is so much horder than it is in UCD, but when you tell people that – OH! MY! GOD! – no one believes you.

Eventually, roysh, Fionn leans over to me and goes, 'I'm going to drop the old Chief Justice here home,' and I high-five the dude and he helps her off the stool and out the door. Hazel, roysh, she shows no sign of following, so obviously I'm there thinking, I'm well in here. I go, 'So, where are you living?' still playing it Kool and the Gang, and she goes, 'Sandycove,' and I'm like, 'I've been known to find myself in that particular vicinity. Can I drive you home? We're talking Golf GTI. Black. *With* alloys,' and she goes, '*Oh* my God! Cool.'

So there we are in the cor, roysh, heading out towards her gaff, and I decide it's time to put on the old *Pretty Woman* tape, but I can't remember whether I've, like, rewound the tape to the stort of 'Fallen'. If I haven't, roysh, she's going to get an earful of Roy Orbison giving it, 'Whoooah-hoh, Pretty Woman,' which is actually a pretty good song, but a bit of a passion-killer.

So I'm basically taking a bit of a chance hitting the play button, roysh, but it's cool because the next thing I hear is, like, Lauren Wood's voice and Hazel goes, 'OH! MY! GOD! I don't believe it,' and I'm like, 'What?' cracking on to be all surprised. She goes, '*Oh* my God, this *has* to be fate. This is, like, my favourite song of all time,' and I'm like, 'Really? Who is it, Samantha Mumba?' She goes, 'It's from *Pretty Woman*. Is this a tape?' and I'm there giving it, 'No, it's just the radio,' and she goes, 'OH! MY! GOD! then this *has* to be fate. Every time I hear this song I'm going to think of you now.'

If only she knew how many locks I've picked with this tape.

So we pull up outside her gaff, roysh, massive pad, her old man must be minted, and she goes, '*Oh* my God, I said I wouldn't let this happen,' and I'm like, 'Let what happen?' and she goes, 'I promised myself that I wouldn't fall so easily again. Especially after Cian.' I'm like, 'Who's Cian,' as if I give a fock. I'm just getting ready to bail in here. She goes, 'You don't want to know,' and she's bang-on there.

She looks away and she goes, 'I got really hurt,' and of course I'm like, 'Hey, just go with the flow,' and I move in for the kill, roysh, but as I go to throw the lips on her she goes, 'What are you doing?' and I'm like, 'Hey, a little bit of what you fancy is good for you.' I hate myself for using Oisinn's chat-up lines, but it's fock-all use anyway because she pushes me away, just as Roy Orbison comes on as it happens. I'm wondering has she fallen to the communists, but she says it's just that she wants to, like, take things a bit more slowly. It looks very much to me as

though this could be a two-day job, which, under normal cir-
cumstances, roysh, would be enough to put me off completely,
but she asks me what I'm doing tomorrow night and, of course,
now I've got to face the old dilemma: do I cut my losses now
and just tell her I'm emigrating to Outer Mongolia, or do I go for
a second crack at it?

One thing is certain, roysh, this whole taking-things-a-bit-
more-slowly shit sounds like she has a potential relationship on
her mind, and even though I know it's a mistake, roysh, I end
up giving her my number, my actual *real* number, and she says
she'll, like, give me a call the next day. Which she does, the sad
bitch, she rings me at, like, eleven the next morning, roysh, a bit
too John B, and asks me whether I fancy going, like, bowling.
I'm like, Bowling? *Hello?* Is this bird a knob or what? Of course
I'm still in the scratcher when she rings, having skipped my
eleven o'clock, and I'm pretty much half-asleep, which is why I
end up agreeing to meet her in Stillorgan.

So that afternoon, roysh, I'm pulling into the cor pork, thinking, If any of the goys find out I'm bowling with a bird, I'm to-
taled. And this is where it all goes pear-shaped. Unbeknownst
to me, she's bringing her whole focking class with her, we're
talking a school trip here, with me roped in as a focking child-
minder for the day. We are talking total mortification and we are
talking TOTALLY.

I'm in such a Pauline, roysh, that I end up having a row with
the bird who gives out those crappy shoes. First of all, roysh,
she says I can't wear the old Dubes, even though they've got,

like, white soles. She goes, 'You have to use the house shoes,' namely these half-red, half-blue things that make you look like a complete knob. And then, roysh, she tells me she needs a deposit of, like, five bills. I'm like, '*Hello?* I've just handed you a pair of shoes that cost eighty bills. Do you honestly think I'm going to run off with these focking things?' and I point down to my feet, roysh, but she just goes, 'That will be five pounds, Sir,' like she's a focking robot or something.

And the kids, roysh, they're all little shits, brilliant at bowling of course, every focking one of them, probably part of the, like, curriculum, if that's the roysh word.

And Hazel, roysh, she keeps coming up to me going, '*Oh* my God, you are so good with kids,' obviously morking me down as future marriage material. I'm there going, Do not even *go* there, girl.

She obviously didn't see me whacking one of the little spoilt shits around the ear. The little focker kicked me, roysh, and told me I was rubbish at bowling, so I hit him a sly little slap around the head, the kind the referee never sees, then bent back one of his fingers and told him he was a spoilt little brat and, of course, he goes bawling his eyes out to Hazel, who is such a sad bitch she actually believes me when I tell her he caught his fingers in the bowling ball, and the kid stays out of my way for the rest of the day, the clever boy.

Then, roysh, it's all across the road to McDonalds, me trying to talk to Hazel, to find out, obviously, if I've any focking chance of getting my bit at the end of all this, and her reminding me to keep my eyes on the ten or eleven little shits who are walking behind us. I feel like the old woman who lived in the focking shoe, sitting there in McD's with all these little fockers running around me. And they're all going, 'Are you Hazel's boy-friend?'

And this one kid, roysh, he sucks a load of Coke up into his straw, roysh, and I swear to God the little bastard's about to, like, spit it at me, and I go, '*Don't* even think about it.' And Hazel all of a sudden jumps up and goes, 'NO, ROSS!' and I'm like, 'What?' thinking, I haven't even hit the little focker yet. She goes, 'You're not allowed to use the D-word to the young peo-ple.' I'm like, 'What D-word?' She goes, 'The D-O-N-Apostrophe-T word. You're not supposed to say *Don't* or *Can't* to the young people. They're negatives, you see.'

I'm like, 'So what do you do then, just slap them?' and she looks at me totally horrified, like I've just shat on her Corn Flakes. She goes, 'You *never* hit young people, Ross. Nobody should live in fear of violence. When you're trying to stop a young person from acting in an anti-social way, you have to ac-knowledge that emotions are involved. So to stop Lorcan from spitting his drink at you, what you should say is, 'I understand *why* you want to do that and I understand that you are upset that I'm asking you *not* to do it, but I really feel that ...' And as she's saying this, roysh, the little focker sitting next to Lorcan is squashing a bit of gherkin into the table.

I just get up and head for the door, roysh, wave at Hazel, and I go, '*Arrivederci*,' which, I remember on the way home, isn't actually Japanese, but I'm sure she got the message anyway.

✳✳✳

I'm in Stillorgan Shopping Centre, roysh, doing a bit of shopping, actually looking for a new pair of rugby boots, and I'm backing out of a porking space when the phone rings and it's, like, Keevo, a Blackrock head but sound anyway. He's like, 'Ross, I've a good one for you.' I'm there, 'Keevo, now is not a good time, my man,' and he's like, 'It won't take long.' I'm there going, 'What is it?' and he's like, 'Think of a number between one and ten.' And I'm like, 'Okay, hang on … roysh, got one.' He goes, 'Roysh, add four.' I'm like, 'Okay.' He goes, 'Now, double it.' And I'm like, 'Hold on, hold on … roysh.' He's there, 'Now, halve it. And I'm like, 'O-kaaaay.' Then he goes, 'Take away four,' and I'm like, 'Yyyeah,' and he goes, 'And you're left with six.' I'm like, 'No. I'm left with four.' He goes, 'Oh, roysh. No, it doesn't always work.' And he hangs up. And this so worries me, roysh, because Keevo is, like, second year theoretical physics.

✳✳✳

To whom it may concern,

Many thanks for your letter. It was a pleasant surprise to hear from you again. Please accept my apologies for the delay in replying. The college was closed for three weeks for Christmas holidays and I was off work for an extra week due to salmonella poisoning, which I contracted from a piece of turkey which hadn't been thoroughly re-heated.

I note with interest your threat to send *Eros* back to us 'in pieces'. Personally – and I'm not speaking for the entire Department here – I do not see this as a particularly bad thing. I'm not sure whether you have had a chance to view the *Venus de Milo* in the Louvre in Paris, but it has both upper limbs missing and this has merely added to not detracted from its charm.

You will also notice that *Eros* is already missing an arm, the consequence of a similar Rag Day prank, in 1978 I think I'm right in saying. The missing arm, I believe, has given it that classic, ancient look.

Notwithstanding all of this, I must repeat my earlier assertion that the Department does not have sufficient finance to become involved in a project such as this at this time. Incidentally, if you are experiencing financial hardship, as many students do, you might like to know that the college bookshop is currently having a sale. There's up to 30% off some titles.

Happy new year, and regards to *Eros*.

Francis Hird,
Classics Department, UCD

✳✳✳

Sophie takes five minutes to chew one mouthful of popcorn, roysh, and it is, like, seriously storting to wreck my head, and we're talking TOTALLY here, and when I ask her what the fock she's doing, roysh, she says she read in some magazine, maybe *Cosmo* or *InStyle*, that you don't put on as much weight if you, like, chew your food for longer. Chloë, who's, like, second year International Commerce with German, SO like Heidi Klum it's unbelievable – scored her at the Traffic Light Ball – she asks Sophie whether she's seen Valerie lately and Sophie goes, 'Valerie as in first year Strategic Morkeshing in LSB?' and Chloë nods and says she has put on SO much weight and, she's not being a bitch or anything, but OH! MY! GOD! she's actually a size sixteen, and Sophie asks her how she knows and Chloë tells her that she's storted working in Benetton, just to get money together for Australia if she decides to go for the year, and Valerie came into the shop last week. Sophie goes, '*Oh my God!* she used to be SO gorgeous. She brought Alex Gaffney to the Holy Child Killiney debs,' and Chloë's there, 'I SO know.'

I knock back the rest of my Coke, roysh, and I get up to go and Sophie asks me whether I've got a lecture this afternoon. I'm like, 'Had a ten o'clock, but I skipped it. I'm just going off to practice my kicking for a couple of hours.' She asks me whether I've been talking to Sorcha. I say no, roysh, so she tells me the plan for Saturday night has changed, that Gisele has decided to have her going-away somewhere in town, because the problem with Clone 92 is that if the bouncers, like, turn you away, then that's your night over, you're stranded in Leopardstown. She says that Erika won't go there anyway because she reckons it's full of skobies.

I bump into the goys at the Blob, we're talking Christian and Oisinn, and they're about to go on the serious lash with Fionn. Christian already reeks of drink and I'm not sure if it's from this morning or last night. Oisinn goes, 'Where are you going?' and I'm like, 'Training.' Oisinn's there, 'Training? What are you *training* for?' I'm like, 'Rugby. *Hello?* We are all doing *sports* scholarships, remember?' And Christian's there, 'Is this because of what it says on the door of the jacks?' Oisinn's there, 'Leave it, Christian,' and I'm like, 'What does it say in the jacks?' Oisinn goes, 'Just something about you being finished. Past it. You have had a lot of injuries, Ross. I know you were breaking your balls to get back.' Christian goes, 'They call you Tampax, Ross. One week in and three weeks out.' I'm like, 'They call me that?' and Oisinn, roysh, he looks off into the distance and goes, 'Some do. You've had very bad luck with injuries, though.'

So I head down to the gym, roysh, do some stretches, and then do half-an-hour on the treadmill, after which I'm, like, to-tally shagged. But I am so determined to get fit, roysh, that I go roysh through the pain barrier. I do, like, half-an-hour on the bike and a few weights and then I head out with a ball to, like, practice my kicking. It's focking pissing rain. I basically hate January.

When I get to the field, roysh, who's there before me only Matthew Path, the knob whose place on the team I'm about to take, and he's, like, practicing his kicking as well, roysh, and when he sees me he storts totally gicking himself. I stand there and watch him for, like, twenty minutes, really psyching the goy out of it and in the end, and I'm not being a bastard here or anything, the goy couldn't hit a donkey's orse with a banjo. He's taking kicks from, like, different angles, roysh, and even in front of the post he goes and misses and he's getting, like, totally flustered, doesn't have the big-match temperament, as Sooty, our old coach, used to say. It's no wonder UCD are focked.

When he finally gets one between the posts, roysh, I just stort clapping, sort of, like, sarcastically, if that's the roysh word. Then I head over and stand in front of him and I've got my old Castlerock jersey on, roysh, and I point to the badge and go, 'You know what this means, don't you?' and he goes, 'It means you went to a school for wankers,' and quick as a flash I'm like, 'It actually means that you can go home now,' and then I go, 'You're excess baggage,' which, I have to say, I'm pretty pleased with, roysh, even though I don't know where I got it from.

He goes, 'You're living on past glories,' and I'm there giving it, 'Your girlfriend didn't seem to think so,' and then I push him out of the way and go, 'Learn from the master.' I stort spotting the balls, roysh, and kicking them at the goal he's been using and he stands there and watches me putting ball after ball straight between the posts from, like, every angle you can think of. I'm on focking fire. Doesn't matter what I do, I can't miss. He watches me for, like, ten or fifteen minutes and then I decide I've punished him enough and, as I'm leaving, I turn to him and go, 'Thanks for keeping my place warm, orsehole.'

I have my shower and get changed and it's, like, only three o'clock, so I phone Christian on his mobile, roysh, and he tells me they all ended up heading into town and they're in The Bailey, so I drive in, pork the cor on Stephen's Green and head down. I am in *such* good form. I walk in and I'm like, 'I'm back, goys. I am SO back,' and Oisinn goes, 'Pint?' and of course I give it, 'Orange juice.' And Oisinn makes this, like, wolf-whistling sound and then high-fives me. Christian, who's *totally* shit-faced, he grabs me around the neck and goes, 'Remember, if you choose the quick and easy path as Vader did, you will become an agent of evil. You must complete your training,' and I'm like, 'My training is complete, Obi Wan,' sort of, like, playing along with the dude. Then I go, 'I'm going to kick orse, Master.'

I knock back a couple of glasses of orange juice, roysh, but the goys are on a totally different buzz from me, so I end up heading off after a couple of hours and I'm in such a good mood I even think about phoning Erika on the way back to the cor, but it's, like, early days yet.

Fock this for a game of soldiers, my cor – we're talking my brand new Golf GTI here – has been focking clamped and I'm just there going, that is SO not on. I get onto the old man, roysh, and I go, 'Need your credit cord number. Now.' He goes, 'What for?' and I'm like, 'No time to go into all that. Just gimme the focking number.' The dickhead, roysh, he actually goes, 'It's a bit of an awkward time, Ross. I'm in a meeting,' and I'm like, 'Well just give me the focking number then and stop blabbing on,' which he does, the focking tosser.

I phone up the number on the notice that's stuck to my windscreen and I go, 'Yeah, you've put a clamp on my cor. Take the focking thing off. Here's my credit cord number. You've got fifteen minutes, otherwise I'll take you to the focking cleaners.' The dude on the other end of the phone, he takes down the number, roysh, and I go, 'And make sure you get all the glue off my windscreen, or I'll sue your focking orses.' He goes, 'Can I just take your name, Sir?' And I'm like, 'My name? It's Ross O'Carroll-Kelly. And if you haven't heard it before, don't worry. You will.'

✳✳✳

When we were in, like, first year in school, roysh, Christian's old pair split up for, like, six months or something, and though Christian never really spoke about it, pretty much everyone knew it was because his old man was basically knocking off this other bird who was, like, a portner in the same company as him, she was a barrister, or something. Anyway, roysh, while all this shit was going down, Christian was sent to, like, Castlerock to board, and his sister, roysh, we're talking Iseult, she boarded at Alex., just for, like, the year, while the old pair were working things out.

Christian said it was, like, the most amazing year of his life, but I knew he hated it. A couple of the goys I knew from the junior cup team said he used to cry pretty much every night when the lights were off and he thought, like, no one could hear him.

I used to stay back after school for a couple of hours, roysh, supposedly to do supervised study, that's what I told my old pair, but it was basically so me and Christian could hang out, mostly chatting about rugby and birds we'd snogged and birds we wanted to snog and birds who wanted to snog us, and *never* about his old pair. And even though, roysh, technically I shouldn't have still been on the school grounds at, like, half-seven at night, the priests never said anything to me because, well, basically I think it was because they knew the shit that Christian was going through and having his best mate there just, like, made it better for him. Sounds a bit gay, but it wasn't.

Anyway, roysh, this sounds a bit gay as well, but I hated going home because it was like he was in prison or some shit, and I was just, like, visiting him, and every night, roysh, when it was time for me to head off, he'd ask me to stay a bit longer and when I'd tell him that I had to get my bus, he'd say that there was a 46A every, like, ten minutes.

Seems so long ago now. I remember this one time, roysh, and this is going to sound totally weird, but we were hanging out at the rugby pitch next to the dorms, basically lying on the grass, watching the sky get dark, again talking about birds, probably Karyn Flynn and Jessica Kennedy, these two Mounties we were into. This thing, roysh, had been on my mind for about a week, so I turn around to him and I'm like, 'Christian, can I ask you something?' and he goes, 'What?' and I'm there, 'You know that thing they say about magpies? That it's, like, one for sorrow, two for joy, three for a girl ...' I can see him now, roysh, all of a sudden sitting up, so he's, like, leaning on his elbows, and he goes, 'Yeah. What about it?' And I went, 'I saw four the other day ... does that mean I'm ...' And he broke his shite laughing. Absolutely cracked his hole. He went, 'You are so focking weird, Ross,' and he broke his shite laughing again. Then I broke mine.

***

STOP FOCkiNG Us aRound this iS one of His feathers WEll accepT 500 lIDs pay or the stAtue gets iT

***

What happened between me and Christian's old dear wasn't actually my fault. Okay, I didn't exactly fight her off, roysh, but basically she was the one who made a move on me and I'm the one, of course, who, like, ends up the villain. Christian's old man is basically an orsehole, roysh, who was doing the dirt on her for years and not just with that bird he worked with, there was also this other bird he played tennis with in Riverview and then this other one who was, like, Christian's old dear's best friend since they were, like, ten or something. Doesn't excuse what happened, roysh, but Christian's old man is basically a focking hypocrite if he tells Christian about it.

It happened at Iseult's twenty-first, roysh, we're talking Iseult as in Christian's sister here, about three years ago. The porty was in their gaff on Ailesbury Road and it was obvious that the old pair had had a massive row earlier in the day, you could tell from the atmosphere and the way the old dear was putting away the sherry. Basically, I don't know what Christian's old man had said to her, roysh, but the shit was *totally* hitting the fan.

I went to use the downstairs jacks and there was someone in there. I couldn't hold it. Knocking back the beer all day, my back teeth were floating, so I headed upstairs. The door wasn't locked, roysh, but when I pushed it there was something blocking it, a pair of legs, basically Christian's old dear, sitting on the side of the bath, bawling her eyes out.

I was a bit embarrassed, roysh, probably should have focked off back downstairs instead of going in. She was, like, off her face and suddenly she storts pouring out her whole, like, life story to me – what Christian's old man was *really* like and *that woman* who had the cheek to come into her home on this of all days, and I wasn't sure who she was talking about, though I presumed it was someone she'd found out the old man was rattling on the side. And that's probably what the row was about, him inviting her.

It's funny, roysh, I'd always had a bit of a thing for Christian's old dear. She was always a bit of a yummy-mummy, not quite as nice as Simon's, but I wouldn't have said no.

I sat on the bath beside her, roysh, and the next thing – it's focking stupid, I know, but I'd a few on me as well – we're suddenly, like, hugging each other and there's a bit of kissing going on and, well, I'll spare you the details, but basically one thing led to another and we did it, there on the floor of the bathroom, and there's me gicking it in case Christian, or his old man, or, fock, his granny even, came up to use the can.

When it was over she said it was lovely, she goes, 'That was lovely,' but I knew it was bullshit. It was too quick and too sleazy to have been lovely.

And that was it, roysh, we both got dressed and headed back downstairs to the porty and it was never, like, mentioned again. Even when I was in the gaff after that there was no, like, awkwardness about it. Sometimes I wondered whether she was too pissed to even remember because she basically acted like it had never happened and shit.

That was until this night, about three weeks ago, when she phoned me up, roysh, and says she told Christian's old man what had happened between us. She was really sorry, it was all bound to come out now, she said. I asked her why she had to say anything. I'm like, 'It was three focking years ago, for fock's sake.' She goes, 'And we're separated now. I know it shouldn't matter. But there's so much stuff going on. So much bitterness. So many bad things coming out. I found out today about this woman he was seeing. Two years it was going on. Right under my nose as well. We had a row about it. On the phone. And in the heat of the moment, I mentioned what happened between you and me.'

I asked her did she think he'd tell Christian and she said not for now, roysh, because Christian was refusing point-blank to see him or even, like, take his calls because he was, like, blaming him for the break-up and shit. But she was sure it would come out eventually. He would use it to try to worm his way back into Christian's good books. Nothing focking surer.

✸✸✸

The old man calls a meeting of KISS, roysh, what with all the stuff in the papers about rugby going to, like, Croke Park and shit, and you should see our driveway, it's like focking Maxwell Motors, we're talking Beamers, Mercs, Rovers, the whole lot. The old man's, like, in his element, of course, crapping on about the Berkeley Court and how the heart and soul of the game belongs at Lansdowne Road. He's there giving it, 'I don't care whether it's Abbotstown, Croke Park, or Áras-an-blooming-Uachtaráin, rugby will *not* be moving to the northside, certainly not as long as I have breath in my lungs and I'm chairman of Keep It South Side.'

I warned him not to make a focking knob of himself again, but of course the old dear was straight on my case, going, 'Please be on your best behaviour, Ross. Today's a big day for your father,' and it must be, roysh, because she's got the focking gourmet coffee out again and it's, like, I don't know, French Vanilla Supreme all round, and the old man's giving it, 'It's far from Wedgwood that Bertie Ahern was reared,' which gets a laugh off all his dickhead mates, and the old dear, who's standing there with the tray, goes, 'I say, how clever, Darling,' and she kisses him – on the *actual* lips – and I'm thinking, *Oh my God!* I am going to focking vom.

She lays the tray down on the dining-room table and she gives it, 'For heaven's sake, that man can't even speak properly, that Bertie Ahern.' And Alan, this total orsehole who's, like, president of Castlerock this year, he goes, 'You're right, Fionnuala. It's all Dis, Dat, Deez and Doze with that chap.' And Alan's wife is like, 'C as M. The man is simply C *as* M.'

The old man goes, 'But we're not allowed to say that, unfortunately. Not politically correct, quote-unquote. That's why we have to think out our strategy carefully. You mention unmarried mothers, tracksuits and satellite dishes and you're immediately labelled a snob. With a capital S.'

I'm standing at the door of the sitting room, listening to this shite and going, 'What a bunch of sad bastards,' under my breath. Eduard, this knob the old man knows from the golf club, he bangs his fist on the table and goes, 'What are we going to do then?' and Richard, this other complete and utter dickhead who's supposed to be helping the old man get his handicap down, goes, 'That's the frustrating thing, Eduard. We know what this is about. It's about Bertie Ahern getting votes in these Northside hellholes. That's what it's about ... I mean, some of these young girls, they're having these babies just for the money. Are we just going to sit back and accept that that's right?'

The old man goes, 'I think you've gone off on a bit of a tangent there, Richard, but your point will be noted in the minutes. But if we're to accept that we can't include anything about sovereign rings, little moustaches, or spice burgers in our argument, then I believe there's only one way for us to fight this nonsense. And that's by using the only language Fianna Fáil understands.'

Hennessy goes, 'I can raise a few hundred thousand. Might mean going to Guernsey, but it's feasible.' Eduard goes, 'You'd do that?' and Hennessy's like, 'This is an attack on our way of life, Eduard. I'd do that and a lot more besides.'

Richard goes, 'I've known Frank Dunlop for many, many years, and something tells me that simple bribery isn't going to work this time.' Eduard, roysh, he loses it then, jumps up and goes, 'Well, what do you suggest we do? For thirty-five years I've been going to rugby internationals. Thirty-five years. It's the Berkeley Court. It's the Dorsh. It's ... it's ... I mean, where is Abbotstown anyway?' Hennessy puts his orm around him, trying to calm the looper down, and he goes, 'Who knows, Eduard? Who knows ...?'

The old man's there, 'Can I just call this meeting to order for a moment and say that I think we've gone off the point slightly. This Abbotstown business, it's still some way down the line. The real, immediate danger at the moment comes from the GAA. If they vote to open up Croke Stadium, we could be in real danger. We'll be travelling out to north Dublin for our matches quicker than you can say, "What do you mean, you don't sell Courvoisier around here?" Now I think Richard is right. Frank Dunlop has been keeping his head down lately, and who can blame him?'

Hennessy goes, 'Kerrigan. He hates anyone with money,' and the old man's like, 'Let me finish, Hennessy. What I'm saying is, let's deal with the GAA *first*. If we need to bribe anyone, we've got to get a few of these Gaelic Association of … what does it stand for? Gaelic … I don't know, these GAA chaps. What I'm saying is, let's put together, say, £50,000 each and try to bribe a few of them. Get them to vote against it.'

Hennessy goes, 'Just think of all the bacon and cabbage and, you know, sports coats they could buy with that kind of money.'

And Richard's like, 'We can offer it to them, but they'd never go for it, would they?'

✱✱✱

JP asks me whether it's true I've been texting Lana, this Daisy Donovan wannabe who's doing fock-knows-what in Bruce. I go, 'I wanna say this just one more time. I did *not* have textual intercourse with that woman,' and everyone at our table cracks up, including Erika. Probably the funniest thing I've ever said.

✱✱✱

Usual crack in college, doing fock-all, just basically chilling, taking it easy and shit. I hit the sports bor in the morning, roysh, read Wardy's report on the Clongowes match, play a few frames of Killer with, like, Oisinn and Christian, head down to 911 for the old rolls, then to the computer room for the two hours of free internet access, which is mostly spent downloading pictures of Rachel Stevens, Carmen Electra and Lisa Faulkner.

After that, roysh, the afternoon's basically my own, so me and the goys are, like, sitting around in Hilper's with Chloë, who's, like, first year B&L, and Clodagh, who's repeating first year Orts, and everyone has, like, their mobiles, their car keys and, in the girls' case, lip balm on the table, and Oisinn's talking about some goy in first year Business who, he says, is a total faggot and we're talking a *total* faggot here, and all of a sudden, roysh, Chloë goes, 'What have you got against gay people?' and Oisinn's like, 'Nothing,' and Chloë goes, 'You better not have, because I've got *loads* of friends who are gay.' Clodagh says she has too, but Chloë says she doesn't have as many as she has and they argue about this for, I would guess, fifteen minutes.

I have to say, roysh, that Chloë is a total honey, we're talking really well-stacked here, former Virgin on the Rocks, so like Emmanuelle Béart it's unbelievable, while Clodagh is a complete focking moon-pig, though Christian told me in Annabel's last Friday night that he'd be prepared to take a bullet for me if I'd any chance of being with Chloë.

So we're sitting there, roysh, and Chloë is SO flirting her orse off with me it's unbelievable. She's there going, 'Ross, would you be a complete dorling and go and get me a cup of boiled water?' and I ask her why boiled water and she says that it's, like, good for your skin and anyway cold water just, like, slows down your metabolism. I have to say, roysh, she looks totally amazing in her pink Ralph with the collar up and a baby blue sleeveless bubble jacket. She goes, 'Would you be a complete dorling, Ross, and get it for me? And a packet of Marlboro Lights as well,' and of course I'm there, 'Does the Pope shit in the woods?'

After lunch, there's, like, fock-all happening, so the five of us decide to head out to Stillorgan to, like, see a movie for the afternoon. Clodagh says she really wants to see *Cast Away*, roysh, and Chloë says that is SO a good idea. Clodagh says they actually filmed it in two sequences, roysh, and that Tom Hanks basically lost three stone in eight months to play the port of a goy who's, like, shipwrecked on a desert island, and Oisinn says that three stone in eight months is nothing, that anyone from the cast of 'Friends' could do that in a long weekend, and even though I think it's, like, really funny, roysh, I notice that Chloë isn't laughing, so I tell him he's a knob.

So we're about to head off, roysh, when all of a sudden this goy, Dowdy, who's, like, second year Sports Management, ex-Clongowes boy and a total dickhead, he comes over and storts, like, chatting to the birds, asking them how they're fixed for the exams and shit. Clodagh says she hasn't done a tap all year and SO has to get her finger out of her orse it's not funny, and then he turns around and asks us the same question, roysh, and we all, like, totally blank him.

He's there, 'Oh, I get it, the old school-rivalry shit. All I'm saying, goys, is don't leave it too late to stort studying. I should know,' and I go, '*Hello?* We're doing Sports Management.' He goes, 'I know. You've still got exams,' and I'm like, 'I've been training my orse off for, like, two weeks. I cannot *believe* they are pulling this shit on me now. How many exams are we talking? There's only, like, three subjects on the course.' He goes, 'Well, there's actually seven subjects on the course, goys. You must have done exams at Christmas?' *Oh my God,* roysh, I'm storting to feel seriously dizzy. I'm like, '*Seven* subjects? Christmas exams?' He's there, 'Yeah, we're talking physiotherapy, computers, psychology ...'

Me and Oisinn are there, 'OH! MY! GOD! you know what this means? If we've missed the Christmas exams, we're going to have to sit the summer repeats.' I'm there, 'I am SO not cancelling Ocean City.'

So we tell the birds, roysh, that we're going to have to postpone the flicks because this is, like, a major emergency, and me and Oisinn end up hitting the sports bor and knocking back a few pints, to get over the shock more than anything, and by seven o'clock we're totally shit-faced. We hit the M1 for a few more, then head into town to Mono.

Pretty much the next thing I remember is being out on the dancefloor, giving it *loads* to 'Beautiful Day', roysh, and the bouncers telling me and Oisinn that if we can't control ourselves we're going to have to take it outside, and I look around, roysh, and I notice that Fionn's here as well. That geeky-looking focker doesn't have to worry because he's doing Orts and he's focking brains to burn and he's chatting up this bird, blonde hair, big baps, a little bit like Stacey Bello, though not up close, and when I get up close she's asking him where he's from and he says Killiney and she's, like, totally disgusted all of a sudden and she goes, 'I am SO not getting involved in another Dorshline relationship,' and she focks off.

And that's pretty much the last thing I can remember, except I think I ended up being with this bird Carol, who's, like, first year accountancy in Bruce, really good-looking, so like Estella Warren you would actually swear it was her, but I wasn't with her for long because I could hordly stand, and I was so off my face I ended up giving her my number – we're talking my *real* number here – though that isn't the thing I was most worried about the next morning.

I don't know whether I imagined this because I was so horrendufied, and I can't get through to the goys to find out whether it really happened, but I could have sworn, roysh, that I was walking down Grafton Street, just before I blacked out, and I bumped into Hendo, the UCD coach, who said he'd been trying to contact me all day and seeing the state of me now he's wondering why he bothered at all, but I'm on the team for next week's match if I can manage to stay off the drink for that long and I'm a disgrace to the game of rugby and it's a pretty sad day for UCD that the team has to rely on the likes of me and I should get myself sobered up and get my act together and this is my, like, last big chance. And maybe it was the drink, probably was, but I could have sworn that he said the match was against, like, Castlerock RFC.

And of course I'm like, 'Fock.'

CHAPTER FIVE
'Ross thinks he's, like, too cool for school.'
Discuss.

JP, roysh, he persuades Oisinn to borrow his old man's cor, we're talking a big fock-off Beamer here, and they head out to Tallafornia and drive around these real skanger estates, with JP sticking his head out through the sunroof, shouting, 'AFFLUENCE! AFFLUENCE!'

✳✳✳

Valentine's Day was the usual crack – got four cords, two from, like, secret admirers, roysh, one from Jessica Heaney who's, like, second year Actuarial and Financial Studies in UCD, a big-time flirt and SO like Natasha Henstridge you'd swear they were twins, and one other addressed to 'The goy with the smallest penis in UCD,' which is obviously from Keeva, or Amy, or some other bird I've given the flick to and is having a problem getting over it, maybe Emma, or Sinéad. Or Cara, or Jill. One of those orseholes. Or Sadch. Or Abhril. Or Teena with two Es.

Anyway, roysh, the good news was that Fionn got his hands on tickets for the Valentine's Ball, so there I am in my gaff getting ready, roysh, looking pretty well, I have to say, in my new beige chinos, light blue Ralph and Dubes, when all of a sudden there's this, like, ring at the door. I open it, roysh, and surprise sur-focking-prise, who is it only Sorcha, who hands me this cord, roysh, and this present and goes, 'Friends?' and I just, like, shrug my shoulders and go, '*What*ever,' thinking, *Hello?* Has this girl no, like, self-respect? Then she gives me a hug and goes, 'You smell SO nice. What are you wearing?' Everything with this girl comes with a focking hug. I'm like, '*Emporio He*,' and she goes, 'Giorgio Armani?' and I just, like, nod at her.

She's totally dressed to kill, roysh, and we're talking totally here, and she's there giving it, 'You going out tonight?' and I'm like, 'Going to the Valentine's Ball,' and she goes, 'Oh my God, where is it on this year?' and I just go, 'Town.' She is SO trying to get back with me it's embarrassing. She goes, 'Are you not going to open your present?' so I tear open the wrapping and it's, like, the new Radiohead album, which I've basically wanted for ages, and she goes, 'I hope you haven't already got it,' and I'm like, 'Yeah, I have actually,' and she says, OH MY GOD! she'll change it, but I tell her not to bother, that I'll give it to Megan, and she's like, 'Who's Megan?' and I go, 'This bird I've been seeing. She's, like, first year B&L. You wouldn't know her. Looks like Holly Valance,' completely making it up, and the sad bitch nearly bursts into tears.

The next thing, roysh, the old dear decides to stick her focking oar in, she comes out to the hall and goes, 'Sorcha! Come in, come in. Ross, why have you left her standing at the door?' and the two of them air-kiss each other and then, like, disappear off into the kitchen together, talking about the sale in Pamela Scott and whether or not Ikea will ever open up a branch in Dublin. I'm just glad the old dear has managed to tear herself away from Dick-features. They actually bought each other Valentine cords, roysh, how focking twisted is that, they're in their, like, fifties. It's that focking statue, I know it is.

I just, like, grab the cor keys. The old dear tells me to drive carefully and I tell her to focking cop herself on, and as I'm leaving I notice that Sorcha has actually got, like, tears in her eyes and she's hordly even touched the cappuccino the old dear's made for her and I'm like, *What* a total sap.

The Coyote Lounge is totally jammers, roysh. There's, like, a queue halfway up D'Olier Street when we arrive and everyone's there going, 'WE HATE C&E. WE HATE C&E,' and the Commerce and Economics Society goys are, like, *totally* bulling. After about an hour, roysh, we finally manage to get inside, but I end up having a pretty shit night, probably because I'm only drinking Diet Coke, what with me back playing serious rugby and all.

The only bit of crack I actually have, roysh, is watching Oisinn totally crash and burn when he chances his orm with Phenola, this complete fruitcake who's, like, second year B&L. He's chatting away to her, roysh, giving it loads, and that Destiny's Child song comes on, roysh, 'Independent Women', or whatever the fock it's called, music for cutting men's mickeys off to, and all of a sudden he makes a lunge for her and she slaps him across the face and tells him that trying to be with a girl while that song is on is SUCH a no-no. It's, like, SO funny seeing this big six-foot-five, seventeen-stone prop-forward getting slapped across the face by this little, like, squirt of a bird.

But then I end up getting cornered by Kate, roysh, this total knob who's, like, first year Orts, and we end up having one of those pain-in-the-orse conversations which storts off with her asking me who I know in Orts and I go, 'Lisa Andrews,' and she goes, 'OH! MY! GOD! I can't *believe* you know Lisa Andrews. She's one of my, like, best friends. Who else?' and I go, 'James O'Hagan,' and she goes, 'OH! MY! GOD! I can't *believe* you know James O'Hagan. I was with him at the Freshers' Frolic.'

I'm storting to lose the focking will to live when Fionn comes over and rescues me, roysh, and he points over to this bird, I think it's Bláthnaid, who's, like, repeating first year Counselling and Psychotherapy in LSB, and she's wearing half-nothing, and Fionn turns around to me and goes, 'Gardaí at Harcourt Terrace are seeking the public's help in tracing the whereabouts of Bláthnaid Brady's clothes.' I laugh, roysh, but I tell him that I'm going to fock off home because I have to be, like, up early the next morning.

The next day's a pretty big one for me. Castlerock College are playing their first match in the Senior Cup against the Logue, and Father Feely asked me to go back and give the goys on the S a pep-talk. I have to say I'm pretty nervous going back, roysh, especially with all the shit that's going to come down about next week.

The thing is, roysh, by some focking miracle the goys don't know this yet, but I'm making my debut for UCD next week and it's against Castlerock RFC, with mid-table mediocrity in Division Two of the AIL at stake. Someone at the school is bound to have heard. It's a mare. A total mare.

Anyway, as it turns out, roysh, I'd nothing to worry about, because I get an amazing reception at the school the next morning. I'm there giving the goys on the team my speech, roysh, all like, 'THIS IS THE GAME OF YOUR LIVES' and 'KICK ORSE, ROCK,' and as I'm leaving the stage, the whole assembly is there singing 'Castlerock Über Alles' and it's, like, really focking emotional.

But then, roysh, over comes Magahy, this total dickhead, he's one of the geography teachers, and he comes up to me, roysh, and asks whether it's true that I'm going to be playing against Castlerock in the AIL next week. Now this goy, roysh, is a total orsehole. He coached the Junior Cup team when I was in, like, first year, a total club man, he goes to all the matches and sits up at the bor thinking he knows everything about rugby when in fact he knows fock-all.

I *totally* hate this goy and there's, like, history between us as well. When I was in second year, roysh, I missed a pretty simple penalty and we ended up getting knocked out of the Junior Cup by focking Pres. Bray of all schools, and Magahy goes to me, as I'm leaving the pitch – now I probably should say I was a bit heavier in those days – he goes, 'You're going to be huge, Ross … especially if you keep eating the way you do.'

I so haven't forgotten that.

Anyway, roysh, he asks me if the rumours are true and I'm like, 'What's it to you?' and he turns around and goes, 'You're going to be a turncoat, then?' and I just, like, put my baseball cap back on, roysh, and go, 'No, Magahy, you dickhead. I'm going to be focking sensational.'

✳✳✳

The cor, we're talking the black Golf GTI, *with* alloys, it's in the garage at the moment – just thought if I'm getting serviced on a regular basis, roysh, then my wheels deserve the same pleasure – but the only downside is that I have to use the old public transport, the dreaded 46A. I'd totally forgotten how many Paddy Whackers use it. I'm sitting upstairs, roysh, and there's this, like, total fleck beside me, and he's smoking away there, roysh, and I'm thinking of saying something to him, not that I've any objection to smoking – Sorcha smokes, so do most of the birds – but I just want to basically say to the guy, Are you gonna be a knacker all your life?

I don't get a chance to say anything, roysh, because past the shopping centre in Stillorgan, he suddenly jumps to his feet, reefs open the window and shouts, 'Oi, Plugger. I fooked your mudder,' and this Plugger goy, roysh, he's standing near the bus stop looking up at the top deck, trying to spot who it was who shouted it, no doubt half of him thinking it's probably true, then he sees the goy and he goes, 'Alroy, Anto. Storee?' and the two of them give each other the thumbs-up. Then Anto sits back down and lights up again.

What the fock is the deal with these people?

✹✹✹

A few months ago, roysh, before I decided to lay off the sauce and go back training, me and the goys – we're talking Christian, Fionn, Oisinn, all those – we were out on the lash, roysh, a Monday night in Peg's, pound a pint, the usual crack and when it was over we all headed back to Oisinn's gaff on Shrewsbury Road to get, like, food and a Jo Maxi. So there we were, like, in the kitchen, roysh, and I looked over at Oisinn – he's had, like, thirteen or fourteen pints at this stage – and the goy's eating a block of lard. We are talking focking *lard* here. At first, roysh, I thought it was the usual crack, you know, absolutely storving but too shit-faced to cook, I mean the goy would eat focking anything as it is, but then he tells us, roysh, that he's in training, and of course we're all there, 'What for?' and says the Iron Stomach contest that the C&E are holding.

To cut a long story short, roysh, Oisinn decided to enter after he met a bunch of Andrews dickheads in the Ass and Cart the previous weekend, all first year Commerce heads who recognised him and storted giving him loads about what a shit school Castlerock was, roysh, brave men it has to be said because Oisinn is a big focker. But it was all like, 'How many points did you get in the Leaving?' and, 'How many former *taoisigh* went to your school?' and what with one thing and another this goy, Keyser, who Oisinn came pretty close to decking, he ended up, like, challenging Oisinn to see who had, like, the strongest stomach.

So the day of the competition arrives, roysh, and we're all there in our Castlerock jerseys, giving it loads, and there's, like, seven people in the competition, all sitting in a row, a few from Commerce, a couple from Science, but all eyes are on Oisinn and Keyser, who are the big-time favourites, and we're all there giving it, 'You can't knock the Rock. You can't knock the Rock,' *totally* intimidating the Andrews goys.

So first, roysh, all the contestants are given a can of Holsten, which is, like, six months past its sell-by date and, while they're drinking that, they have to eat a Weetabix with, like, soy sauce and lemon curd on it. One of them, roysh, we're talking one of the Science goys, he borfs straight away, so there's only, like, six of them left and we're all there giving it loads as they hand out the next thing they have to eat, which is, like, a pot of cold custard with a spoonful of baked beans stirred into it, we're talking cold here, and a spoonful of treacle as well. *Oh my God*, I thought I was going to vom myself.

More Holsten. Then it's, like, a double shot of tequila, roysh, and then they all have to hit the deck and do, like, twenty sit-ups each. The next thing is a cold mince-and-onion pie with, like strawberry jam and Bonjela gum ointment on it, and this girl sitting beside Oisinn, a real Commerce head, she just goes totally green, roysh, and we're talking *totally* here, and she spews her ring up all over Oisinn, all over his chinos, all over his Dubes, all over everything. At this stage, I'm convinced that Oisinn is going to borf as well, but he manages to keep it in.

Then, roysh, we see one of the Andrews goys in the crowd, Henno, this total dickhead who's going out with Emma, not hockey Emma, we're talking Institute Emma, who I was sort of seeing when I was doing grinds. I look over at him, roysh, and give him the finger and he comes over and goes, 'Your goy is going to lose,' and of course I'm there, 'You seem pretty sure of yourself,' and he goes, 'There's something you don't know about Keyser. He has no taste-buds, man. Lost them a couple of years ago. An unfortunate accident involving a flaming Sambucca. Tragic really. He can't taste any of that shit he's eating.'

I'm like, 'OH! MY! GOD! that is *it*,' and I storm up to the front and tell Oisinn that me and the goys are pulling him out of the competition. He's like, 'No *focking* way.' When he says this, roysh, he has a mouthful of, like, beetroot and yoghurt, most of which ends up all over my jacket, we're talking my red Henri Lloyd sailing jacket here. I go, 'Oisinn, Keyser's a freak. The goy has no taste-buds,' and he thinks about this for, like, five seconds, roysh, swallowing what he has in his mouth, and goes, 'So? We're Castlerock, remember? We never quit.'

I have to say, roysh, I feel pretty emotional at that moment, but then I have to take a few steps backwards because all the other contestants stort, like, spewing their guts up all over the place, and suddenly there's only, like, Oisinn and Keyser left in it, we're talking a two-horse race. More Holsten. More tequila. A twenty-second squirt of, like, ketchup into each of their mouths. *Oh* my God, how they don't borf there and then, I don't know. Another double shot of tequila. Hit the deck, twenty press-ups and then, like, twenty sit-ups. Then they've got to, like, put their heads back while one of the C&E goys comes up behind them and feeds them, like, a raw fish. He holds it by the tail and just, like, drops it down their throats.

Keyser is looking so cocky at this stage, roysh, dancing to the music and everything. A glass of cooking oil with a squirty cream head. Pickled onions with ice cream. Mussels. A catfood sandwich with toothpaste and ketchup on it. Down they go. Keyser looks like he could go on at this all day, but Oisinn looks in trouble.

He's knocking back the beers, though, probably to take the focking taste out of his mouth, and when he finishes another – it's, like, his eighth – he turns around to Keyser and goes, 'Are you not drinking?' So Keyser, roysh, he's suddenly handed two cans by one of the C&E goys, who's noticed that he's only drunk, like, six, and Keyser decides he has to show off, he can't be seen to be drinking less than a Rock boy, so he shotguns the two cans and downs them.

Next thing, roysh, you can actually *see* that the goy is going to borf, his face goes white and it's like he can't catch his breath, roysh, and he just leans over and spews his guts up, we're talking all over the gaff, we're talking all that shite he's just eaten, and we're talking undigested here.

We all just, like, mob Oisinn, singing 'Castlerock Über Alles', the whole lot, then we're like, 'SPEECH! SPEECH! SPEECH!' and eventually, roysh, when he's, like, composed himself, Oisinn goes, 'Thank you very much. I have to tell you that I knew all along about Keyser having no taste-buds. It didn't bother me. For I also knew that Andrews goys can't drink for shit, therefore I believed that I could eat more than Keyser could drink. It was a gamble, but it worked.'

Christian turns to me, roysh, and goes, 'The goy's a focking legend, Ross. A *legend.*'

Oisinn heads off to Vincent's, roysh, and we peg it into town and tell him we'll meet him in the Temple later on. Ten o'clock, we're all still sitting around waiting for the man of the moment to arrive, and I think Fionn speaks for us all when he goes, 'How long does it take to pump a goy out?'

There's, like, loads of birds hanging around our table and shit and it's just like the night we won the Senior Cup, except they're actually wrecking our heads a bit because this should be, like, a night for the goys. And I'm just pretty much savouring this moment, roysh, because it's only a matter of time before the goys find out I'm going to be playing against Castlerock next week and I get the feeling that things are going to change.

The second Oisinn arrives, it's definitely going to be a case of ditch the bitches. The saps are actually, like, in competition with each other to see who's going to end up being with him when he arrives. Sarah Jane, who's, like, repeating first year Law in Portobello, she goes, 'My cousin actually knows Oisinn's sister *really* well.' And the other bird, Bryana I think her name is, looks a bit like Naomi Watts, she goes, '*Hello?* I was in Irish college with Bláthnaid for two summers. She's one of my *best* friends.'

Chloë, roysh, who's, like, second year International Commerce with French in UCD and, like, really good friends with Sorcha she asks me what Oisinn had to eat and I tell her, roysh, about the cold custard, the beans, the Weetabix and the raw fish, the mince-and-onion pies and the strawberry jam, and she goes, 'OH! MY! GOD! that is SO gross. Can you *imagine* how many points that is?'

✳✳✳

I bump into Erika in Finnegan's Break and she's, like, sipping a glass of hot water, roysh, I ask her what she's doing for the afternoon and she throws her eyes up to heaven and says she's going to the orthodontist, and I'm like, 'Have you heard I'm back playing serious rugby?' and she stubs out a Marlboro Light and goes, 'This affects me how?'

I ask her what time she's going to be finished at the dentist, and she says it's the orthodontist and I'm like, 'Same thing,' and she just looks me up and down and goes, 'Hordly.' Then she focks off.

I ring Oisinn on his mobile but there's, like, no answer. I ring Christian and it's, like, switched to his message-minder. I get the *Star Wars* theme tune and then it's like, 'A long time ago, in a Galaxy far, far away … was a man with a message to leave. Beep.' I don't bother leaving one. I phone Fionn and he's not answering either. And it's obvious. Basically, the goys know about the match.

✳✳✳

Simon is the first one over. Feel a bit sorry for Simon. He was captain of the S the year we won the cup and now he's the youngest ever captain of Castlerock RFC at, like, twenty years of age. The club is his life, and we're talking *totally*. But he comes up to me, roysh, and he goes, 'So it's true then?' and I'm like, 'What's true?' and he's there, 'You *are* stabbing us in the back.' I'm there, 'You are SUCH a sad bastard,' and he goes, 'I seriously didn't think you'd play. I knew you were training with UCD, but I presumed this was a game you'd skip. Out of loyalty. Looks like I was wrong,' and then he, like, pushes me in the chest, roysh, and calls me a turncoat and I switch my gearbag to my other shoulder, basically getting ready to deck the focker if he touches me again.

He goes, 'Whatever happened to Castlerock above all others? *"We'll shy from battle never. Ein volk, ein Reich, ein Rock"*?' I'm just there, 'We're not at school anymore, Simon. I'm playing for UCD now.'

He storts, like, shaking his head, roysh, going, 'No, no, no,' we're talking tears in the stupid sap's eyes here, the whole works, and he's giving it, 'You *never* leave Castlerock, Ross. And *it* never leaves you.'

I'm trying to reason with the goy, roysh, telling him that playing for UCD is, like, one of the conditions of my scholarship and shit, but he keeps bullshitting on about how pretty much all of my old team-mates off the S went on to sign for Castlerock and now, just when they're looking like pulling themselves out of the bottom four of the Second Division of the AIL, along comes one of their own to stab them in the back. He goes, 'You haven't played rugby all season, Ross,' and I'm there, 'That's why I've got a point to prove. Show them that the old magic is still there.' He goes, 'But why *now*? Why *this* game?' and I go, 'I've grown up, Simon. I think it's about time you did, too,' and I stort, like, heading towards the dressing-rooms and he shouts after me that I'm totalled, we're talking totally totalled and he's talking TOTALLY.

I get into the dressing-room and all the other goys are already there and Hendo, our coach, is giving this, like, major pep-talk about how we've, like, striven all season to finish mid-table and we can't let it slip through our fingers now.

I'm getting changed into my gear, roysh, when Hendo storts, like, looking at me and he goes, 'Any divided loyalties here today?' and I'm there, 'Are you talking to me?' and he goes, 'I saw you talking to Simon Wallace out there. Just want to know whether you're with us or against us today.' I'm just there, 'I'm kicking focking *orse* today,' and the whole dressing-room goes ballistic, roysh, everyone banging on the lockers, kicking the walls, giving it, 'YOU THE MAN, ROSS. YOU THE MAN.'

It's just like the old days, roysh, except that outside the door there's a couple of hundred Castlerock fans giving me total filthies when we go out, instead of, like, cheering me on, but I do see one friendly face in the crowd and it's, like, Christian, and I walk up to the dude and go, 'Hey, Christian. Looks like I'm public enemy number one around here.' He goes, 'Anyone hurts you out there today, man, and I'll focking kill them.' I go,

'I knew you'd understand. Us college heads have to stick together, eh?' and he's there, 'No, that doesn't mean I'm on your side, Ross. I won't stand by and watch you get hurt, but that doesn't mean I agree with what you're doing.'

I'm like, 'What am I doing, Christian?' and he goes, 'You're turning to the Dark Side.' Then he unzips his jacket, roysh, we're talking his red-and-blue Armani sailing jacket here, and underneath it he's got his old Castlerock jersey on and he just looks me up and down and goes, 'The Emperor has won,' and he walks off.

I can see, like, Fionn and JP and Oisinn, all my so-called mates, over the other side of the pitch and they're, like, giving me filthies, and we're talking total filthies here.

Out on the pitch, roysh, all the old goys are there, all my old mates off the S, we're talking Eunan, Jonathon, Brad, Evan, Terry, Newer, Gicker, and I try to shut it out of my mind as the game storts. And I manage to do it pretty well, roysh, getting seven out of my eight kicks in the first half-an-hour and putting in what I have to say is an amazing tackle on Simon when he's, like, pretty much clean through for a certain try.

At half-time we're, like, 21-13 up, but the Castlerock goys stort to tackle me really hord in the second-half, there's total focking hatred there, and I sort of, like, go off my game a bit, miss a couple of, like, pretty easy kicks and suddenly Castlerock stort to get on top of us. Simon's having a focking stormer.

So to cut a long story short, roysh, two minutes to go and it's, like, 33-27 for them and we pretty much need a seven-pointer to win it. We're pressing, pressing, pressing in the last few minutes and suddenly the ball breaks to me, roysh, and I get over for a try roysh under the post and there's all this, like, booing roysh the way around the ground. All the goys on our team are coming up to me congratulating me, roysh, but also reminding me how important the conversion is, as if I need reminding. This is to win it.

As I'm walking back to take it, roysh, Christian runs onto the field, comes roysh up to me and goes, 'I know there's good in you. I've felt it,' and a couple of stewards come on and drag him away.

The kick is a piece of piss. I blow hord, take three steps backwards and three to the left, run my hand through my hair, blow hord again. I look over at Simon and Eunan, who have their hands on the crests of their jersey, we're talking tears in their focking eyes here. I look at Christian, roysh, who's got his eyes closed, like he's praying, probably trying to use the focking Force or something. I look at them all and think about all the great times we've had together and I think about how much I love those goys, without wanting to sound gay, like, or anything.

I run my hand through my hair and, like, blow hord again.

Then I send the kick high and wide and in the direction of the corner flag.

✱✱✱

Aoife says that Graham, some dickhead she knows from Annabel's, is SO good-looking that every girl in her year wants to be with him, but Sorcha says he is SUCH a Chandler when it comes to commitment, and I am already beginning to regret meeting the birds for lunch and my eyes, roysh, they keep, like, wandering over to where Erika is sitting with this really bored expression on her face, like she basically hates everyone at the table, no, everyone in the world.

I get out my phone, roysh, and text her and it's, like, **WAN 2 TLK?** and a couple of seconds later her phone beeps and she, like, reads the message and tells me, in front of everyone, that I'm a sad bastard. I can feel Sorcha staring at me, roysh, so I try to change the subject by asking Aoife how her brother's getting on with Clontorf, but before she can answer this waitress comes over and tells Emer that people aren't allowed to eat their own, like, food on the premises.

Emer just goes, 'Hello? It's *only* a bag of popcorn,' and the waitress is like, 'It doesn't matter. House rules,' and Emer puts the bag away really slowly, roysh, while giving the waitress a total filthy and the waitress goes again, 'I'm sorry, it's house rules,' but Emer doesn't answer, just carries on staring her out of it.

The conversation suddenly moves on to some bird called Allison with two Ls, who's, like, second year Tourism in LSB and is, like, SO thin, according to Emer, and Aoife goes, 'OH! MY! GOD! did you see the dress she wore to Melissa Berry's 21st?' and Sorcha asks her what it was like and Aoife says it was a Chanel. Emer says that Allison is thinking of going to Australia for the year and so, apparently, are Caoimhe Kennedy, who I'm pretty sure I was with at the Traffic Light Ball, and Elaine Anders, who I've never focking heard of. Aoife tells Sorcha she should go to

Australia for the year herself and Sorcha tells Aoife she SO should go as well.

Emer was in Lillies on Saturday night, but there was, like, no one really in there, unless of course you call Amanda Byram and the lead singer from OTT someone, which she doesn't. Sorcha goes, 'OH MY GOD! I forgot to tell you, Claire is thinking of entering the Bray Festival Queen competition,' and Erika all of a sudden perks up and she goes, 'Oh, your little friend, the one who thinks coleslaw is cosmopolitan?' Everyone's looking for somewhere else to look. Erika goes, 'Yes, that would be SO her alroysh,' then she gets up, roysh, picks up her bags, we're talking Carl Scarpa, Morgan and Nue Blue Eriu, and just, like, walks out of the place, leaving her lunch on the table and her Marlboro Lights.

Aoife says that girl has SUCH an attitude problem and Sorcha tells her not to worry, she's sure Ross won't mind paying for her Caesar wrap, seeing as he's SO fond of her, and, to be honest, I've no problem with that at all. Emer says the new series of 'Ally McBeal' is SO not as good as the last one.

✳✳✳

The traffic on the Stillorgan dualler is a mare, and we are talking total here. I open the glove comportment, roysh, to get out my Eminem CD and it's, like, gone. So I ring the house, roysh, and the old man picks up the phone and he can tell from my voice that I'm seriously pissed off about something and he goes, 'I take it you've read it then?' Of course I'm like, '*What* are you focking talking about?' but he goes, 'To think I almost invited that man over here for New Year. I suppose he's never been a friend of schools rugby. We knew that.' I go, 'I don't even want to know what you are bullshitting on about. Just put the old dear on.'

So he gets her, roysh, and I'm like, 'Answer me one question and do *not* bullshit me. What have you done with my Eminem CD?' and she goes, 'I took it back to the shop, Ross. It was disgusting, some of the things he was singing about. It was eff this and you're an effing that, mother this and mother the other.' I'm like, 'It's none of your *focking* business what I listen to,' and she goes, 'You left it in the CD player in the kitchen, Ross. I thought it was my Celine Dion album. Delma was here for coffee.' And she's there giving it, 'I'm not the only one who brought it back, by the way. The young lady in the shop told me it's the most returned record they've ever sold. I would worry about the influence that that kind of thing might have on you, Ross.'

I'm like, 'Bitch, I'm a kill you,' and I hang up, roysh, and punch the *focking* dashboard and and and … FOCK*!*

And to cap it all the traffic is actually getting focking worse, and how many focking gears does that cor in front of me have? I turn on the radio, roysh, but – again – I can't get a decent song, it's all Christina Aguilera and Ronan focking Keating and I'm flicking from channel to channel, but it's like, 'normal lending criteria and terms and conditions apply', and 'regular savings and higher returns with personal investment plans', and 'help bridge the recruitment gap by skilling up your existing workforce'. 'And the slip light is out of action on the main streesh in

Bray and there's bad flooding around Baker's Coyner and elec-
trical cables are dain on the Belgord Raid and there's the usual
delays on all routes out of the city, including the Naas Raid, the
Navan Raid and the South Circular Raid ...'

✳✳✳

Me, Christian and Oisinn, roysh, we're bored off our tits in the
bor, so we head over to the Orts block, roysh, see if Fionn's
around. Turns out he's got no lectures this afternoon but – get
this, roysh – he's actually gone to a philosophy lecture, the
dude's not even doing the course, roysh, but you know who is?
Exactly. That focking kipper from Galway. He's giving her a
rattle, no doubt about it. Me and the goy, roysh, we're curious,
so we head into the lecture hall ourselves, sit down the back
and OH! MY! GOD! I have never seen so many amazing-looking
birds in my life. They're actually better looking than the birds on
our course, which is saying something, roysh. I remember
Fionn telling me before that all the, like, bimbos who do Orts
always choose either philosophy or psychology because they
think they pass for, like, depth, but I seriously didn't think
there'd be this many crackers.

I turn around to Christian to tell him that if I could have a
fourth shot at the Leaving, maybe aim for points this time rather
than just trying to pass the thing, I'd try to end up in here. I go to
tell Oisinn the same thing, roysh, but he's already talking to this
bird beside him, Elinor I think her name is, I know her to see
from Club Shoot Your Goo, looks a little bit like Maria Grazia
Cucinotta, and I hear her asking Oisinn if he heard that Kelly is

thinking of going to Australia for the year, and I wonder whether she's talking about Kelly who was in the Institute with us last year – tall bird, amazing bod, always has, like, sunglasses in her hair. Then I hear Oisinn asking her if she's wearing *Fifth Avenue* by Elizabeth Arden and it looks like he's clicked.

I still can't see Fionn. I'm looking around for him, roysh, and the lecturer's blabbing away, all I can basically hear is blah blah blah, but then I suddenly cop the fact, roysh, that everyone's looking at me and the lecturer's going, 'Well?' Of course I don't know what the story is here. I'm like, 'Sorry, what was the question again?' and he goes, 'I didn't ask you a question. I asked you to expound, for the rest of the class, if you'd be so kind, your understanding of the term metaphysics.'

Of course, I should tell the goy to go fock himself, roysh, but obviously I don't want to look stupid in front of the class, so I do what I always did at Castlerock, which is close my eyes, look as though I'm really in pain and keep going, 'Oh my God, I so know this. It's on the tip of my tongue,' but the focker lets me carry on doing this for, like, ten minutes before he finally throws the question to someone else.

He asks this bloke, roysh – he's a total howiya – and the goy goes, 'Well, metaphysics is one of de foyiv branches of philosophy. Dee udders are logic, ethics, aesthetics and epistemology. De term was coined by complete accident. It's de title of a buke written by Aristotle after he completed wurk on his *Physics,* and dis was sort of put at dee end of dat body of wurk. Now dat particular buke, *Physics*, dealt wit what you'd call dee observable

world and its laws, whereas metaphysics deals wit de princi-
ples, meanings and structures dat underlie all observable real-
ity. It's de investigation, by means of pew-er spekelation, of
the nature of being, de cause, substance and de purpose of
everyting.'

Of course I'm nodding through all of this, cracking on that
that's what I was going to say. The lecturer goy's like, 'So metaphysics might ask, what?' and this cream cracker goes, 'What are
space and toyim? What is an actual ting and how is it diffordent
from an idea? Are humans free to decide der own fate? Is der a
God dat's put everyting in motion?' The lecturer goes, 'And because the answers to such questions cannot be arrived at by ob-
servation, experience, or experiment ...' and the skanger goes,
'... dee must be products of de reasoning moyind.'

Everyone's impressed, you can basically tell. I turn around to
this bird behind me – the image of Asia Argento – and I go, 'Bit
obvious when you're given time to answer,' then I turn around
to Christian and I go, 'They're letting skobies into UCD now?
When the fock did this happen?' and Christian shakes his head
and I go, 'Let's get on the Internet, check out the website. There
must be something in the terms and conditions about this.'

Then up the front, roysh, we suddenly hear all this, like, sniggering and there's these four Nure goys we know – they're
sound even though they're, like, Gick – and they're sitting behind this bird in a pink Hobo top. Anyway, they've slipped
something into her hood, a photograph or something. Of course
we find out later, roysh, that the goys had gone on a knacker

holiday, we're talking a real 'Ibiza Uncovered' job, after the Leaving, roysh, and the picture was of Kenny's dick, which the rest of the goys took when he was locked. So this little item ends up in this bird's hood, roysh, and of course she's the last one in the whole focking lecture hall to cop it, but when she finally realises there's something going on, she reaches back, pulls the picture out, jumps up and goes, '*Oh my God! Oh my God! Oh my God!*' and pegs it out of the place, basically in total shock.

Then it's, like, high-fives all round.

***

To whom it may concern,

Many thanks for your recent letter and the small piece of masonry, which, a cursory inspection would suggest, is indeed a feather from one of *Eros*'s wings. Thanks also for the kind offer to cut your ransom demand by some fifty per cent.

Unfortunately, we still do not have the finance available to get involved with this project and this will remain the case until we contact you again. However, the summer is approaching and I am confident you will find casual work that will help alleviate whatever financial difficulties you are currently experiencing.

Apologies for the delay in replying, incidentally. I was off on paternity leave for four weeks. My wife gave birth to our third recently, a boy. He weighed eleven pounds at birth. Mother and baby are both well.

Love to *Eros*, if you'll pardon the Classics Department in-joke.

Kind regards,

Francis Hird,
Classics Department, UCD

✳✳✳

I'm on the 46A, roysh, *trying* to have a conversation with Fionn, when all of a sudden we're going through Stillorgan, roysh, and all these knobs from Coláiste Iosagáin get on and stort, like, talking in Irish, or that's what Fionn said it was anyway. It's, like, so head-wrecking. I'm there, 'What the *fock* are they trying to say?' and Fionn goes, 'They're talking about the teachers' strike,' and if that's the case I can't understand why they look so focking miserable. They actually seem disappointed that the Leaving might not be going ahead, the sad bastards.

I'm just wishing there was a focking lecturers' strike. I am so going to have to repeat at this stage it's not funny, which is why I'm going out on the lash tonight, to try to forget about it. I'm telling Fionn that I'm so not cancelling the States, roysh, I'm going on a J1er one way or the other and I'm not coming back to sit repeats, no *focking* way, I'll probably end up repeating the whole year instead, maybe actually going to a few lectures next year.

I'm trying to get my head around all of this, roysh, but all around me it's all, *Tá me, tá me, conas atá tú*, blah blah blah, and I turn around to these two knobs behind me and I go, 'There's no focking Leaving Cert this year. Get over it,' and one of them, roysh, she goes, 'Sorry, would you mind your own business, please?' And quick as a flash, roysh, I turn around and go, 'Only if you get a life,' which I'm pretty happy with. I'm like, 'Talking in that stupid focking language on the bus. School's over. *Hello?*'

I turn around, roysh, expecting Fionn to, like, back me up, but instead he's chatting away to these other two birds in front of us, telling them that it's the students he feels sorry for and that he's thinking of applying to become an exam supervisor and the birds think this is 'SO cool', and the goy thinks he's a stud.

I don't know which of the two he's trying to be with, roysh, but I can't watch and I decide to get off in, like, Donnybrook and see are any of the goys in Kiely's. As I'm heading down the stairs, roysh, I can hear him arranging to meet the girls in some bor in town after the Institute. The focker hasn't even noticed I've gone.

✳✳✳

Sophie phones me up, bawling her eyes out, roysh, telling me she failed philosophy and her parents are going to go ballistic and OH! MY! GOD! her old man is SO not going to give her the money to go skiing now, and it's all because of that complete dickhead of a lecturer who set *such* a hord paper, everyone said so, even Wendy, whoever the fock she is, and he was *such* an orsehole to her when she went to him to try to get her grade changed. And I can just picture her going in to see him in a little titty-top, trying to sweet-talk the goy. She tells me she SO needs someone to talk to and can I call over, roysh, and I'm pretty much certain I'm going to get my bit here, so I go, 'Is the bear a Catholic?'

I'm actually on the way back from Christian's gaff, roysh, and I'm pretty much home, but I turn the cor around and head for Glenageary. *Oh* my God, she goes, it wasn't like she was looking for a 2.1, or even a 2.2, all she wanted was a scabby pass and he was too much of a focking orsehole to give her that and – OH! MY! GOD! – now her points have, like, *totally* gone out the window because she's eaten, like, three bars of Dairy Milk, which is eighteen points in itself and that's all she's supposed to have in an entire, like, day and that's not even counting the Weight Watchers' lasagne, we're talking the beef one, not the vegetarian, which is, like, five-and-a-half, the four pieces of Ryvita, which is, like, two, and the bowl of Fruit and Fibre, which is, like, one-and-a-half, or five-and-a-half if you have it with full milk, which she did.

She goes, OH! MY! GOD! It was bad enough failing without going into that *dickhead* and making a complete tit of herself. She tells me she asked the goy what he would suggest she do, roysh, and he told her to, like, set her sights lower, maybe get a job with FM104 or one of the other radio stations, driving one of those big four-wheel drives around town. He said he was sure that a girl with her talent would be snapped up quickly.

I give her the old Ross O'Carroll-Kelly Hug, one hand stroking her hair, sort of, like, consoling her, and the other hand on her orse. Not blowing my own trumpet or anything, but I don't think I need to spell out what happened next.

CHAPTER SIX
'Ross has, like, SUCH commitment problems.'
Discuss.

'Ross, I cannot believe you're wearing a polo-neck in this weather. And a *black* polo-neck at that.' The old dear says this to me at the dinner table, roysh, and I'm just there, you know, yeah *what*ever, but the stupid bitch won't let it go, roysh, it's like she *knows* the focking reason I'm wearing it and she's trying to, like, embarrass the shit out of me. She's giving it, 'The hottest day of the year and you decide to wear something like that. In the middle of May. Charles, say something to Ross, will you?' The old man is just, like, staring at the back page of the *Sunday Indo*, going, 'Kerrigan … what's he *after*?'

The old dear goes, 'Put away the paper, Darling. Come on, it's salmon-en-croute,' and she kisses him on the forehead and I go, 'You two stort that lovey-dovey shit again and I'm getting my own gaff. You make me want to vom, you know that?' She totally ignores this, goes, 'Come on, Charles. Don't let that man upset you,' then turns to me and she's like, 'and Ross, why don't you go upstairs and change into a T-shirt. I've ironed your

Ralph-what-do-you-call-it. Much more appropriate for a day like today. Get some colour into you,' and I'm just there, 'Will you just shut the *fock* up going on about it. You are SUCH a knob, do you know that?'

I get up from the table and, like, storm out of the house and I get into the cor and check out my neck in the rear-view. There's only two types of people who wear polo-necks – one, total knobs, and two, anyone unlucky enough to have a big dirty Denis on their neck.

This Monday-night-in-Peg's thing basically has to stop. I should have seen it coming, of course, but I was completely off my face, bank-holiday weekend, roysh, why not? Originally went out for a few scoops, ended up, like, knocking back beers until, whatever, maybe two in the morning, and what with one thing and another I ended up being with Auveen, this total babe who's, like, second year Orts, roysh, and a little bit like Piper Perabo, except with, like, braces on her teeth.

Anyway, roysh, the goys – well, Fionn mostly – he calls her The Hound of the Baskervilles because when she's, like, shit-faced, roysh, she basically storts, like, sucking the neck off you. Of course, Monday night, I'm too off my face to fight her off, so I wake up this morning, roysh, in Christian's gaff – Ailesbury Road, focking amazing pad – and I am absolutely reeking of, like, toothpaste. Christian comes into the room, roysh, and I'm like, 'What the fock is that smell?' Of course, he goes, 'You must rest. You've had a busy day,' and I'm like, 'Will you quit it with that *Star Wars* bullshit. Why am I smelling of toothpaste?' and he's, like, all offended.

He goes, 'I put it on your neck last night. To try to get rid of the ...' and the whole night suddenly comes rushing back to me. Of course, it had to happen on the one weekend of the year when the sun is, like, splitting the trees, and I am focking burning up in the cor as I head for Kiely's and, by the sounds of it, roysh, the weather's going to hold for, like, half the focking summer. Some knob on the radio says there's a heatwave on the way because, I don't know, Fungie the Dolphin is wearing shades and a focking sombrero.

All I can say is that I'm glad I'm heading to the States in June, by which time the thing will probably be yellow, or some focking colour. I pork the cor around the corner, roysh, take fifty notes out of the old Drinklink and hit the battle-cruiser, feeling really, like, self-conscious and wondering whether the focking thing is visible. I get a pint in and head over to the goys. Zoey and Aoife are sitting with them and they're, like, locked in conversation, which is sort of, like, unusual because those two usually hate each other's guts.

Aoife asks Zoey why she didn't go out last night and Zoey says she did, roysh, and Aoife goes, 'Oh my God, how come you're looking so well then?' and Zoey says it's Radiant Touch and Aoife goes, '*Oh my God*, YSL,' and Zoey nods and says, OH MY GOD, it is *such* a life-saver.

Judging from his body language, JP is going to try to be with her, roysh, while Oisinn is definitely going to chance his orm with Aoife. JP asks Zoey whether she was in Reynards last night and she says no, she was in Lillies, and Aoife asks whether Bono and Matt Damon really were in there and she says no, that was only a rumour, and that the only famous people in there were two newsreaders off TV3 and the Carter Twins. Then she says she's going to the toilet, roysh, and when she's gone Aoife says, 'OH! MY! GOD! Not meaning to be, like, a bitch or anything, but Zoey looks like *shit*.'

When Zoey comes back from the toilet, roysh, she looks at me and goes, 'Oh my God, Ross, what the *fock* are you wearing?' and everyone looks at me, roysh – we're talking Fionn, JP, Simon, everyone – and I'm wondering whether they know what happened, whether Christian has, like, told them. I presume he hasn't and I just go, 'It's a polo-neck. What's the big deal?' and Aoife goes, 'You do look a bit of a knob in it, Ross.' I tell her that polo-necks are in and Zoey thinks for a minute, roysh, and goes, '*Oh my God*, they are. I read that in *Marie Claire*. They're the new, em, shirts, I think.'

I can see Simon sort of, like, sniggering, roysh, and also JP, who I think was actually in Peg's last night, can't remember, but I'm pretty sure now he knows the story, and basically all of a sudden, roysh, he tells me that I look like the goy off the Milk Tray ad and everyone storts breaking their shites laughing.

And then Fionn, roysh, he goes, 'And all because the lady loves … Ross's neck.' And Fionn high-fives JP, and JP high-fives Christian, and Simon high-fives … Let's just say that everyone high-fived everyone else.

Focking dickheads.

✳✳✳

Amanda, roysh, this bird who, I have to say, has the total hots for me – a friend of Eanna's sister – I saw her this morning at the bus stop in, like, Stillorgan, waiting for the 46A, so I pull over, roysh, ask her does she want a lift into college and she's like, '*Oh* my God, you are SUCH a dorling,' and I'm there, 'Hey, it's a pleasure to have such a beautiful girl in my car,' playing it totally cool like Huggy Bear.

We're getting on really well, roysh. She tells me all about this huge row she's just had with her old pair because her old man – a complete tosser apparently – is refusing to pay her cor insurance, and then about some friend of hers who's on the permanent guest list in Reynards. Anyway, to cut a long story short, roysh, we get to UCD and she says she so has to, like, buy me lunch later to say thank you for the lift and for listening to her problems, basically giving it loads, TOTALLY gagging for me, so I arrange to meet her in the Orts block, roysh, at, like, half-twelve.

She's in first year, we're talking Philosophy and, like, Linguistics, which is what she had that morning. I know because I basically just hung around waiting for her, roysh, but then I got bored so I ended up going into her lecture. She's sitting in the back row, roysh, with a couple of her mates, one of them I recognise from Knackery Doo, the old Club d'Amour, and she sort of, like, mouths the word 'Hi!' to me and I scooch up beside her.

The lecturer, roysh, he is SO boring it's unbelievable. He's like, 'In English, a double negative is a positive. In some languages, including Russian, the inverse is also the case, but there is no incidence in the English language where a double positive forms a negative.' I'm like, 'Yeah, roysh!' And everyone breaks their shites laughing, and I didn't even realise I'd, like, said it so loud, and I look at Amanda and her head is turned the other way and I can hear her going, '*Oh my God, oh my God, oh my God*, I am SO embarrassed.'

✳✳✳

I'm in my room, roysh, listening to a few sounds, bit of Eminem, bit of the Snoopster, when I'm suddenly, like, thirsty and I hit the kitchen for glass of Coke. When I get there, roysh, I'm just like, *What* are these two focking weirdoes up to now? The old man's standing outside the laundry room, roysh, holding the door shut and the old dear's standing behind him with the wok and she's holding it up in the air, roysh, as if she's getting ready to, like, whack someone over the head with it. I just ignore the two of them and open the fridge. The old man's shouting through the door, giving it, 'The guards are on their way. They'll put a stop to your fun and games, with a capital S, you mark my words.' The old dear goes, 'We're taxpayers,' and the old man looks at her over his shoulder and he's like, 'That's not *technically* true, Darling.' The old dear goes, 'And don't you touch my underwear in there. Unless you want another ten years on your sentence, you monster.'

Of course, the curiosity is storting to, like, get to me at this stage, roysh, so I go, 'What the fock are you two on?' The old man's like, 'Ross, you *are* home. Didn't you hear your mother screaming?' I'm there, 'Considering I was listening to music in my focking room, no, I didn't. What were you screaming about, you stupid wagon? Another halting site planned for Foxrock?' The old man goes, 'Would it were that simple, Ross. No, we've got an intruder. Your mother caught him in the laundry. In the *laundry*, if you please.'

I go, 'If there *is* an intruder, and the Feds are on their way, why isn't he trying to get out of there?' The old pair look at each other, roysh, and the old man's like, 'There's a point, Darling. How hard did you hit him with that thing?' She goes, 'Pretty hard. He was naked, Charles. Kept waving his ... thing at me. Oh the thoughts of it.' The old man goes, 'It'll be a bloody nuisance if he's dead. The police'll probably try to blame *us*. You saw that chap in England. Killed those four yobbos who were trying to steal his lawnmower and suddenly *he's* the one in the wrong.' She's like, 'What are you saying, Charles?' and he goes, 'There's all kinds of loopholes in the law to protect these people, Fionnuala. We're going to have to dispose of the body.' The old dear storts crying, roysh – the stupid focking sap – and the old man goes, 'Hennessy knows people who can take care of it.'

I'm bored listening to this crap, roysh, so I just push the old man out of the way and shoulder-charge the door and it, like, flings open, roysh, and what do I see – I should have focking guessed – *Eros* lying facedown on the floor with a big focking chunk, about the size of a wok, taken out of the back of his head. I break my balls laughing, roysh, while the old man leans up against the wall and goes, 'Thank heavens. Thank heavens for that.'

I stand the statue up again and ask Dick-features if he has any Pollyfilla, but he goes, 'What's that blasted thing doing here, Ross?' I'm there, 'If you must know, I stole it from the Classics Museum. Me and Oisinn are trying to extort a grand out of

UCD.' The old man goes, 'I say, what fun.' The next thing, roysh, the doorbell rings and, of course, it's the Feds, so I have to, like, stick the thing in the cupboard under the stairs.

The old pair go to the door and I can hear the old man giving it, 'Sorry, chaps. False alarm,' and the Feds saying something about wasting Garda time and the old man going, 'Well, I presume that's what they want me to pay my taxes for,' and he slams the door. And the old dear, roysh, she goes, 'Gosh, Charles, you sounded just like Spencer Tracy then.' The old man's like, 'I did?' and she's there, 'Yes. In *Bad Day at Black Rock*. Let's go upstairs, Darling.' I'm there, 'Hey, cut that shit out. You two doing it? The focking thought of it makes me wanna borf.'

The statue has got to go. I phone the goys and tell them.

✶✶✶

Still no word from, like, Sorcha.

✶✶✶

The old man's solicitor recommended that he reach a settlement with the Revenue Commissioners, roysh, so he's heading out to Portmarnock to discuss it with him over an early-morning round of golf. Anyway, roysh, he asks me to drive him, obviously planning to have a few scoops, and I tell him it's no problem at all, even though it sticks in my throat to be nice to the focker, but I'm heading off to the States in a few weeks and I'm gonna need seven or eight hundred notes to bring with me.

So there we are, driving along, roysh, and the old man's boring the ears off me, giving it, 'Hennessy wants me to settle for a hundred thousand pounds, Ross. Or a Rezoning, as he calls it. You know how he likes to joke about this tribunal nonsense,' and I'm seriously fighting the urge to call him a wanker and tell him to shut the fock up. Being up at, like, seven o'clock on a Saturday morning is bad enough without having to listen to his bullshit.

So anyway, roysh, basically what happens is that I end up breaking a red light at the bottom of, like, Stradbrook Road and suddenly, roysh, this old dear in a red Subaru Signet comes around the corner and, like, ploughs into the side of me. It's a good job I'm driving the old man's Volvo and not my Golf GTI because this thing has side-impact bors, it's like a focking tank, and even after the crash there's fock-all wrong with it. Which is more than can be said for the other cor, which is, like, pretty badly damaged and shit. The second it happens, roysh, the old man goes, 'Leave the talking to me, Ross. The first line here is all-important.'

The two of us get out and walk up to the driver's side of the other cor, roysh, and the bird winds down the window and straight away the old man goes, 'Is your neck alright?' and the woman, roysh, she's a total AJH, she goes, 'Me neck's grand.' The old man turns around to me and goes, 'You heard that, Ross. Nothing wrong with her neck. Little trick Hennessy taught me. Cuts off any possible spurious claim for whiplash at source,' and then he, like, whispers, 'Don't get me wrong, I've nothing against working-class people. Quote unquote. Hit one of them in your car, though, and one visit to their solicitor later, they're wearing a surgical collar and trying to sting you for fifty grand.'

The old man goes to the creamer, 'Well, let's be thankful there's no real damage done here. We'll bid you *adieu*,' and he goes to walk off. Of course the slapper's like, 'No damage? What about me car?' and she gets out. *Holy fock!* Leggings are SO focking unattractive. Why *do* poor people have to wear them? She's pointing to the front of the cor – a Subaru Signet, for fock's sake – and she storts getting a bit smart then, roysh, going, 'Someone's going to have to pay for this,' then basically accuses me of breaking a red light, which I totally deny, even though it's true.

The old man, you have to admire him even though he's a total knob, he goes, 'Am I to take it from your tone that you intend to claim from my insurance company for this accident?' and the woman's like, 'Course we bleedin' do.'

I go, 'Easier than holding us up with a syringe, I suppose,' and she's like, 'What d'ye mean by dat?'

Never mentioned it before, roysh, but she's got her daughter sitting in the cor beside her and she's an even bigger knick-knack than her old dear, and of course she decides to get involved herself then. She, like, rips open the cor door and storts giving me loads – ice blue denim mini and black tights, very focking tasteful – saying we better hand over our inshoorice details or there'll be moorder, fookin moorder. She says there'll be even wooorse if she misses her floy t'Englind, so there will.

I'm just there giving it, 'Fock off back to Knackeragua,' but the old man turns around to me and goes, 'Let me handle this, Kicker. I haven't kept my insurance premium so low for so many years without knowing a trick or six.'

He turns around to the daughter, roysh – rings all over her

fingers, looks like she's focking mugged Doctor Dre – and he asks her what time her flight is at, and she says that she's supposed to be checkin' in at half bleedin' seven, so she is. The old man looks at his watch and he goes, 'It's already a quarter past seven, you do know that, don't you?' and the daughter goes, 'So bleedin' wha'?' The old man – he's loving this, roysh – he's like, 'What I'm saying is that you're late for your flight. And you were obviously in too much of a hurry to watch the road in front of you.'

And she just loses the plot then, telling the old man he's this and that, then actually saying the crash happened because I was on my mobile. Basically, roysh, I wasn't on my mobile when I crashed the light, but I *was* checking my messages to see if Sorcha had replied to my text, though I wasn't going to admit that, not with the old man running circles around them.

He goes, 'I'm not saying that you were speeding to try to make the flight. That's just how a judge might look at it.' She hasn't a focking clue what to say then, the daughter. The mother, roysh, she goes, 'A judge?' and the old man goes, 'But of course. If you think you're sending my premium soaring through the roof for this bucket of bolts, you can think again.'

He goes, 'You're no stranger to the court system, I'd wager. Spot of shoplifting, perhaps. Handling stolen credit cards, that type of thing. Off to England then, were we?' Mummy skanger goes, '*She* is. She's off to see her fella,' and daughter skanger goes, 'Tell dem nuttin', Ma.'

The old man goes, 'Bit of a send-off last night then?' and the mother, roysh, she shrugs her shoulders and goes, 'The local,'

BOTH TRADBROOK
STRA OOK ROAD

CLARKE.

real defensive, like, and she's there, 'Have ye a problem wit dat?' obviously not realising that the old man's going to blow her out of the water in a minute. He goes, 'Had a few drinks, did we? A few pints of this *lager,* perchance?' She goes, 'I know what yer getting at. I only had tree glasses,' but the old man's like, 'Did you know you could still actually be over the limit?'

The daughter, roysh, she jumps back in then, giving it, 'Are you sayin' me ma's locked?' and he goes, 'I'm not in any position to judge that. I'm going to call the Gardaí. They can breathalyse her.'

He storts, like, punching the number into his phone, roysh, then he stops and goes, 'There is another alternative, of course. You could get back in your little banger there and be on your way.'

Who knows what the Feds have on these two, roysh, because they only think about it for, like, ten seconds, roysh, then they fock off, calling me and the old man every name under the sun as they get back into their little shit-bucket and fock off.

The old man asks me whether I think he should still call the cops, roysh, maybe report them for leaving the scene of an accident, just so they don't have any second thoughts about claiming. It's tempting, roysh, but in the end I tell him not to bother.

✳✳✳

I would so love to know what Sorcha's game is. She hasn't returned any of my texts for the past, like, two weeks, roysh, then she sends me one today and it's like, **drnk 2moro queens @ 8**. She is so focking with my head at the moment.

***

Sorcha gives me this look, roysh, we're talking total disgust here, and she goes, 'Spare me the character dissection,' and I go, 'I only asked what you thought of my baseball cap,' and she goes, 'Can we *please* change the subject?'

I nod at the borman, roysh, and he takes this as a signal that we want the same again and the lounge girl brings over a pint of Ken and a Diet Coke. I'm there, 'It's really nice to see you, Sorcha,' and she goes, 'We're friends. When Dawson and Joey broke up, that didn't stop them having their movie nights, did it?' and I'm like, 'Course not,' even though I haven't a focking clue what she's talking about.

She tells me she's, like, so chilled out these days and it's SO because of the music she's been listening to. She tells me she had Tchaikovsky's 'Scene from Swan Lake' on in the cor on the way in and Bizet's 'Au Fond Du Temple Saint', and even though the third CD takes a lot of getting used to, she's really storted getting into Strauss, Holst, Prokofiev and Copland. I tell her I've been mostly listening to Eminem, the new U2 album and a bit of Oasis, and she tells me my taste is SO up my orse it's unbeliev-able, and she offers to lend me her *Saving Private Ryan* sound-track, which she says is SO easy to listen to and SUCH a good way to get into classical music, especially 'Hymn To The Fallen', 'Wade's Death' and 'Omaha Beach', and I'm there going, 'Cool.'

She stubs out a Marlboro Light, lights up another. I'm there trying to think of a way to bring up Australia, roysh, to ask her not to go. She goes, 'You heard about Sophie's exams then?' and I'm like, 'Yeah, she was a bit freaked.' She goes, 'She said you called over to her that night. Said you were very nice to her,' and I'm like, 'Em, yeah.' She goes there, 'How nice, Ross?' And quick as a flash, roysh, I'm there, 'What do you care?' and she storts breaking her shite laughing and goes, 'Don't flatter yourself, Ross. Do *not* flatter yourself.'

She takes off her scrunchy, slips it onto her wrist, shakes her hair free and then smoothes it back into a low ponytail again, puts it back in the scrunchy and then pulls five or six, like, strands of hair loose again. I go, 'So you're still heading to Australia?' and she's like, 'In two weeks.' I'm there, 'With what's-his-face?' and she goes, 'Cillian. You know his name's Cillian.' I go, 'What's he like, this goy?' and Sorcha goes, '*Amazing*. He works for PriceWaterhouse Coopers,' and I'm like, 'Just want to make sure he's treating you properly, that's all,' and Sorcha's there, 'For as long as we've known each other, Ross, you've treated me like shit. Why do you all of a sudden care?' There's no answer to that. I'm there, 'I don't sup- pose–' and she goes, 'I'd cancel my plans if you asked me? No, Ross. I wouldn't.'

Sorcha changes the subject, asks me if I heard about Sadbh and Macker and I tell her no, and she says they broke up, which is, like, *such* a pity, she goes, because they looked SO cute to- gether, even though they SO weren't suited, and I can't work out whether Sadbh and Macker are real people, or, like, television characters, it's so hord to tell with Sorcha, but I agree with her because when we're getting on like this she is just SO easy to talk to.

I ask her whether she wants another drink and she says it's

her round and when she comes back from the bor she asks me how Christian is. I tell her his old man's moved out and she goes, 'Mum said he's living in Dalkey, in the aportment they own.' I'm like, 'Christian won't go and see him,' and she goes, 'That is SO unfair on his dad. From what I hear, his mum wasn't exactly blameless,' and I'm like, 'What is that supposed to mean?' maybe a bit too defensive. Sorcha goes, 'I'm just *saying*, Ross, that it takes two people to make a relationship and two to break one.'

When I think about Christian, it makes me sad. I'd love to have a big, deep conversation with the dude, but I find it, like, hord to talk to goys about shit like that when I'm sober, roysh, and whenever I'm locked Christian is always twice as bad as me and pretty much impossible to talk to. I've thought about sending him maybe, like, a text message, sort of like, **R U OK?** but it just doesn't, like, seem enough or something. I'm there, 'The States will take his mind off it, I think.'

She tells me he's SO lucky to have a friend like me and it's nice to hear, even if it is total bullshit. I tell her she's looking well and she tells me that's the third time I've said that tonight.

✳✳✳

The old dear asks me whether it was me who broke her John Rocha signature votive, roysh, and I'm like, '*Oh my God,* you are SUCH an orsehole. I cannot wait to get out of this country.'

✳✳✳

I was never so loaded in all my life, roysh, as I was when me and Oisinn muscled in on the fake ID racket in UCD. The whole of, like, first year was heading to the States for the summer, roysh, and they all needed fake driving licences and shit to get served over there. Of course we end up totally up to our tits in work so it was, like, no surprise to me that I didn't make it into any of my summer exams, although it was to the Dean of our course, who is SO trying to get me focked out of college it's unbelievable. I'm like, 'Hey, had things to do. People to see,' and he goes, 'I think you need to sit down and re-evaluate whether you're serious about a career in Sports Management or not,' and I'm just there, 'Get real, will you?'

I basically didn't give a fock, roysh, because I knew I was going to have to repeat anyway and suddenly I've got, like, eight hundred bills in my pocket and it's, like, money for old rope. A couple of knobs from Ag. Science were actually doing it first, roysh, but Oisinn goes up to them in the bor – they were, like, playing Killer – and he goes, 'You the goys dealing in the fake IDs?' Oisinn had picked up a focking pool cue at this stage, roysh, and the goys are like, gicking themselves, giving it, 'What do you mean, fake IDs?'

Oisinn goes, 'Maybe I'm not making myself clear enough. What I'm asking you is whether they're your flyers I saw stuck up in the Orts block? Outside Theatre L?' You can see, roysh, that these goys are totally bricking themselves, and we're talking TOTALLY. One of them goes, 'Yeah … em, they're ours,' and Oisinn's there, 'Well, what I'm telling you goys now is that there's a couple of new faces on the scene.' He points over at me and I'm, like, trying to look really hord, even though there's no need really because Oisinn is such a big bastard he could handle all of them on his own if he had to.

He goes, 'Time to take early retirement, boys. Enjoyed it while it lasted though, haven't you?' I turn around, roysh – and I have to say I pretty much surprise myself with this one – I go, 'Unless you want to face … involuntary liquidation.'

So basically that's it, roysh. We put the word around the Orts block that we're the men to see for all your fake ID requirements, then spend most of March and April in the bor, playing pool, knocking back beers and taking orders from people.

And fock, I've never been so popular in my whole life. Everyone *loved* us. The babes would come in, roysh, and we'd be giving it loads, looking at their passport photographs and going, 'You look too well in this picture to put it on a passport,' and, 'You must do modelling, do you?'

We're talking The Palace, Annabel's, Mono, I have never seen so much action in my life and, like, not being big-headed or anything, but that's really focking saying something. We'd get bored snogging one bird, roysh, and the next one was already queuing up behind her.

The goys loved us too, and I don't mean in a gay way. We were, like, celebrities. I'm walking through the library, or I'm heading down to 911 for the rolls and total strangers are coming up to me and high-fiving me, telling me they're getting the shekels together and they'll be in touch.

And I'm like, 'Yeah, *what*ever.'

Me and Oisinn, for six weeks we're, like, totally Kool and the Gang. And it wasn't only respect, roysh, there was a bit of fear thrown in as well. Every time Oisinn would hand over an order, he'd go, 'You breathe our names to the NYPD and you're fish food. *Capisce?*'

Sometimes, for a laugh, roysh, we'd print the words, *Póg mo thóin*, in, like, really official-looking writing on the fake driving licences, roysh. *Póg mo thóin* is actually Irish for All Cops Are Bastards, which basically completely rips the piss out of them without them actually knowing. Everyone loved that little touch. They were like, 'OH! MY! GOD!'

The work was a piece of piss. Oisinn, who knows a bit about computers, he downloads this thing off the internet, roysh, said it was a template for a driving licence, and he gives it to me on, like, a disk. So I go home, roysh, get onto the old man's computer, add in the customer's name, date of birth and all that shit, print it out, Pritt Stick the photograph onto it, then take them down to Keeva, this bird I know who works in the local video shop and she, like, laminates the thing.

We didn't cut her in on any of the profits. Oisinn said it was to protect her, roysh – he really gets off on that whole gangster thing – but the real reason was that she didn't want any money. Not being vain here, roysh, but the girl did it for love. She's been mad into me for years, ever since transition year actually when we both did our work experience in her old man's architect's firm. She's actually pretty alroysh lookswise, a little bit like Jennifer Love Hewitt, from a distance.

So for six weeks, roysh, me and Oisinn, well, we have it all. We're talking money. We're talking babes. We're talking fame. But all good things have to come to an end. As Christian always says, there's always a bigger fish. So this day, roysh, we're sitting in the bor, knocking back a few beers with this goy from second year Law, who we brought on the lash for being our five-hundredth customer, when all of a sudden these five Chinese goys come in and say they want a word with us.

Oisinn plays it totally Kool and the Gang, roysh, telling me he'll handle this on his own, then following the goys over to a table in the corner and talking for, like, five or ten minutes. Then the Chinese goys fock off.

Oisinn comes back over, roysh, takes a long swig out of his bottle of Probably and goes, 'We're folding the business, Ross,' and of course I'm like, 'Who were those goys? And why did they all have their little fingers missing?' He goes, 'Why do you think, Ross?' and I go, '*Oh* my God, they're not from Newtown-mountkennedy, are they?' He shakes his head and goes, 'We're not talking genetics here, Ross. Those goys are Triads.' I'm like, 'Triads! *Fock!*' He gets three more beers in and goes, 'You don't fock with those goys.'

I'm there, 'Good while it lasted though, wasn't it?' and he just, like, stares off into space. Eventually he goes, 'Involuntary liquidation. I liked that. Have to hand it to you, Ross, you're a stylish bastard.'

✳✳✳

I meet Chloë in the Frascati Shopping Centre, roysh, and I ask her if she's going to Sorcha's going-away and she says OH! MY! GOD! she is, she SO is. She asks me whether I went out at the weekend and I tell her I was in Annabel's and she goes, *Oh my God*, she was in The George and she had the most amazing time, and she went with Julian and Kevin, two friends of hers who, she says, are *actually* gay, but they're, like, really, really good friends of hers, and that's the thing about gay goys, they're, like, so easy to talk to and she says that even though she's not, like, gay herself, roysh, going to The George is *such* a good night out if you're a girl, because you're not, like, getting constantly hassled by goys all night, and I'm thinking, You should be so focking lucky.

✳✳✳

Sorcha has her going-away porty, roysh, and – typical of the Lalors – it's a big, fock-off, black-tie affair in Killiney Golf Club, we're talking free bor, the whole lot. Anyway, roysh, I only found out the night before that my old pair were, like, invited as well and of course I went ballistic. I'm there going, How the fock am I going to score with the old man and the old dear in the same room? I'm like, 'You're not *actually* thinking of going, are you?' and the old dear's there, 'Mr and Mrs Lalor want us there. They're friends of ours, Ross,' and then she's like, 'I hope you've bought Sorcha something nice,' and I go, 'What I bought Sorcha is my business,' which basically means I bought her fock-all, because I totally forgot, what with me going to the States in a couple of weeks and having to go to the embassy to sort out my visa and shit.

So I head out to Stillorgan that afternoon, roysh, and I end up getting her a fake Burberry bag in Dunnes, which is a bit scabby I know, but I only have, like, ten bills to spend, and I don't want to break into my America money.

That night I meet the goys in the Druid's Chair for a few scoops beforehand, roysh, and then we head down to the golf club, and there's Sorcha's old pair at the door of the function room, roysh, welcoming everyone as they arrive, and Sorcha's sister, Afric, or Orpha, or whatever the fock name she has, she's collecting all the presents and making a list of who gave what, which will no doubt be discussed in detail at the Lalor breakfast table tomorrow morning.

I'm, like, standing in the queue behind this bird, Becky, roysh, who's, like, second year Commerce in UCD, a little bit like Jaime Pressly when she's wearing her contacts, and she's says she's, like, SO bursting to go to the toilet, roysh, and she asks me to mind her place in the queue for her and her present. A big fock-off present it is as well. So she goes off looking for the jacks, roysh, and I'm standing there with this little scabby present from me and this, like, massive one from Becky, and all of a sudden I'm at, like, the top of the queue and Becky still isn't back, so I switch the two cords, put her one with my present and my one with hers.

Sorcha's old dear air-kisses me, roysh, and looks over her shoulder to some friend of hers, maybe from the ladies' golf club, and goes, 'This is Ross. He was on the Castlerock team that won the cup,' and Sorcha's old man shakes my hand, real, like, formal and shit, and then Afric – I think that's her name – kisses me on the cheek and storts giving me the serious eyes, obviously jealous that her sister's getting all the attention tonight and deciding that being with me again would be the best way to piss her off. I hand her Becky's present, roysh, and I go, 'This is from me,' and she's there, '*Oh* my God, what is it?' and obviously I haven't a focking bog, but I go, 'Something special,' and she's like, 'Full of surprises, aren't you, Ross?'

And she looks at the other present, roysh, the wrapping paper all ripped and just, like, turns her nose up at it. The goys were, like, focking the thing around on the way down from the Druid's Chair, practicing their line-outs with it and shit. I'm like, 'That one's from Becky. I think she was too embarrassed to give it to you herself.' Afric says she doesn't blame her and, as I go to head inside, she puts her hand on my orse and tells me I SO have to promise to dance with her later.

I get inside, roysh, and even though it's, like, totally jammers, who's the only person in the room I can see? Sorcha. I can't take my eyes off her. She looks in-*focking*-credible. She's wearing this little black dress, roysh, which I heard Emer say is a copy of the one that Jennifer Lopez wore to the Grammies and, I have to say, I've never seen her looking so well. Every goy in the place is, like, hanging out of her, but she comes over to me, roysh, and she air-kisses me and *oh my God* she smells amazing, *Issey* focking *Miyake*.

She goes, 'I didn't know if you were going to come ...' and I'm like, 'You look amazing,' and she goes, '... I'm glad you did.' I look into her eyes, roysh, and I'm like, 'Did you hear I might be playing for Blackrock next year?' and she turns away and goes, 'Don't, Ross.' I'm there, 'Jim Leyden invited me down to Stradbrook. Check out the facilities.' She's like, 'You're wasting your time. I'm going out with somebody. I don't want any trouble.'

Off she storms, roysh, and 'Stuck In A Moment' comes on and Oisinn comes over and grabs me in a headlock and goes, 'She is *gagging* for you tonight, Ross,' and I'm like, 'Told her I'm not

interested, but she just can't seem to get her head around it.'
Fionn goes, 'Would anyone with any information on the whereabouts of Ross's self-respect please contact Gardaí at Shankill,'
and I just give him, like, daggers.

So we're there for the night, roysh, knocking back the pints,
and about eleven o'clock Zoey and Sophie come around telling
us all to go and 'get food' because there's, like, loads of it there
and we can't let it go to waste, which, as Fionn says, is a bit rich
coming from Calista Flockhart and Geri focking Halliwell. But
we join the nosebag queue anyway, roysh, and who's standing
roysh in front of me only the old man and he's chatting away to
some total knob about, I don't know, the federal reserve, whatever the fock that is. He sees me and goes, 'Ross, have you met
Cillian? He's with PriceWaterhouse,' and the goy – a knob in a
suit – goes to shake my hand, roysh, but I just look him up and
down and go, 'Wow, Sorcha's done *real* well for herself,' and I
turn around and join in a conversation with JP and Oisinn, who
are talking about Formula One.

I'm heading back to where I was sitting with my food, roysh,
and I pass the old dear and she's engrossed in conversation
with Sorcha's old dear about Stella McCartney and some place
in Greystones that is, like, the only shop in Ireland that sells her
stuff, and they see me as I'm trying to squeeze past and the old
dear goes, 'Ross, did you meet Cillian? Sorcha's new boyfriend.
An absolute darling. He's with PWC,' and I tell her she's a sad
bitch.

It's, like, an hour later, roysh, and I look over the far side of
the bor and the old man is still there talking to the goy, and I

feel like going over and asking him whether he still considers me his son at all. Christian is basically off his face. He keeps reminding me that we've been best friends since we were, like, five years old, roysh, and that I'm a great goy and that's not the drink talking, and I'm the best focking friend any focker could hope for, and even though I turned to the Dark Side for a little while, he always knew, blah blah blah.

I knock back the vodka and Red Bull that JP bought me and then this bird, Gemma, who's, like, repeating in Bruce, passes by looking pretty amazing, and I can see what the goys mean when they say she looks like Ali Landry, and all of a sudden I look up and Sorcha is, like, standing next to me again. She goes, 'She's seeing someone, Ross,' and I'm like, 'Gemma? I wasn't actually–' She's there, 'I'm only kidding. She broke up with Ronan ages ago. Do stay away from her, though, and I'm telling you that as a friend. The girl has a serious attitude problem.'

I look over, roysh, and now Fionn and JP are talking to this knob of a boyfriend of hers, and I'm wondering do I have any loyal friends left. Sorcha goes, 'How was the Florida salad? Mum made it. It's, like, a secret family recipe.' I go, 'Sorcha, you didn't come over here to ask me about Florida salad,' pretty confident at this stage that deep down she wants to be with me as much as I want to be with her. That dress …

She's there, 'You're right, Ross. I came over because I wanted to say sorry to you,' and I'm like, 'It's cool.' She goes, 'You don't even know what I'm saying sorry for yet. I misjudged you, Ross. I've just opened your present.' I'm like, 'Okaaaay. Go on,' obviously not knowing what the fock I gave her. She goes, 'Those suitcases are SO expensive, Ross,' and I'm like, 'Just a little token of my affection,' and she goes, '*Little? Hello?* They're Louis Vuitton.'

I'm like, 'Forget about it. By the way, what did Becky get you?' and Sorcha goes, 'Do *not* even talk to me about that girl. Anyway, Ross, the reason I was so happy about your present is that you seem to have accepted what's happening,' and I'm like, 'Happening?' She goes, 'Me and my boyfriend? Going away for the year? That's why you bought me the case.' I'm like, 'Yeah, of course. When, em … when are you going?' She's there, 'The day after tomorrow. Though this is going to have to be goodbye, Ross. I have *such* a lot of packing to do, and she kisses me on the cheek, roysh, and she tells me she is SO going to miss me.

Fionn and JP arrive back over and stort going on about Cillian and how sound he is and how much money he's earning and how he has an offer to play for Mary's when he comes back. Christian throws his orm around my shoulder and asks me whether I know how long it is since we've been best friends, and I can feel tears in my eyes. And JP looks at me, roysh, and he asks me if I'm crying and I say of course I'm not focking crying, it's the dry ice getting in my eyes, and he goes, 'What dry ice?'

✳✳✳

The radio's going, 'If you're paying your home insurance to your mortgage company you could be paying too much,' and all of a sudden this complete orsehole in a red Corsa, roysh, he pulls out roysh in front of me, no indicator, nothing, and I have to hit the brakes and drop down to something like third gear or whatever, roysh, and I am going to be SO late because 'there's focking raidworks in operation on the Rock Raid and the saithbaind carriageway of the M50 between Scholarstown Raid and the Balrothery Interchange is still claised, causing severe delays on all approaches to the Spawell randabite,' and I'm wondering when the *fock* they're actually going to sort out the roads in this country, and all of a sudden we're stopped at lights, roysh, and I get out to have a focking word with the total penis in the red Corsa, and he sees me coming and, like, winds down his window and he goes, 'I'm really sorry about that,' and I'm like, 'If you don't know how to drive, you should have a focking L-plate on your cor, orsehole.'

✱✱✱

Emer goes OH! MY! GOD! she cannot *believe* that Rachel slept with Ross again, especially after Monica warned her off, the girl is SUCH a bitch it's unbelievable, and Fionn throws his eyes up to heaven and asks whether anyone's, like, going to the bor. Emer says that if anyone is, would they get her, like, a pint of Budweiser and Sophie shoots her this filthy, roysh, and Emer goes, 'You are *not* going to make me feel guilty about having a pint,' and, of course, Sophie's there, 'I'm just wondering what happened to your diet, that's all. You had a latte this morning,' and Emer's giving it, 'So?' Sophie's like, 'So … that's, like, eight points or something. *And* a packet of peanut M&Ms.' Emer's like, 'You are SO not going to make me feel guilty about having a pint,' but when JP brings it over, roysh, she hordly even touches it.

Fionn, roysh, he stands up and goes, 'Look at this, everyone,' and he grabs the waistband of his chinos and, like, pulls it out and there's enough room to fit Sophie *and* Emer in there. Sophie goes, 'OH! MY! GOD! that is, like, SO unfair. You eat like a pig,' and Emer's basically like, 'How come your trousers are falling off you?' and Fionn's like, 'I just moved up from a 34" to a 38",' and he, like, cracks his shite laughing, roysh, and high-fives Christian and JP and then goes to high-five me, and when I don't respond, Fionn goes, 'Anyone with any information on the whereabouts of Ross's life, please contact Gardaí at Harcourt Terrace.'

JP goes, 'Yeah, what gives, goy? You're very quiet,' and I'm like, 'I'm cool. Leave it.' Then he goes, 'Hey, let me run something past you guys. Your reactions are requested. Why don't I call the old man, tell him that Hook, Lyon and Sinker is going to have to function without my considerable presence tomorrow, and the lot of us can go on the serious lash tonight. You goys are going to the States the day after tomorrow. Last chance.' Everyone nods, roysh, and Christian goes, 'I knew I should have put a toilet roll in the fridge.'

JP looks under the table, roysh, to see are any of us wearing, like, runners, then he says he thinks he could get us all into Lillies, he knows one of the bouncers, and Emer says OH! MY! GOD! we will never guess who was in there last Saturday night, we're talking that goy off 'Don't Feed The Gondolas', and Emer goes, 'And don't forget Niamh Kavanagh.'

Erika, who's in a snot as usual, says she's not going anywhere if Beibhinn is going to be there and Emer asks what her problem with Beibhinn is and Erika says it's because she's an orsehole and because of that stupid skanger accent she puts on. She goes, 'That whole knacker-*chic* thing is, like, SO sixth year.'

I'm having a mare of a night, and I really can't bear any more of this shit, so I tell the goys I'm hitting the bor, roysh, but I don't, I actually just fock off home.

Sorcha has been gone for, like, ten days and I never thought I'd miss her so much. I spend the rest of the night at home, basically going through old stuff, looking for the Mount Anville scorf she gave me one of the first nights I was with her. We'd beaten Clongowes in the cup, roysh, and her and all her friends came over to me after the game. It's like it was yesterday. We were all like, 'Here they come, goys. Mounties, looking for their men,' but she seemed so, like, sincere, if that's the roysh word. She goes, 'Congrats, you'd a great game,' and of course I'm like, 'Thanks,' playing it totally Kool and the Gang. She goes, 'Did you hear I got onto the Irish debating team?' and I'm like, 'Yeah,' even though I didn't.

I go looking for the Valentine cord she sent me last year, telling me she would always love me no matter what, but I can't find it, though I do find the menu from her debs, the one that she wrote on saying she'd never met a more amazing person than me before and if there was, like, one goy she'd like to spend the rest of her life with, then it would be, like, me. It's funny, roysh, I don't actually remember ripping it in half, but I must have at some stage because it's in, like, two pieces.

I check the time, roysh, and it's still only seven o'clock. I decide to drive out as far as the Merrion Centre. It's, like, Thursday evening, we're talking late-night shopping. As I pull into the cor pork, I'm thinking about the morning she went away, when I called up to her and made a complete tit of myself asking her not to go and she just, like, put her head in her hands and went, 'Ross, I cannot deal with the soap-operatic implications of what you're saying right now.'

I get out of the cor and go into the shopping centre. Don't know why, roysh, it's not like I'm going to see her or anything, but I walk by her old dear's boutique and have a sly look in. Her old dear's not in there either, just some other bird who works for her.

I wander around, not knowing what the fock I'm doing here, maybe it's just to feel close to her. I go into the chemists, roysh, head down the back to the perfume counter and pick up a bottle of *Issey Miyake*. I spray some on the palm of my hand and stort, like, sniffing it, roysh, and the woman behind the counter goes, 'Can I help you, Sir?' and of course I just blank her.

I spray some on my other hand, roysh, and it's weird. So many memories suddenly come flooding back and the bird in charge of the perfume suddenly comes out from behind the counter, roysh, and goes, 'Excuse me, Sir, do you know that that's ladies' perfume you have there?' and I'm like, 'No shit, Sherlock,' in no mood for this bullshit at all, but then she tells me to leave the shop or she'll, like, call security. Of course I'm there, 'I'm going nowhere,' but then this big fock-off security goy comes in, so I basically stort heading towards the door, and he tells me he never wants to see me hanging around the shopping centre again.

I really can't wait to get out of this country.

I mosey back downstairs to the cor pork and I think about texting Sorcha. But of course it's too late for that.

***

I turn off the engine and check the time and it's, like, four o'clock in the morning. I ask Oisinn whether he's planning to talk all night and he goes, 'I'm having a conversation here,' then turns back to Christian and goes, 'Not a bad question, Christian. I would say Padme Amidala would be a Nina Ricci kind of bird. Probably something like *L'Air du Temps*.' Christian goes, 'Explain that to me,' and Oisinn's there, 'It's a floral, spicy fragrance that emanates a mysterious power of seduction. Hauntingly sensuous,' and Christian nods his head really, like, slowly and he goes, 'Like Her Highness herself.'

I go, 'Is that it, goys? Or is there any more of this shit?' and Oisinn's there, 'Hey, Ross, take a chill pill. You're lucky we agreed to come at all,' and I go, 'Sorry. Just a bit stressed, that's all.' Christian goes, 'I still don't see why we've got to fock the thing off Dún Laoghaire pier. Can't you just stick it back in the Classics Deportment when nobody's looking?' I pull the balaclava down over my face and go, 'Too risky. And anyway ...' and Oisinn straight away goes, 'Now don't stort with all that focking juju nonsense again,' and I'm like, 'I'm telling you, Oisinn, that thing has put a spell on my old pair. It's making me vom. It's put a spell on me as well. It's like I'm focking jinxed or something.'

We get out of the cor, roysh, I open the boot and the three of us look in. I pull back the blanket and *Eros* is there, smiling up at me. I'm sure that thing had a sad face when I robbed it. I go, 'It's brought me nothing but bad luck, goys. Look at Erika. Six months ago, I'd have been in like Flynn there. But she doesn't want to know me. Explain that.' Oisinn goes, 'Maybe she thinks you're a penis,' and I stare at him, roysh, give him total daggers, and he goes, 'Might come as a shock to you, I know, but not every bird in the world wants to sleep with Ross O'Carroll-Kelly.'

I go, 'Are you two benders just gonna stand there, or are we gonna get rid of this focker and split?' Oisinn grabs one end and me and Christian grab the other. Oisinn goes, 'Seriously, though, Ross. You heard what Fionn said. Eros is the Fertility God. If anything, he's going to *help* you get your rock and roll.' I go, 'That's another reason to get rid of it then. The old pair don't need any more focking encouragement, and I'm certainly not splitting my trust fund with some mistake of a focking brother or sister. This thing weighs a focking tonne. Probably should have porked closer to the end of the pier.'

Christian says that Padme wasn't born a Royal, roysh, she was in fact the daughter of common parents from the mountain village of Theed and she never forgot her roots, fair focks to her, she used to take off her make-up and dress down to roam around her old village anonymously, see how the other half lived. I go, 'Cool,' because Oisinn's roysh, they're doing me a favour by being here.

We get the thing halfway down the West Pier and I tell the goys we've gone far enough. Oisinn goes, 'Well, let's get rid of it now before someone sees us,' and the three of us grab it, roysh, and – one, two, three – fock it over the edge and – *gloop* – it sinks roysh to the bottom of the sea.

And that's when I stort to feel weird, not weird in a bad way, roysh, just weird in a weird way. Strange things stort happening. The thing is, roysh, suddenly I couldn't give two focks about Erika, but I can't stop thinking about Sorcha. I get this amazing urge to, like, ring her, but then I remember that it's after four and she won't, like, thank me for it.

But I can't stop thinking about her. How she's a ringer for Gail Porter when she's got her hair down. How her mouth goes all, like, pouty when she's trying to be angry with me. How she never, ever orders dessert but always ends up eating pretty much all of mine. How she pays seven lids a week to Concern by direct debit to sponsor some focking African kid she's never gonna meet. The girl is amazing. And now she's ten thousand focking miles away in Australia, with some knob called Cillian. And she might never come back.

I sit down on this little concrete pillar thing, roysh, and I send her a text and it's like, **DRNK 2MORO NITE?** and I sit there for, like, ten minutes, staring out to sea and just, like, thinking about her. She tried to dye her hair once when we were about sixteen, roysh, and it ended up going orange. She used to work at week-ends in some focking animal sanctuary, cleaning the shit out of the kennels, and when I found out she wasn't getting paid, I went, 'What a waste of time.' She used to have a Winnie the Pooh hot-water bottle.

I sit there for ages. It's, like, agony waiting for her to text me back and in the end she doesn't. Then I remember the goys. I walk back to the cor. Oisinn is outside, chatting to some bird by the sounds of it. He's going, 'What are you wearing? No, no. Let me guess. Something totally modern. Totally original. You might almost say a fragrance for the new millennium,' then he sniffs the air and goes, 'I can smell that blend of spicy, floral and Oriental notes from here. Hmmm, hmmm. *Ultraviolet.* Paco Rabanne's finest ever fragrance, in my humble opinion.'

I get into the cor and I look at Christian in the rear-view. I go, 'So focking clear to me now. Christian, I'm in love with Sorcha,' but he doesn't say anything. Oisinn gets into the passenger seat. He goes, 'Don't know why, just felt the urge to ring that bird I was with in Annabels last Friday. Emma Halvey.' I go, 'She was–' and he's there, 'Bet-down, I know. That's how I like them.'

Christian goes, 'Your old man's solicitor, Ross,' and I'm there, 'Hennessy? What about him?' He's like, 'What was that blonde bird's name we met the night of his fiftieth?' I'm like, 'Lauren, wasn't it?' and he goes, 'Lauren,' and he sits back in his chair and goes, 'Lauren,' again and sort of, like, stares off into space.

I stort the engine and I go, 'Something weird has happened here tonight, goys,' and no one contradicts me.

✻✻✻

YoU WErE WarNEd
Not to FOck
wiTh us
eros is SleePing
WITH THE fIsHeS

CHAPTER SEVEN
'Ross so can't hold his drink.'
Discuss.

I'm standing at the check-in desk when my mobile rings and I'm like, 'Y'ello?' And who is it, surprise sur-focking-prise, only Knob Head himself. He goes, 'Hey, Kicker, where are you?' and I'm like, 'The airport.' He goes, 'You never said goodbye,' and I'm like, 'Get focking over it, will you?'

***

Our landlord in the States, roysh, turns out to be a goy called Peasey Pee, which isn't actually his real name, he's called Peasey Pee because basically he does a lot of drugs and PCP just happens to be the drug he does most. I've been told, roysh, on pretty good authority, that it's, like, an animal tranquilliser, but that means fock-all to Peasey, who snorts, like, thirty or forty lines of the shit a day. He's always offering it to us as well, but the goy looks totally wasted – Fionn goes, 'Think Iggy Pop with a coat-hanger in his mouth' – so he's not exactly a good advertisement for the shit.

But Peasey's actually sound, roysh, and we're pretty much talking *totally* here, because without him we would be SO up

Shit Creek it's not funny. We basically arrived in Ocean City, Maryland, with, like, no jobs, nowhere to live, nothing. We had enough money to stay in, like, a hotel for the first few nights – we're talking the Howard Johnson, roysh – but the money soon runs out, especially when you're, like, drinking for Ireland, as we've been. After four or five nights in the hotel, roysh, we check our bills using the old television remote and *Holy Fock!* you should *see* how much we owe for our mini-bars alone. Mine's, like, five hundred and seventy lids. Fionn's is, like, four hundred and eighty. Oisinn's is, like, six hundred and nine. And Christian's is, like, over a thousand. So there's no other alternative, of course, but to peg it without paying.

So there we are, roysh, wandering around Ocean Highway with nowhere to live, place probably crawling with Feds looking for us, and all of a sudden we stumble on this, like, agency, which basically finds accommodation for students. We go in, roysh, tell the dude behind the counter we're Irish lads, just over, like, looking for work for the summer, blah blah blah, and we need somewhere to live. He tells us, roysh, that pretty much all of the accommodation in the town is already gone, that we've left it very late to be, like, arranging anything and I go, 'No shit, Sherlock.'

He goes, 'Are you going to be working while you're here?' and I'm like, 'Eh, you could say that, yeah,' and I just, like, break my shite laughing in the goy's face and Oisinn, Fionn and Christian, roysh, they're, like, cracking their shites laughing as well and they both high-five me, but when we turn around we notice that the goy hasn't got the joke – Americans have basically got no sense of humour – and he's in a bit of a snot now. He tells us that our only hope is this goy, Peasey Pee, who can usually be found down on the beach, flying his kite, and then he's like, 'Next, please.'

At first, me and the goys thought that this whole flying-his-kite thing was, like, slang for something, but we actually end up finding the dude down on the beach trying to control this big fock-off kite in the wind. He's about fifty, roysh, we're talking grey hair down to his shoulders, a big mad pointy nose and these crazy focking eyes which keep, like, darting all over the place. Fionn goes, 'The goy looks like a photo-fit,' which he actually does, roysh. I just march straight up to him and I go, 'We need somewhere to stay.' He doesn't answer me, roysh, just nods his head and carries on looking up at the kite. Fionn steps forward then and he's like, 'We can pay you four hundred dollars a month. We're talking each.'

And the goy, roysh, he looks at us for the first time, his crazy grey hair blowing in the wind, and goes, 'What kind of fricking shakedown merchants are you?' and it's like he's going to deck us, so I turn to Fionn and I go, 'Leave the negotiations to me, my man,' and I'm like, 'We'll pay you five hundred dollars a month each. No more.' He stares at me, no, it's more *through* me, and goes, 'I want three hundred and fifty dollars a month off each of you. No more, you leprechaun focks,' basically haggling himself out of six hundred bucks a month.

And ever since then, it's been more of the same, the dude's, like, the dream landlord. Doesn't give a shit, roysh, that the basement where me, Fionn, Oisinn and Christian sleep is knee-deep in beer cans, condoms and dirty clothes and that it smells like the focking chimpanzee cage at the zoo. We basically only see him, like, a couple of times a week, when he comes in to hide drugs in our cistern and then focks off again, and whatever you say to him, roysh, whether you're telling him that there's a letter for him, or you've accidentally put your foot through another window, he always does exactly the same thing, laughs really loud, shakes his head and goes, 'You goddamn Irish.'

✳✳✳

We all end up getting jobs in this local steamhouse, roysh, peeling prawns and crabs, and life is basically a laugh, except that the whole social side of things is, like, totally hectic, the old buck-a-beer nights really bringing out the pig in me and the rest of the goys. We've calculated, roysh, that we've been on the lash for, like, seven days running, roysh, basically spending every penny we earn on booze, so we decide this one night, roysh, that we're going to, like, crash, recharge the old batteries, whatever, because we are seriously in danger of getting the sack if we're caught falling asleep at work again, and we're talking TOTALLY here.

So there we are, roysh, sitting in, being very good, watching the wrestling, when all of a sudden Christian – who went out for a packet of Oreos four focking hours earlier – comes back to the gaff, off his focking tits, and tells us he's won two hundred bills playing Kino, this, like, lottery game they have down in Pickles. Of course me, Oisinn and Fionn crack on that we're really pissed off with the goy, roysh, and we tell him his tea's out in the kitchen if he wants to lash it in the microwave, and we just, like, carry on watching telly. Scotty Too Hotty is lashing Stone Cold Steve Austin out of it. I turn around to Mad Mal from Monaghan, this Belvo boarder who lives upstairs, and tell him this SO has to be rigged, and he says I'm deluded and he reminds me that Stone Cold never had what you would term 'great technical ability' and was always overrated as a wrestler, principally due to his ubiquity as the WWF's number one poster-boy.

Fionn, in the corner, roysh, he goes, 'Style is no substitute for substance, Ross,' the smug bastard and he pushes his glasses up on his nose and, like, out of the corner of my eye, roysh, I can see Christian still standing in the doorway, all upset because he thinks we're, like, in a snot with him. He goes, 'I was on my way to get the biscuits and one drink just turned into another, you know what it's like. Come on, I've brought you back a present,' and I notice that he's got a shitload of drink in a bag, we're talking Stinger Lager, we're talking twenty-four cans for six bucks or something, we're talking total piss here, but fock it, it gets you shit-faced eventually.

So anyway, roysh, to cut a long story short, the four of us and the three Belvo heads who're sharing the house, we all end up tucking into the cans while we're watching the wrestling, and what happens? Half-an-hour later and the beer's all gone and

Christian's there going, 'Come on, young Skywalker. Let's go to the battle-cruiser,' and I'm like, 'Christian, I am SO not going out tonight,' but, of course, ten minutes later, roysh, just as Stone Cold is talking us through his amazing comeback against Scotty Too Hotty, we're out the focking door to Ipanema, this club where we spend the whole night knocking back bottles for, like, a dollar a pop.

The Belvo goys – we're talking this Mad Mal dude, Codpiece and The Yeti – they're sound, even if they did go to a crap school, and we get a bit of a debate going about the time we lashed them out of it in the senior cup and whether the penalty try we were awarded in the last minute was, like, fair or not. Then we move onto, like, birds we all know and birds we've been with, with me dominating the conversation, of course, and all of a sudden Oisinn has that funny look in his eye. The nose is, like, twitching and Fionn's playing along, going, 'What is it, boy? You smell something?' like he's a dog or some shit. Ois-inn's giving it, 'A fragrance that explores the essence of (*sniff, sniff*) honeysuckle, gardenia and (*sniff, sniff*) ylang ylang. Blended with notes of vanilla, (*sniff, sniff*) nutmeg and, unless I'm very much mistaken, sandalwood. It can only be …'

He suddenly, like, whips around on his stool and goes to this bird sitting behind him, he goes, 'An ode to the eternal woman,' and of course the bird – American, twenty-four or twenty-five, looks a little bit like Kate Groombridge – she's a bit, like, taken aback and she goes, 'I beg your pardon,' and Oisinn's there, 'You're wearing *Organza*. By Givenchy,' and the bird smiles and looks really impressed and Oisinn goes, 'I apologise. I'm a sucker for its velvety and mythical seduction,' the smarmy focker, and he turns around to face her and the goy is in. He is SO in. Fifteen minutes later they leave together and we're all there going, He got over that Emma Halvey pretty quickly.

No such luck for the rest of us. By the end of the night we're too locked off our faces to even think about scoring, no golden goals tonight, we're totally horrendufied, and we end up getting kicked out of the place when Codpiece and The Yeti get up on the tables and stort singing the Belvo song.

We decide to head back to Pickles then, roysh, but we can't get in because one of the goys on the door cops that Codpiece's ID is fake, and as we're walking off, roysh, basically telling the bouncers what a bunch of dickheads they are, I look at Codpiece's driving licence and it's a real, like, Fisher Price effort, and I'm going, 'This is a piece of shit. It's so obviously a fake,' and he goes, 'You focking sold it to me,' and what could I say to that? I go, 'Come on, let's get a tray of the old National Bohemian and hit the Laundromat,' which is what we basically do.

I'm totally in the horrors at this stage, roysh, and I'm there giving it, 'This whole buck-a-beer-night thing is bang out of order. I've a good mind to sue that place,' and Fionn's going, 'It's socially irresponsible to sell drink so cheaply,' always has to try and sound more intelligent than me. But he's even more locked than I am, so to get him back for being such a focking Know-Everything-Glasses-Wearing-Tit, I convince him to climb into one of the spin-driers and have a crack at

Codpiece's long-standing record of forty-two rotations. Never in a million years would he do this sober, but Fionn's a useless drinker and you can pretty much persuade him to do anything when he's shit-faced.

I take off his glasses, roysh, and he goes, 'Someone phone Norris McWhirter,' whoever the fock he is, 'I've a line for his next book,' and he curls up inside the thing and I slam the door, roysh, and The Yeti, who is a big, hairy bastard, as you've probably guessed, he drops, like, four quarters in the slot and the things storts spinning. Fionn ends up lasting what I tell him is a very brave thirty-four rotations – a Castlerock record – before he boots the door open, slides out onto the floor and borfs his ring up all over the place and Codpiece's Dubes. He's going, 'I've laid down a morker.'

I hand him back his glasses and we head off, and all of a sudden we realise that it's, like, bright outside. Ocean City is, like, waking up and we're all sobering up and suddenly everyone has gone really quiet, remembering what a shitty job peeling shellfish is when you've got a hangover, roysh, and you've had no sleep and you've got that skanky smell in your nostrils all day with your dodgy New Delhi. Coming home at that time of the morning, it's a straight choice between heading back to the gaff for an hour's kip or hitting the nearest 7-Eleven for a cup of black coffee and a packet of Max-Alerts, these pills that the long-distance lorry drivers take when they've got to drive, like, coast to coast.

I am seriously hanging, roysh, my head is thumping, I feel like I'm going to focking vom any minute and Christian has his orm around my shoulder and he's telling me he doesn't know why Vader ever bothered with Bossk, he was more of a slave-trader than a bounty hunter and was only ever good for catching Wookies and even at that the three-fingered Trandoshan was in the halpenny place compared to Chenlambec, and I tell him that even though he's my best friend, I need him to shut the fock up roysh now.

I get a coffee and wash down a couple of pills, roysh, then borf my ring up in some random doorway. Then the four of us – we're talking me, Christian, Fionn and Oisinn – we just trudge on with our heads down, none of us saying anything, in the direction of the steamhouse.

✳✳✳

I'm moseying down the boardwalk, roysh, eating a Payday, checking out the scenario, amazing-looking birds wearing half-nothing, we're taking big nids everywhere you look, when all of a sudden, roysh, I cop this bird who's looking straight at me and, like, smiling at me. She's working in this gaff, roysh, making fudge, using this mad shovel thing to turn over these big fock-off slabs of the stuff on this, like, hob. I give her this little wave, which is a bit gay, roysh, but she doesn't seem to mind, just goes, 'Hey there. You from outta town?' She looks like Sofia Vergara except with even bigger bazookas, if you can imagine that. Of course I'm playing it cool like Fonzie. I'm there, 'Yeah, I'm from Ireland. Just having a look around. And I like what I see.'

She goes, 'I'm Candice.' I thought Candice was an STD. I go, 'I'm Ross O'Carroll-Kelly. You from round here?' She goes, 'No, I'm a stoodent. I'm from Jacksonville, Florida. Just came here for the summer to, like, work. You working too?' Of course I didn't want to tell her about the steamhouse, because, let's face it, how un-focking-sexy is shellfish? I'm there, 'Yeah, I'm a dolphin trainer.' Birds *love* dolphins. She goes, 'No shit?' and I'm there, 'Yeah, seriously, I train dolphins. For, like, shows and shit.' She goes, 'That is, like, SO cool.' It's funny, the American accent's just like the Irish one.

I go, 'So what do you get up to at the weekend, Candida?' She goes, 'Well, me and the girls mostly play, like, volleyball down at the beach. Have a couple of beers and, like, hang out and stuff. Hey, you wanna come along this weekend?' I'm like, 'Saturday good?' She goes, 'Sure, Saturday's swell. Bring your buddies. We're dying to meet new people.' I'm there thinking, I bet you are. I go, 'See you Saturday then,' and she goes, 'Sure,' and I'm like, 'Later.'

I have to say, roysh, after that I'm pretty much on top of the world, too cool for school, and I decide to hit the Drinklink, see did Penis Head put that two grand he promised me in my credit cord account. Turns out he did, luckily for him, and I take out two hundred bills, roysh, thinking about maybe going out on the lash later to, like, celebrate.

The next thing, roysh, I'm suddenly getting this whiff, we're talking piss and B.O. and I turn around and there's this, like, goy standing beside me, roysh, looks like a tramp, or vagrant as they call them over here. He tries to shove this, like, book in my hand, roysh, and he goes, 'Have you heard God's news?' I'm there, 'I don't believe in God. I'm a Catholic.' He goes, 'A Catholic? Well, you evah thought of changing ya religion?' I'm like – and I'm pleased with this – I go, 'You ever thought of changing your deodorant?' The goy doesn't know what to say to that. He's like, 'I … em …' I'm there, 'You don't have *all* the answers then, do you? Try this one out. You believe in God. You look like a tramp, you smell of piss and you sleep, I presume, under the boardwalk here. I don't believe in God. On Saturday I've been invited to play beach volleyball with a bunch of supermodels. I suggest you have a word with that God of yours.'

I give the bum a buck and fock off.

✳✳✳

Coming to the States is, like, *such* a culture shock. 'Judge Judy' is actually on in the mornings over here. Fock-all about that in the USIT brochure.

✳✳✳

When we arrived in Ocean City, roysh, I think I mentioned we went on the total lash for the first few days. Anyway, I got up the first Saturday afternoon, roysh, totally hanging, and we're talking TOTALLY here, and somehow managed to write, like, two letters. One was to JP, who I feel a bit sorry for, being stuck at home working for his old man, though he's raking it in so fock him. The other letter was to the old dear, which sounds sort of gay, I know, but the thing is, roysh, I thought that if I let her know straight away that I was, like, settled in and whatever, she'd leave me the fock alone for the rest of the summer and I wouldn't end up hearing from either her or Dick-features again until I needed money sent over.

So the letter, roysh, it was just like:

> Greetings. Having a great time in Ocean City, which is on the east coast of the States. I've had a good look around the place, checked out some of the local history and stuff and found it really interesting. Christian, Fionn and Oisinn are really into it as well. We've been to about twenty museums so far. It really is a beautiful place, much quieter than Martha's Vineyard and Montauk apparently, which suits me because I'm planning to really knuckle down and work hard this summer because, to be honest with you, I'd like to come back with at least a few hundred bills in September. If I'm going to repeat first year, it's not fair that I ask you to pay for it.
>
> Speaking of money, I was wondering was there any chance you could send me some. Not much. Only like four hundred or something, because the rent is due and I've actually been so busy that I haven't even had time to ring Dad's friend about that job. Oh, hey, that's four hundred lids, not dollars. Anyway, I have to go now. We're off to see, I don't know, a castle this afternoon.
> Later, Ross.

About, like, four days later, roysh, I get this e-mail from JP, roysh, and it's like, 'What the fock are you on? What castle? Not fair to ask me to pay your way through college. You guys must be doing some serious drugs over there. Lucky fockers,' which is when I realised, roysh, that I'd actually put the two letters in the wrong focking envelopes and the old dear ended up getting JP's letter, which was like:

Yo, you are missing the best focking crack ever over here. You should have seen the state of us last night. Oh my God, three nights on the total rip and I can hordly remember a thing. Couldn't stand. Couldn't even talk, for fock's sake. I arrived here with the eight hundred bills that the old man gave me and I actually haven't got a focking cent left to my name. Spent the lot in the first three nights. Most of it actually on the first night. The beer is amazing. Total rocket fuel. Milwaukee's Best or, as we call it, The Beast. Twelve pints and I was totally shit-faced and ended up in some focking illegal gambling joint with the goys, lost about four hundred notes on the blackjack table, then got thrown out by the bouncers for singing 'Castlerock Über Alles', giving it LOADS, roysh, really letting Ocean City know we'd arrived.

Ended up hitting this nightclub then to drown our sorrows. Off our focking faces. We're talking totally here. Met these two birds, Barbara and Jenna with a J. They were as shit-faced as we were. They were like, 'So, what do you guys do for a living?' and I'm giving it, 'Christian's an actor, Fionn's a geek and Oisinn's a bouncy castle,' and they're like, 'And you?' and I'm there, 'I'm a Navy Seal. I never talk about it, though. What about yourselves?' And Jenna with a J goes, 'We're the President's daughters,' and we all broke our shites laughing.

Got focking nowhere, of course. Ended up pulling this bird, I don't know if you'd call her a hooker, but the deal seemed to be that I basically bought her drink and fags all night and she came back to the gaff with me for a rattle, no questions asked, no names exchanged, a bit like some of the birds from UCD I suppose.

Anyway, the important thing is I christened the old bed. I was telling the goys I'm joining Shaggers Anonymous. That doesn't mean I'm giving up looking for my bit. Just means I'm doing it under a false name. Must avoid Klingons at all costs. It's a short enough summer and there's a lot of birds out there who need pleasing.

Anyway, must go. I'm about to get pissed again and hopefully laid. There's a lot of beer out there as well and it's not going to drink itself. Rock rules, Ross.

And fock it, the old pair will have a knicker-fit when they read it. I'm not answering the phone and I've told the goys that, if they ring, roysh, I'm not in. They probably won't even send me the money now, wait'll you see.

✳✳✳

I know how to play beach volleyball. I was focking glued to it during the Olympics. Cecile Rigaux. Natalie Cook. Danja

Musch. All those birds rolling around in the sand. Hugging each other. What's the point of the men's event, though? Must be for benders. Anyway, roysh, what I'm saying is I know the ins and outs of the game, though I crack on to Candice that I don't, so she's there with her hands on my shoulders, showing me where to stand and the only thing I'm worried about, roysh, is if she looks down and cops the old Cyclops standing sentry. She's going, 'Okay, guys. This game is, like, *rul* easy,' which it probably is if you could concentrate on the focking ball.

Candice's mates look like they've stepped out of the best wet dream you've ever had. Her best mate, roysh, she says her name is Heather, but there's no focking way, it's Caprice Bourret, I'm telling you. Hello, Liv Tyler. Oh, Leeann Tweeden, nice to meet you. They're all, like, tanned and fit-looking, roysh, and we're a pretty sorry sight by comparison, apart from yours truly, of course. Oisinn really shouldn't take his top off. He's got bigger baps than anyone here and he'll give the birds a complex. Fionn, well he was too hungover this morning to get his contacts in and he's, like, blind as a bat of course, so he had to wear his glasses, and what with them and his skinny white body he looks like what he is: Woody Allen in a pair of Speedos. So Christian is my only competition, which basically says it all.

I can see all the birds checking me and I'm flexing the old pecs to give them a thrill. Leeann Tweeden actually turns to me and goes, 'You work out a lot, huh?' and I'm there, 'Be a sin to be given a bod like this and not look after it,' playing it Kool and the Gang, and I cop the four birds whispering away to each other, roysh, obviously trying to decide which one of them was going to try to be with me.

The mistake me and the goys made, roysh, was having a few scoops at lunchtime. We popped into the New Yorker bor for a few straighteners, then filled this big fock-off Eskie with bottles of the Beast before hitting the beach. The birds say they don't want any booze, roysh, that's how, like, serious they are about the game, but we're, like, half-trousered by the time it storts.

Whoosh! Candice serves an ace. *Whoop!* Then another. *Phissh!* What the *fock*! We don't even get a chance to move. After fifteen minutes of this, I call a time-out and we go into a huddle. I turn to Oisinn and I'm like, 'Sorry, are we the same goys who were the backbone of the Castlerock senior cup-winning team of 1999? Are we a bunch of wusses?' Oisinn goes, 'It's no good, Ross. I'm looking at them when I should be looking at the ball. I tell myself not to but ...' I turn to Christian and I'm like, 'You could have returned that last serve. You hit it straight into the net.' He's there, 'Sorry, young Skywalker. Watching them hugging and kissing each other every time they get a point, I can't get enough of it.' Fionn goes, 'Ross is roysh, goys. Let's show these admittedly attractive birds what we're made of. We're Rock, remember?' and we burst into this chorus of, 'You can't knock the Rock!'

But basically, they could. Ten more minutes it took. It was, like, one ace after another and we're left there, pretty much in a crumpled heap on the ground, roysh, and the birds haven't even broken a sweat, they're cracking their holes laughing and

then they tell us that they all play for, like, the University of Florida, which explains a thing or two.

We sit around talking for a couple of hours, roysh, getting to
know the birds, scoping their racks when they're not looking
and making pretty light work of what's left in the Eskie. Then
the birds announce that they have to, like, mosey and Candice
turns around to me when no one else is listening and goes, 'You
wanna ride?' and of course I'm like, 'What?' thinking, There's no
way it could be this easy. She goes, 'You guys wanna ride somewhere?' and I'm like, 'How about my place?' and she goes,
'That's great, Ross. You wanna give me directions?' I go, 'Are
you sure about this? We've only just, like, met,' and she goes,
'Shees, it's only a ride. No big deal,' and I'm like, 'I SO love
American women. Happy days.'

I go and tell the goys, roysh, that we're in and they're all giving it, 'What a ledge,' and, 'You the man, Ross,' and I'm there,
'Come on, we're meeting them in the cor pork.'

Candice's cor is this big, fock-off soft-top, a beast of a thing,
red with white leather seats. All eight of us fit in it, even though
it's a bit of a squeeze for the lucky bastards in the back. I'm in
the front passenger seat, wondering whether Candice is on the
Jack and Jill and listening to Brucie belting out, '*Born* in the
USA, I was *born* in the USA,' when all of a sudden, roysh, don't
know whether it's the heat, or the running around, or too much
booze – but I actually feel sick. I'm there, 'Candice, em, I'm
really sorry about this, but I think I'm gonna borf.' She goes,
'Shit, Ross, you coulda mentioned that before we got on the

freeway. Can ya hold it?' I'm there, 'No, but don't panic, I'll lean out of the cor and do it. The G-force will take it away from the cor.'

And just as she's going, 'No, wait!' roysh, I lean out and – *weeeuuuggghhh! WEEEUUUGGGHHH!* – stort throwing my ring up. And of course the G-force doesn't bring it away from the cor, it throws it back into the cor and it's like – SPLAT! – all over everyone on the backseat and everyone screams, roysh, and I turn around to, like, say sorry and shit, but then my stomach just opens up and it's, like – *weeeuuUGGGHHH! WEEEUUUUUGGH!* – and it's like – SPLAT!SPLAT!SPLAT! – everyone in the back getting showered with, like, the gallon of beer I drank and the four shots of Wild Turkey and the pastrami-and-mozzarella panini I ate and the bottle of blackcurrant Sunny D. And the birds are all screaming, roysh, and the car swerves in the road and the goys are telling me they're going to focking kill me and eventually Candice pulls off the freeway and we come to a stop and everyone's just, like, silent. I turn around and I look at the goys and the three birds in the back and they're all in, like, shock, roysh, and their faces are all, like, streaked with purple vom, with little bits of, like, half-digested meat and cheese and, if I'm not mistaken, coleslaw dripping from their hair and their faces and I'm thinking, How the fock did I fit that lot in my stomach in the first place?

Candice, roysh, you can tell she's trying to control herself, she's staring straight ahead and doing these, like, breathing exercises, but it's no good, she just goes, '*Out!*' and I'm there, 'Me included?' She goes, '*I'M TALKIN' TO YOU!*' I'm like, 'Sor-ee!' and I get out of the cor and so do the goys. The birds take off and leave us there on the side of the road. None of the goys says anything. They're still in shock. I go, 'Let's see can we thumb a lift back to the gaff. We'll be lucky, though. Look at the state of you three.'

✳✳✳

Z ... Y ... X ... We're talking W ... V ... U ... Oh yeah, you can forget pretty much every bit of advice they give to students going to the States for the summer, roysh, the only thing you really need to know is how to say the alphabet backwards, that and how to walk in a straight line with your finger on your nose. If the cops stop you with a few scoops on you, roysh, and they know you're, like, Irish and shit, they are SO going to bust you unless you can show you're not, like, totally wrecked.

Oisinn is the undisputed master at – what does he call it? – feigning sobriety, and we're actually talking *total* here. I've seen that goy knock back fifteen pints of the Beast, roysh, and then do the whole ZYX thing while walking on a white line in the middle of Ocean Highway, we're talking *with* a full pint on his head. All these cors flying by either side of him, beeping and shit. Doesn't spill a drop. The goy's a legend.

Anyway, roysh, the other night, we're in the gaff and he's teaching me the whole alphabet thing – backwards, I know it forwards – and suddenly I hear this voice giving it, 'Will you two fags shut the *fock* up and go to sleep,' and it's, like, Gavin, who I should explain is a Gerard's boy, The Yeti's cousin and a total knob who arrived the day before yesterday.

He's actually bulling, roysh, because I ended up scoring his bird – or should I say *ex*-bird – Ciara, in Pickles the other night. *Oh my God*, what a *total* focking honey, we're talking the image of Katherine Heigl here. But I suppose I should stort at the beginning.

I go to work yesterday. Miracle of focking miracles, I've been here for three weeks and I'm actually still employed, though only just. Anyway, I'm wrecked as usual, roysh, not having slept for, like, three nights because it's still, like, Porty Central at our gaff and the bod is storting to build up a bit of a tolerance to the old Max-Alerts.

So there I am, roysh, standing over this big smelly barrel of, like, crabs and shit, having the crack with a few of the Haitians who work with me, and one of them – Papa Doc, they call the goy – he goes, 'You no look so good, Ireesh. You whiter than white,' which is when I tell him about the keg porties we've been having, we're talking five of the focking things in the last, like, seven days and the old pace is, like, storting to get to me. He just goes, 'I give you something for that,' and he brings me down to the steamroom, roysh, where he's got, like, twenty-four cans of the Beast stashed away. He goes, 'I believe to you Ireesh this is called hair of dogs?'

Happy days. So there's me and Papa Doc, eleven o'clock in the morning, roysh, in the steamroom, knocking back a couple of quiet, social beers and the next thing, roysh, he pulls out the biggest focking reefer this side of, I don't know, whatever the capital of Haiti is. I have to say, roysh, I've never been into, like, drugs and shit, too serious about my rugby, but this stuff was focking amazing. Had, like, three puffs of the thing and the next thing I know I'm waking up in the middle of the floor and who's standing over me, roysh, only the boss, we're talking Fatty Dunston himself, a complete dickhead, and he's there giving it, 'You focking Irish. This is the last year I employ any of you drunken focks,' and he tells me I'm out of here, which is American for sacked, roysh, and I don't know where I am at this stage and I look up at the clock and it's, like, nearly five o'clock.

Papa Doc comes over, roysh, and he goes, 'Sorry, Ireesh. Thought I let you sleep. You tired, man. You tired,' and I'm there, 'Thanks very much. Now I'm basically unemployed as well.' He goes, 'Don't worry. Fatty sack me many, many time. You come back tomorrow, he give you your job back, man,' and I'm there, 'How can you be so sure?' and he stares off into space for, like, twenty seconds, and just when I think he's going to say something really, like, deep, he goes, 'Who else gonna work in this shithole for six bucks an hour?' which is actually a good point.

I'll probably end up having to spend a week as the Trash Monkey, which is the job everyone hates, roysh, going through all the rubbish bags to make sure no knives and forks have been thrown out. The job is usually, like, rostered between about ten of us, but anyone caught acting the dick always gets given it.

But anyway, roysh, the upshot of all this was that I obviously decided to go on the lash for the night, so me and Christian headed for Hooters, roysh, and the Belvo goys, Mad Mal, Codpiece, The Yeti, are already in there with a few heads they know, and this orsewipe, Gavin, who has just got off the plane and is totally trousered. He keeps going, 'I can hold my drink. It's the jetlag,' and we're all there, '*What*ever.'

This goy is a major pain in the orse with drink on him, and he corners me at one stage, roysh, and storts telling me all about his ex and how he's only really out tonight because he heard she was going to be there and how he loves her, even though he blew it by being with her best friend Jemma at the Muckross pre-debs, and she still hasn't forgiven him for it, even though that was, like, last year, but he's convinced she still has strong feelings for him, which is why he ended up coming to Ocean City for the summer, even though most of his mates were actually going to Toronto, but he wanted to be close to her because he thinks there's still a chance that blah blah blah.

I'm there going, *Hello?* Get me *out* of here. And then he storts focking crying, roysh, going, 'My head is SO wrecked, I focked up my exams and everything.' I think he's first year Commerce, UCD. He's giving it, 'I've got to go back to Ireland to sit the repeats and just the thought that she might be with someone else while I'm away is, like, killing me.'

And while he's saying all this, roysh, I'm not really listening, I'm looking over his shoulder at this bird who is giving me loads, we're talking serious mince-pies here. I have to say, not being big-headed or anything, but I actually look really well at the moment, I always do with a tan.

Gavin's going, 'Will you look after her when I'm away?' and I'm telling him yeah, he can trust me, wondering when he's going to fock off and leave me alone so I can chat up this bird. Eventually, roysh, after crying into my ear for, like, twenty minutes, he goes up to the bor to get a round in, pint of Ken for me and fock-knows-what for him, probably a Baileys what with him being such a focking woman and everything.

So I'm about to go over and introduce myself to this bird, roysh, but she actually comes over and storts chatting to me, and the first thing I notice is that she's actually Irish. She goes, 'Are you a Yankees fan?' and I'm like, 'Sorry?' and she's there, 'Your baseball cap. Are you a Yankees fan?' I'm like, 'Oh that. No, I just liked the cap. I'm not into American football at all. I'm more rugby,' and she goes, 'American *football?* OH MY GOD! *Hello?* I thought they were, like, a basketball team. I am SO dumb,' and I'm like, 'I don't think you're dumb. In fact, I think you're really intelligent. And beautiful,' which is total bullshit because I know her ten focking seconds.

But she sort of, like, blushes when I say that, roysh, and then she goes, 'How do you know Gavin?' which is when I cop it, roysh – this is the bird that the dickhead's spent the last three hours crying into my ear about, and looking at her, roysh, I can understand why. She's Jayne Middlemiss with short hair.

I'm there, 'I actually don't know the dude. We're just living in the same house,' and she goes, 'The goy is like a limpet.' I'm like, 'I didn't know you were actually Irish until I storted talking to you,' and she's there, 'Oh? Where did you think I was from?' and I don't have a focking clue what to say next, roysh, what country would, like, sound good – I'm useless at geography – so I just give it, 'Who cares where you're from, as long as you're here now,' and she must think this is good, roysh, because the next thing I know she's making a move on me and I have to say, roysh, she's an amazing kisser, and I can understand why this Gavin goy is trying to get back in there.

I think I can also understand why he storts going totally ballistic when he arrives back from the bor with the drinks, roysh, and catches me and her wearing the face off each other. All of a sudden I open my eyes and he's standing in front of us, screaming the place down and we're talking TOTALLY here. He's there going, 'I trusted you, Ross. And this is how you repay me?' and he's about to throw a pint over me, roysh, when Oisinn arrives over, grabs him in a headlock and drags him out of the place, and Christian follows them outside going, 'Be mindful, Gavin. Strong is the Dark Side. Seduce you it can.'

Ciara tells me that Gavin SO needed to see her with someone else. I'm like, 'Oh, thanks very much,' and she goes, 'I didn't mean it like that,' and she smiles and goes, 'I'm SO glad it was you.'

I ask her for her number, and she gives it to me.

✹✹✹

The old man rings up when I'm out at work, roysh, and he leaves this message on the answering-machine. This is, like, word-for-word what he said, roysh. Now you tell me whether you think he's losing the focking plot. It's like, 'Hi, Ross. Pick up if you're in … pick up if you're in … pick up if you're in … If not, well, I was just ringing to find out how you are, tell you we got your, em … letter.'

I'm like, 'Fock.'

He goes, 'By the sounds of it, you're, eh … having a good time. Just, you know … be careful. Em, that's what your mother wanted me to say. Condoms and so forth. Oh, I posted you some money. And em … That's it really. No other news. Just boring old work stuff really. Bit of trouble in the office at the moment. With the staff. Nothing for you to be worrying about, though, Ross.'

As focking *if*.

He's like, 'Don't, em … don't be fretting about your old man, I can cope with these things. You keep on … em … you know, enjoying yourself. Okay, I'm not Bill Gates. Not by any stretch of the imagination. But I know how to run my business. That's one thing I do know, Ross. And if I left it to some of the inverted-commas experts who work for me, where would the company be today? Nowhere. That's where. With a capital N. Give these people a screen-break and the next thing you know they want a bloody crèche on every floor of the building.

'Do you remember that management seminar I went to last year, Ross, where you are, in the States? It was New York, I went with Hennessy. It was 'Say Pretty Please and Watch Your Profits Soar'. What a bloody waste of money that turned out to be.

Hennessy and his little fads. Five thousand pounds I paid to hear some so-called authority on employer/employee relations talking about the connection between morale and productivity levels. Rubbish. And I did give it a chance, Ross. Your mother will vouch for that. I stopped referring to the people who work for me as employees and started to call them stakeholders. Quote unquote. But you see the problem was that they thought this new name actually entitled them to something, the grabby so-and-sos …

'I personally had to sack four of these so-called stakeholders when they started campaigning for an extension to the half-hour lunch break, which has been the standard here for years, Ross. Years! Only takes one or two bad apples, of course.

'Anyway, the whole office is up in arms at the moment. Up in arms, if you don't mind, because I had the coffee machine re-moved. Now I don't want to go into the whos, whys and hows of the whole affair, but the word has gone around the office that I did this to save the £60 a month that it was costing me to lease the machine, which is rubbish, Ross. Rubbish. With a capital R.

'Let's not go into the wherefores and the whatnots of the situation, but let's just say that this all started a couple of weeks ago at Heathrow of all places, where I found a fantastic book in the management section called *Are You Being Taken For a Mug?* I've got it here in front of me. It's all about caffeine and the detri-mental effect it has on the performance of a workforce. Quote unquote.

'Now, I know what you're thinking and it did cross my mind, too. Surely caffeine *improves* productivity, acting as it does to increase alertness, enhance sensory perception, overcome fatigue and improve endurance and motor functions. Nice theory, Kicker. But – and I have to emphasise the but here, Ross – the chap who wrote the book, he points out that caffeine is an addictive drug, which has a sedative effect when it's taken in excess. You try operating a company and maintaining profit margins when you've got 400 people on the payroll doped up to their eyeballs on fresh ground medium roast by mid-morning, oh you'd know all about it then, by God you would.

'Didn't need to finish reading, Ross, my mind was made up. Did you know that coffee can cause panic attacks? Panic attacks! I mean we all know about heart disease and peptic ulcers, but panic attacks? And what was the other one, oh yes, insomnia, that was the one that really got to me, because this chap who wrote the book – I'm going to write him a letter, the man has changed my life – he claims that these things account for between eight and twelve percent of all cases of absenteeism. This is America mind you, but I'm sure the figures here are …

'Oh wait, that was the other thing I was going to mention, he says that the average American worker spends, what was it, ah yes, I've got it here in front of me – I marked a lot of the more interesting points with post-its and had Susan type them up for me – here it is, the average American worker spends 114 minutes of every eight-hour day standing around chatting to other employees at the coffee machine or water cooler. And what he's saying is that this quote-unquote downtime costs American industry approximately $177 billion every year.

'Now even when you factor in whatever benefits there are from the stimulant effect that caffeine has on the central nervous system of your average worker – we're talking increased attentiveness, reduction in fatigue, etcetera, etcetera, you're still talking about $98 billion. Then factor into the equation the health problems caused by caffeine addiction and caffeine-related absenteeism and you're talking about losses in the region of $121 billion per year. Not my words, Ross. The words of Mark Finnerty, author of *Are You Being Taken For a Mug?*

'Now I'm not suggesting that I've lost anything like that amount of money, but if Maureen and Deirdre want to sit around for half the day talking about their husbands' vasectomies and the traffic on the Lucan bypass, then they can bloody well do it at their own expense, not mine, thank you very much indeed.

'The machine has been gone for the best part of a week now and I hear you, Ross, I hear you, you're wondering what the net effect of it has been, well I'm coming to that now. Must admit, productivity *is* down – marginally! – though I'm putting this down to the deliberate go-slow that the staff have organised in a fit of pique and which I'm sure will end when the next round of redundancies and wage reviews are announced just before the summer holidays.

'This Finnerty chap who wrote the book – I must ask Susan to get an address or telephone number for him – he says that an initial dip in output is normal, due to the 'cold turkey' effect that the withdrawal of any drug will have. The symptoms, according to the book, are lethargy, headaches and depression, but all are temporary and normal service will resume within four to six weeks.

'My next dilemma, of course, is what to do about the heat in the office. The same chap has written another book that I'm trying to get my hands on about how an overly comfortable working environment can induce feelings of contentment and sluggishness in workers, with a resultant fall-off in efficiency. Says in the blurb I read that cold workplaces tend to keep workers focused and more attentive, which is only common sense when you think about it

'Think I'll wait until the brouhaha over the coffee machine dies down before I start turning down the thermostat, bit by bit, every day, while carefully monitoring its effects.

'Anyway, I'm sure you've better things to be doing than listening to your old dad whittering on. A phone call would be nice, though. Your mother would love to hear from you. In fact, em, we both would, em … me and your mother. We'll be in tonight if you want to, em … you know, call us. Don't worry about the time difference, it's fine. So, em, talk to you soon.'

The thing is, roysh, I don't even know how he got the focking number. I certainly didn't give it to him.

✳✳✳

Christian has totally forgotten about this Lauren bird he was in love with before we came away, roysh, and has the hots for this

Chinese bird who works at 7-Eleven, we're talking the one on Ocean Highway here. Pretty much every night he goes in there on his way home from work for, like, M&Ms, or Peppermint Patties, or whatever we're having for dinner, and storts, like, chatting her up, giving it loads with the old, 'I feel a disturbance in the Force which I've not felt for a long time,' and even though most birds think he's a complete and utter weirdo, roysh, this one thinks he's, like, the funniest goy she's ever met. Or she did. Until two weekends ago, roysh, when he decides to go into the shop totally shit-faced, with a traffic cone on his head and his schlong in his hand, and ask her to the Film Ball next year. Her old dear went totally ballistic, focked a price-gun at him. It was really, really funny at the time, roysh, but of course we're all, like, borred from the shop now, and considering it's the only gaff around here that sells the old Max-Alerts, that's a problem, a *major* problem, as in how the fock are we going to porty *and* work?

Christian's answer, roysh, when I put this question to him the next morning was, 'Don't centre on your anxieties, Obi Wan. Keep your concentration here and now, where it belongs,' which is obviously a lot of focking help.

In the end, roysh, me, Fionn, Oisinn and Mad Mal from Monaghan, we sit down to discuss it, roysh, and between the four of us we decide the only answer is to, like, break into the shop and steal enough tablets to keep us going for the rest of the summer. We'll, like, climb up onto the roof, roysh, smash the skylight, and one of us will be winched down into the shop on a rope. At first, roysh, when Oisinn suggests it, we're all like, *Hello?* but as the night wears on, and we *are* drinking seriously fast, it becomes the best idea that any of us has ever heard.

At, like, three o'clock in the morning, roysh, Peasey Pee calls around to hide more shit in our cistern and we ask him if he has any rope, and he just, like, shakes his head, chuckles to himself and goes, 'You crazy, cattle-rustling Irish,' and a few minutes later he comes back with a huge length of rope, which is, like, four inches thick.

So there we are, roysh, half-three in the morning and we're all wearing our black 501s and our All Blacks' jerseys with the collars turned up, and we're climbing up on the roof of the shop. We're tiptoeing around on the slates, and I'm just about to ask how we're actually going to smash the skylight, roysh – did anyone bring, like, a hammer or anything? – when all of a sudden Oisinn marches straight over and puts one of his size-four-teens straight through the focking thing – *CRASH!* – and we're all waiting for the alorm to go off and the Feds to arrive and, like, throw us in the slammer.

But the alorm doesn't go off and when we're finished telling Oisinn what a complete focking dickhead he is, we lash the rope around Mad Mal's waist, make sure it's secure, and then stort lowering him down through the broken skylight into the shop. The goy's quite small, roysh, but he weighs a focking tonne and it takes the four of us to hold his weight.

And everything's going very smoothly, roysh, until the second he hits the floor and then the alorm – which we'd presumed mustn't have been working – suddenly goes off, though fair play to the goy, roysh, he doesn't panic, just uses the map that I drew him to find the roysh shelf, then he storts throwing packets of pills up through the skylight to us and we stort stuffing them into our pockets.

Oisinn reckoned beforehand that, if the alorm went off, we had, like, two hundred seconds to do the job before the cops arrived, though he said this wasn't based on any *actual* reconnaissance work he'd done on local police response times, but rather the way it always was in the movies. So Mad Mal's down there, like, three minutes, roysh, and we're all, like, telling him to hurry the fock up, but he goes, 'Wait, I just want to grab a few magazines,' and we're there, 'What the fock do you want magazines for?' and he looks up through the skylight at us, roysh, his face all blacked up with shoe polish, which he's obviously taken from one of the shelves, and he goes, 'For the long, lonely nights.'

Oisinn goes, 'Good one, Mal, see have they got *Hustler*,' but of course we should have known better. When we pull the little focker back up – it takes a good five minutes because we, like, drop him twice – he's got, like, three WWF magazines, all the same as well.

Anyway, roysh, we manage to get back to the house before the Feds are on the scene, and we empty all the tablets into a big bowl on the kitchen table and, like, burn all the packets in the garden. So that's grand, roysh. Had a couple more cans, ended up going to bed at five, set the alarm clock for seven to get up for work.

We've only been asleep for, like, half-an-hour, roysh, when there's all this, like, hammering on the door, and I look out the window and there's, like, a cop cor outside, and I'm there, 'Fock, it's a bust, goys!'

I wake up all the others, roysh, and we're all standing there in the sitting room, *totally* bricking it, and the banging's getting more and more, like, impatient, and it's obvious that someone's trying to boot the focking door down. We manage to convince Christian to go and answer it, roysh. We're there, 'Just play it cool like Huggy Bear,' so he goes and opens the door, and he's still totally jarred at this stage, roysh, so what does he say? At the top of his voice, he goes, 'WE'VE GOT FOCKING RIGHTS! YOU CAN'T SEARCH THIS PLACE WITHOUT A WARRANT!'

We hear this, roysh, and we decide there there's nothing else we can do except eat the evidence and suddenly we're all there, like, shovelling the pills into us. We must swallow, like, twenty or thirty each, roysh, when all of a sudden we hear the goy at the door go, 'How many times do I have to tell you, I'm not a fricking cop. I'm a friend of Peasey.'

Turns out he's, like, telling the truth. The goy says his name is Starsky, so-called because of his love of, like, cop cors. The one porked outside he stole from the cor pork of a bank in Salisbury, 'the chicken capital of the world' he kept calling it. He said he needed shit, roysh, and he asked whether Peasey had left anything for him, and when we said no, he goes, 'Always the fricking same, that goddamn long-hair,' and he focks off.

Of course we're all in the horrors now, having just, like, over-dosed on Max-Alerts, and we are talking TOTALLY here. Four nights later, roysh, we're all still totally hyper, you know that feeling when you're, like, focking wrecked but you still can't sleep a wink?

The following weekend, roysh, we still haven't come down, so the whole lot of us decide to head for the hospital, we're talk-ing the casualty deportment here, because it's getting, like, majorly scary by this stage. So we get a Jo down there, roysh, me, Fionn, Oisinn and Mal – fifteen dollars it cost us – and we burst into the place and I grab one of the doctors and I go, 'We've taken about thirty Max-Alerts each and we haven't slept for days.'

And he looks at me, roysh – this is no bullshit – and he goes, 'Sorry, we're not looking for ward staff at the moment.'

CHAPTER EIGHT
'Ross is, like, SUCH a no-good loser.'
Discuss.

I've made a bit of a habit, roysh, of trying to get home from work in the evenings before the rest of the goys, just so I can get to the answering-machine first, make sure Dick-features hasn't left any more of his stupid messages, because the slaggings are pretty bad at this stage. Here's the one he left this afternoon:

'Hey, Kicker, guess what … Oh, by the way, pick up if you're in … hello? Hello? Pick up if you're in, Ross … Oh, never mind. Promised I'd keep you abreast of developments *vis-à-vis* the withdrawal of the coffee machine and any improvements or otherwise in productivity pertaining therefrom. Nothing to report, I'm afraid to say, Ross, or rather, nothing positive. What I can tell you is that in a fit of what I can only describe as pique, with a capital P as well, Maureen – lippy little madam from accounts – went out yesterday and bought a kettle and four large drums of Nescafé Gold Blend. They were sitting there, Ross, on the draining-board in the canteen, brazen as you like, when I passed by there on Tuesday morning. Gold Blend, thank you very much indeed.

'All the girls from accounts were in there too, sitting around and sipping their coffees without a by-your-leave, wittering away among themselves, house prices in Shankill and Deirdre's going-away party. I'm paying for all of this, of course. And you know me, Ross, I'm not what you would call a quote-unquote vindictive man, but I don't mind telling you I headed straight for the petty-cash tin to see if these drums of coffee had been purchased from company funds. Gross misconduct. Instant dismissal. Capital I. But of course, Maureen's much too clever for that. Don't mind admitting the resolve was tested, Ross. The resolve was tested.

'Went home and couldn't sleep. Had a couple of brandies but they only gave me heartburn. Your mother tried to help, of course. She's a rock, your mother. Just give them their machine back and be done with it, was her advice. Just trying to be helpful, of course, but that'd be a climbdown I told her. They see one sign of weakness in me and we'll have that minimum wage nonsense all over again. Wouldn't be a climbdown, she said. You don't have to say anything. Just put it back and say it was being repaired.

'And then she said something that got me thinking. It got me thinking too much if the truth be told. She said, "Charles, I'm sure it takes longer to make a cup of this – what did you call it? – instant coffee, than it does to make a cup of the real thing." And that was me awake for the night. Couldn't get this blasted conundrum out of my head. Which takes longer to make: instant or machine coffee? Couldn't let it go. I had to know.

'By the way, Ross, if you're in pick up, it's unfair to leave me talking into a, em … where was I? Oh yes, which is quicker? Well, I remembered that a few months earlier I had chanced upon a couple of girls from the marketing department lounging around in the canteen, middle of the morning, drinking coffee without a care in the world. So I asked them what they thought they were up to. "Screen-break," they said. Screen-break, quote-unquote. So I asked Susan to launch a bit of an investigation, you know how she likes all that cloak-and-dagger stuff, to find out how long it actually takes to make a cup of coffee – using the machine, you understand.

'So, my curiosity having been pricked by your mother's earlier statement, I remembered that I had a copy of Susan's report in the study. Sleep was out of the question at that stage, so I went and ferreted the thing out. Made for very interesting reading. *Very* interesting. She estimated the time it took to brew the coffee first thing in the morning at eight minutes. Each cup made thereafter took approximately thirty-six seconds, adding five seconds for milk and seven seconds for each sachet of sugar used.

'So, armed with this information, I decided to head straight for the office. My pulse was racing, Ross, I don't mind admitting that to you. It was racing. I looked at the clock. It was four in the morning. The traffic wouldn't be bad for another half-an-hour yet. Made town in good time, parking the car on Stephen's Green, then letting myself in. Headed for the kitchen. Looked around. No one else in. Checked my watch. Waited for the second hand to reach twelve, then filled the kettle. Switched it on. And then as coolly as you like – or as coolly as my shaking hands would permit – I started to make a cup of this instant stuff, just as I'd seen it done once. Tried to remember the process as best I could. One-and-a-half teaspoons of coffee. A drop of milk. Two sachets of sugar. Add the hot water. Stir it until the granules dissolve.

'Well! Instant coffee, my eye. Took almost *twice* as long to make as the proper stuff. I went back home then, considering my findings in the car on the way, though in the end I decided to sleep on it and, well, it was such a stressful night I was out as soon as my head hit the pillow anyway.

'Still didn't know what to do when I went back in the next morning. Then when I got back into the office, who was there only these two scruffy-looking chaps with long hair, absolutely stinking they were, wearing sandals and God knows whatever else, hanging around the reception area.

'"Don't worry," I told Una, our telephone girl, "I'll handle this," and I turned to them and I said, just like this, I said: "There are bloody good support services out there for people like you. You'll not be getting a penny from me. Now leave before I call the Gardaí." You'll never guess what happened next, Ross. "You don't understand," one of them said. "We're from SIPTU. We're here for a meeting."

'Well, you could have knocked me down with a feather. SIPTU, if you don't mind. Maureen had only dragged one of these wretched trade unions into the whole sorry business.

And, well, that's what's really bothering me, Ross. Don't want those people hanging around. Could spell trouble and spell it with a capital T. There's been a lot of changes in employment legislation in recent years that I haven't really kept abreast of.

'Rang up Hennessy, see could he do anything about it, but he's keeping his head down. The word out at Portmarnock is that he's gone to the States. Not surprised with the hard time he's been getting at that tribunal. Happy with yourself now, Mister Cooper?

'But I think I might have bitten off more than I can chew with this union business. But don't you come rushing home, Ross. No charging off to the airport at a hundred miles an hour. No, I'll fight this battle myself. The gloves are off. I'm not giving in to the unions. Oh, no. Give them back their blasted machine and it'll be breast-feeding stations and gluten-free bread for the world and his mother next. Better go and think through my next move. Oh, by the way, ring your mother, will you? You know she worries.'

✳✳✳

We get shit-faced in Hooters one night, roysh, and me and Christian take a cab, we're talking forty miles out of town, to go to this, like, lap-dancing club. And what a waste of focking money. The bird takes fifty bucks off you, tells you not to touch her and keeps asking you if you've got a credit cord. I turn to Christian and I go, 'This is a bit too much like having a focking girlfriend.'

✳✳✳

Fionn and Oisinn, roysh, they end up quitting the steamhouse, without even telling me and Christian, the sly fockers, and they get jobs at, like, Ocean Pines Golf Club, porking cors and shit. They're actually amazing jobs as well, the bastards, the tips are supposed to be pretty amazing, though the uniforms are a bit skangery, we're talking grey Farah slacks, purple jacket and a black pointed cap. One of the Belvo goys told them they looked like two gay usherettes heading out for the night, and Oisinn basically decked the goy.

Anyway, roysh, we're in the gaff this day, we're talking me and Christian, both on a day off, both totally broke, and I mean TOTALLY, sitting in watching 'Judge Judy', knocking back the last of the cans, when all of a sudden this, like, envelope drops through the door and it's, like, a letter from Dick-features himself, full of the usual bullshit, roysh. It's like, 'Did you manage to see any of the Lions games over there?' and 'Hope you're working hard and putting a bit of money aside for college next year,' and I'm about to burn the focking thing, roysh, when all of a sudden – OH! MY! GOD! – there's, like, a cheque in the envelope and I *cannot* believe how much it's for, we're talking five hundred focking bills here, and I'm so happy I could nearly sit down and actually finish reading his stupid letter. I said nearly.

The old man is a dickhead and everything, roysh, but the money comes bang on time because we've been basically living on Cheerios (stale) and Raisin Bran (disgusting), we're talking breakfast, dinner and tea here. So me and Christian, roysh, we sit down and talk over how we should, like, spend the shekels.

Should we head down to Foodrite and stock up on provisions, or should we go on the complete lash? Should we pay off the electricity bill before they discover that Oisinn has put, like, a magnet inside the meter, or should we go on the complete lash?

We go and get changed. Christian decides we need something pretty strong to get the ball rolling, roysh, so he disappears under the stairs and comes back out with a bottle of the old Mad Dog 20/20, which he said he was keeping for a special occasion. We knock it back, roysh, do a couple of lines of this new shit that Peasey got from his Detroit connection, hit the bank, cash the chicken's neck and then mosey on down to Hooters.

The place is fairly packed, I have to say, for four o'clock in the afternoon and we're already pretty buckled by the time we get there. It's actually an amazing bor – we're talking Bap City, Arkansas here – and the waitresses are, like, practically naked and they flirt their orses off with you.

I get chatting to this bird, roysh, this American bird, who I thought looked like Jenny McCarthy, until I got up close and realised she was more like focking Mick McCarthy, but I was actually getting on alroysh with her, I could tell she was seriously interested in me and, of course, I'm there giving her the old chat-up lines – 'Let's not do what happened here today an injustice by pretending there's not an attraction between us' – basically giving it loads, but then she asks me what I'm doing for the summer, roysh, and I'd usually make something up just to impress her, but I'm too shit-faced to think of anything, so I tell her

I'm slaving away in the steamhouse and she immediately loses interest. She goes, 'I *thought* you were in IT or something,' and walks away, giving me this filthy look.

I fock off and look for Christian. It takes me, like, half-an-hour to find him, roysh, and when I do he's sitting up at the bor with Sophie and Chloë, as in Sophie and Chloë from home. They're in Montauk for the summer, but I had heard a rumour they were coming down here for a holiday. The last thing we want, though, is a couple of Klingons from home cramping our style for a couple of weeks. We've both scored both of them back home, loads of times as well, and there's, I don't know, a billion other birds in the States who we haven't been with. I'm over the other side of the bor, roysh, trying to get Christian's attention without the birds seeing me, but he's telling Sophie that the big mistake Grand Moff Tarkin made in the Battle of Yavin was deploying so many TIE fighters, whose surgical strike potential against ground and deep-space targets was rendered irrelevant by their basic lack of speed and poor manoeuvrability and that if Tarkin was half the military strategist that the Emperor thought he was, he'd have used more TIE interceptors, which you girls will, of course, recognise from their distinctive dagger-shaped solar panels. The birds are just looking at him blankly, going, 'Cool.'

I can't get the focker's attention so I have to go over, roysh, and Sophie and Chloë both go, 'OH! MY! GOD!' seven or eight times and air-kiss me and then they go, 'OH! MY! GOD!' a few more times. And even though I'm cracking on to be happy to see them as well, I'm pretty pissed off here, roysh, because I'm going to have to get them a drink. I slap a twenty and my fake ID on the bor, roysh, and get them in – two bottles of Ken for me and Christian and vodka and Diet 7-ups for the birds – and Sophie storts bitching about some girl who was on the organising committee for the Foxrock pre-debs with her and used to be so nice but has *such* an attitude problem these days and it's all since she got the jeep.

Chloë takes a Marlboro Light out of the box and she goes, 'Tell me about it. Her phone went off once in the middle of German. Me and Ultan were both like, duuhhh,' and Sophie goes, 'I know, it's like, ahhhh,' and Chloë goes, 'Oh, TOTALLY.' Of course I'm looking at Christian and eyeing the door, but he doesn't cop it, he asks Chloë who Ultan is and she goes, '*Oh* my God, he is SUCH a good friend of mine. He's actually gay,' and I don't know why I say this, roysh, probably because she's bugging the shit out of me at this stage, I go, 'What the *fock* has that got to do with anything?' and Chloë stops, like, fumbling around in her jacket for her lighter and she goes, 'Sorry, does that make you uncomfortable, Ross, talking about people who are gay?' and I'm there, 'No, I just don't see what him being gay has to do with the story. It's like if you said, you know, "He's a really good friend of mine. He's actually got red hair." I mean, what does it have to do with the story? That's all I'm saying.' Chloë stares at me for ages, roysh, not saying anything, then she goes, '*Oh* my God, you are SO homophobic,' and she finally finds her lighter in the pocket of her jacket.

Christian gets a round of drinks in then and Sophie asks me whether I've heard from Sorcha and she's basically being a bitch to me. I'm there, 'Why would I have heard from her?' and she goes, 'We all got postcrods from her. She's having an amazing time. Cillian's trying to get her to do the bridge climb,' and Chloë goes, 'Oh yeah, and they went out for dinner in Dorling Harbour. She said it was SO romantic,' and I'm there going, 'Do I *look* as though I give a shit?' and the two of them just, like, smile at each other, all delighted with themselves.

Anyway, roysh, four or five pints later, the old beer goggles are on and basically Sophie and Chloë are the best-looking birds we've ever seen in our lives, and it's pretty obvious that Christian's going to end up being with Sophie and I'm going to end up scoring Chloë, who, I think I mentioned earlier, actually looks a bit like Heidi Klum. Especially after what I've drunk.

So ten o'clock, roysh, Christian offers the birds a lift back to their hotel and I pull him aside and I'm like, 'We can't focking drive in this state and – *Hello?* – we don't have a cor.' He goes, 'No, but we know where we can get one,' and he tells the birds we'll be back in a minute, roysh, and we ended up catching a cab up to Ocean Pines Golf Club, bang on time as it happens because Fionn is about to pork this big, fock-off, eight-litre Viper.

This cor, roysh, is an animal and we're talking TOTALLY here. I walk up to Fionn and I'm there, 'We're taking this beast for a little joyride,' and Fionn's like, 'No *focking* way, man,' and I look at him and I go, 'You either let us take this, or I break every pane of glass in your face.' He goes, 'There is no *focking* way you are driving this cor out of here, Ross,' but then I offer him a little persuader, roysh – we're talking a hundred bucks here – and he says alroysh, we can go for a spin, roysh, but only if *he's* doing the driving. I'm there, 'Hey, Kool plus guests.'

So the next thing, roysh, we've picked the birds up and after they've, like, air-kissed Fionn for, like, twenty minutes – 'OH! MY! GOD! How oooor you?' – we're pegging it down Ocean Highway, burning the orse out of the thing, me and Buddy Holly in the front, Christian and the two birds in the back, heading back to their hotel for a night of passion, knowing we're guaranteed our bit. We'll get Fionn to drop us off, then tell him to fock off.

But then all of a sudden, roysh, we hear this, like, siren and the Feds are behind us, telling us through this, like, megaphone to pull over and, of course, Fionn is shitting it because he knows he's going to end up, like, losing his job over this. For about ten seconds, roysh, he actually considers trying to outrun them, but then Sophie says something about Rodney King, and at first I think she's asking me to put on a CD, but Fionn goes, 'Shit, you're roysh,' and pulls into the hord shoulder.

Sophie goes, 'OH! MY! GOD! If I get deported my parents are SO going to go majorly ballistic.' Two cops get out. We are totally cacking it. One of them walks up to the driver's window, roysh, while the other one storts looking the cor over. The cop's like, 'Do you know what speed you were doing?' and Fionn goes, 'I'm going to guess here and say forty.' The cop goes, 'Are you Irish?' and Fionn's there, 'Yeeaahhh,' like this is a good thing, but the cop goes, 'So was my fawtha, so I know goddamn blarney when I hear it. You were going ninety-frickin'-five miles an hour. In a forty zone.' He goes, 'Now, let me see your identification.'

And Christian, roysh, he leans forward and waves his hand in the cop's face and goes, 'You don't need to see his identification.' I'm thinking, We're going to end up in focking Sing Sing here. The cop goes, 'What?' Christian waves his hand again and goes, 'These aren't the droids you're looking for.' The cop goes, 'You, out of the cor. *Now!*' but Christian goes, 'Move along.' The cop reefs open the door, roysh, and he's about to drag Christian out. The birds are, like, screaming their heads off, but then the next thing, the cop, he gets this, like, message on the radio, roysh, and it's like, 'Armed robbery in progress on Hudson and Atlantic. All units proceed,' and him and the other cop, they don't say anything else to us, they just go, 'Hoooly shit!' and peg it back to their cor, and they're gone. Christian's there, 'They must have been Tridarians.'

Fionn tells us that that is it, that is SO it, he's bringing the cor back to the golf club roysh now and he doesn't give a *fock* how we get back to the hotel with the birds and, not wanting to piss him off any more than he already is, I tell him it's alroysh, if he drops us off at his work, we'll phone a cab from reception.

We turn off into the golf club, roysh, which is up this big long driveway. Sophie's telling Chloë that dieting and exercise won't get rid of cellulite on their own and that Kylie – I presume she means Minogue – swears by dry skin-brushing, hot water with lemon in it and salt baths, and Chloë says she knows, but she also SO has to stop drinking water with her meals because it just, like, bloats the food in your stomach and Sophie goes, 'I know, it's like, aaahhhh.'

Oisinn is standing in front of the clubhouse, looking pretty focked-off. He's there, 'Fock it, goys, the dude who owns the cor, he came back for it, his wife's gone into focking labour. Kept telling me to fetch his goddamn cor fast. I tried to stall him, but he knew something was up. I told him it was stolen. He's gone to see the focking manager.' Fionn goes, 'We are SO fired.'

But Oisinn, roysh, he goes, 'Well … maybe not. I've an idea,' and of course Fionn goes, 'Shoot.' Oisinn's like, 'We'll just tell the manager that the goy's a drug trafficker. And we were just trying to buy some time until the Feds arrived.' Doesn't sound very convincing to me. Fionn goes, 'He's never going to buy that.'

But Oisinn, roysh, fair focks to him, he pulls out this massive bag of, like, green powder, roysh – it looks suspiciously like the stuff that Peasey had stashed in our cistern – and he opens up the dash and throws it in and then goes, 'OH! MY! GOD! look what I found when I went to look for a cloth to wipe the inside of the windscreen … goys, call 911.'

✳✳✳

When we arrived here first, roysh, there were, like, eight goys staying in our gaff, but of course as the summer wears on, roysh, more and more stort arriving, goys who came over after sitting the repeats, friends of friends who were focked out of other gaffs for portying too hord, blah blah blah. Suddenly, roysh, we ended up with, like fifteen goys in the gaff, or sixteen if you count Blair, which we never really do because he's always so out of it, we're talking a total pisshead here. Out of the four weeks he's been here, roysh, I'd say he's spent, like, three of them lying unconscious on the floor of the kitchen, which is how he got the nickname Lino Blair.

Come home from work the other night anyway, stinking of fish as per usual, and I go to grab a beer, but the goy's lying on the floor in front of the fridge and I can't get the door open without whacking it off his head. So I open the door, roysh, whacking it off his head, and he doesn't even wake up, no movement out of him at all. But, roysh, the second he hears the ring-pull going, he's like, 'Ross, you stole my place on the Leinster Schools team two years ago. You steal one of my cans and I'm beating the shit out of you,' and I'm basically there, 'Chill out, Clongowes boy. This is my beer I'm drinking,' and he's so lucky he's lying on the ground because if he wasn't, I'd deck the focker.

Anyway, roysh, I'm far too busy for his shit because I've got this bird, Jenni with an i, coming round, second year B&L in UCD, chambermaiding in some focking hotel or other for the summer, we're talking pure quality here, a little bit like Jessica Alba except better looking, if that's possible. She's also doing waitressing three nights a week in Secrets, roysh, which is where me and the goys first saw her and, of course, they're all totally bulling that I was the one who actually ended up getting in there.

Went out for a drink with her the night before last, roysh, then made the mistake of inviting her round to the gaff tonight to grab a bite to eat, listen to some sounds, totally forgetting that our gaff is a complete shithole, we're talking empty beer cans, used johnnies, cigarette butts and squashed mince-pies strewn all over the shop and a big pool of beer, we're talking an inch thick here, covering the whole floor of the kitchen. But of course by the time I remembered this I'd already asked her round, roysh, and it was far too late to try to clean the gaff up.

I decide to go for the old damage limitation instead, roysh. I end up borrowing a brush from work and I sweep most of the, like, debris, out of the sitting room, my plan being to try to contain her to just the one room while hoping against hope that she doesn't notice the smell. Of course, the first thing she says when I open the door and show her in is, '*Oh* my God, *what* is that smell?' and – quick thinking, roysh – I go, 'Oh, it's just something I was cooking,' and she looks at me sort of, like, searchingly, if that's the roysh word, probably wondering whether I'm some kind of Jeffrey Dahmer freak.

She storts to relax, though, when I lash on the old *Pretty Woman* tape, me slyly fast-forwarding it to the end of 'Real Wild Child' and then, halfway through 'Fallen', giving her the old, 'I've never felt so close to anyone in my life,' bullshit as we both try to get comfortable on the futon. She says OH! MY! GOD! that song is, like, SO one of her favourite songs of all time, but

progress is slow, roysh, and by the end of 'Show Me Your Soul', we're still far from naked.

Basically, it turns out, roysh, that she has a boyfriend back home, some knob called Ryan, who's, like, second year Social Science in UCD and who, she tells me, is working in Cape Cod for the summer, as if I actually *give* a shit. She ends up boring the ear off me for, like, half the night about this dickhead, it's like, 'Oooh, he's *such* a good sailor, even I feel safe on the water with him and I can't swim,' and it's, 'Oooh, he's so romantic, you should have seen what he did for my eighteenth,' which is when I cop it, roysh, she's actually trying to convince herself that she's *not* going to do the dirt on him, but at the same time the bird wants me bad. The head's saying No, but the body's saying Go.

So there I am, roysh, basically changing my approach all of a sudden, going, 'What's he doing in Cape Cod, this Richard tosser?' and she goes, 'You mean Ryan? He's working. His best friend's uncle owns, like, a country club.' I raise my eyebrows and I go, 'And *you're* in Ocean City?' She's there, 'We just de- cided to take a break from each other. For, like, the summer. We're going to New York afterwards for a holiday. *Oh my God*, I am so looking forward to seeing him again.'

I'm like, 'And do you think *he's* being faithful?' and she goes, 'Of course he is,' though she doesn't sound, like, convinced. She changes the subject, storts asking me about my exes, some of whom she actually knows. Then we stort having this whole discussion about, like, relationships and love and shit. And that's when I decide to make my move. It's like rugby. You see a space and you exploit it. I'm like, 'Do you love Richard?' and she's there, 'Ryan?' and I'm like, 'Yeah, whatever,' and she hums and haws for ages, roysh, blabbing on about how you can never really know whether someone is, like, the roysh person for you, and how she so knows that now, especially after what happened with Andrew – whoever the fock he is – and at the end of all this babbling, roysh, she goes, 'I suppose I do love him, but I'm not *in* love with him, if you know what I mean.'

I know what she means alroysh. We're talking green light for go here and it comes not a minute too soon, because at this stage, roysh, the futon is seriously storting to hurt my orse, and I remember that Fionn told me that 'futon' is actually the Japanese word for torture, which might be bullshit because he's always, like, taking the piss out of me for being, like, thick. I just go, 'All I know, Joanne,' – I actually call her Joanne and she doesn't cop it! – 'all I know is, if you were *my* girlfriend, I wouldn't want to be away from you all summer. I wouldn't want to be away from you for five minutes,' and the next thing I know, roysh, she's pulling my baseball cap off and we're playing tonsil hockey, *totally* wearing the face off each other, roysh, when all of a sudden she jumps up and says she has to use the bathroom. Of course, I know what this is all about. Ten minutes of, like, agonising in front of the mirror, trying to decide whether this Ryan dickhead's doing the dirt as well and whether she'd be a fool to pass up this opportunity to be with yours truly. Only one answer to that, of course.

I nip into Oisinn's room, roysh, to see has he any of the old love zeppelins left, and he's in bed watching SVU. He goes, 'Can you two keep it down out there. You're making me borf,' and I go, 'That girl is SO gagging for me,' and he's there, 'Sounds like an edge-of-the-bed virgin to me. Twenty bucks says she just wants to talk tonight.' I'm like, 'Quit the shit, Oisinn. I need johnnies.' He goes, 'We don't have any. We used them all last week. At the keg porty? The water fights?' and I'm like, 'Shit, yeah. Hey, some porty wasn't it? Fock, but what the fock am I going to do?' He's like, 'You'll just have to get off at Sydney Parade, my man,' and I'm like, 'No *focking* way,' but all of a sudden, roysh, Christian, who I presumed was asleep, he goes, 'There's a six-pack in my grey Diesel jeans, Skywalker. They're hanging on the back of the chair,' and I'm like, 'Thank you SO much, Christian. Thank you SO focking much.'

To cut a long story short, roysh, I'm heading back into the hall when suddenly I hear all this, like, screaming and shit, and the next thing Jenni with an i comes pegging it out of the bathroom and she's having a major knicker-fit – and we're talking MAJOR – bawling her eyes out, the whole lot. I'm like, 'Calm down, calm down. What's wrong?' and she goes, 'The bath, OH! MY! GOD! it's, it's, it's dis*gust*ing.' I'm like, 'It's only Mad Mal's home-brew. Didn't have a container big enough for it so he just made it in the bath.'

But she's not listening, roysh, she's there, 'I'm going. Get me a cab. Now.' She's *totally* losing the plot and I just want to basically get the hysterical bitch out of the gaff at this stage. Of course we can't make outgoing calls, roysh, so I have to grab Fionn's mobile to ring the local cab firm. She calms down a bit, but still doesn't say a word to me while we're waiting for the Jo to arrive.

I know enough not to bother asking if I can see her again. As I'm seeing her out, she goes, 'Well, this was certainly a night to remember,' and she gets into the back of the cab, winds down the window and she's like, '*Oh* my God, just to think, I was actually going to let you be the first.'

I head back inside, open all the condoms and leave the silver wrappers on the floor beside the futon, basically for the goys to see in the morning, though I know that makes me a sad bastard. Then I go into the jacks to flush the unused johnnies down the pan, roysh, and I'm still wondering why she reacted the way she did, and that's when I look down to my roysh and see this big fock-off rat swimming around in Mal's home-brew. And that's basically when I decided that we seriously needed to clean up the gaff.

✸✸✸

The phone rings, roysh, and I'm actually in the middle of having a shave, but no one else is bothering to answer the thing, and of course I'm cacking it in case it's Dick-features again, so I have to peg it to it before it switches onto answer-machine and half the house hears what a total knob he is. So I answer it, roysh, and I'm like, 'Y'ello?' and I hear the voice on the end of the line and – oh, *fock it* — it's, like, Christian's old man.

I go, 'How are you?' and of course he's there, 'You don't care how I am. Put Christian on the line.' I'm like, 'Look, I just wanted to explain–' and he's there, 'I have nothing to say to you. Go and get my son.' I go, 'He's, em, not in,' and he's there, 'Do you want me to ring your parents with my news instead?' and I'm there, 'I'll go and get him.'

I put the receiver down on the table, roysh, and head down to the basement. Christian's lying on his bed with his Walkman on and it's 'Stuck In A Moment', I can hear it, and when he sees me he takes off his headphones and goes, 'Hello there, young Skywalker,' and I tell him that his old man's on the phone. I'm, like, totally crapping it. I'm just surprised he can't, like, hear it in my voice.

He just goes, 'I'm not in,' and I'm like, 'I think I might have already told him you were here,' and he goes, 'Well just tell him I don't want to *focking* speak to him then.' I'm like, 'Okay, man. Take a chill pill,' and I go back upstairs to the hall, roysh, and pick up the phone and I go, 'Em, he says he doesn't want to talk to you.'

His old man doesn't answer for ages, roysh, and eventually I go, 'You're not going to tell him about–' but suddenly the line goes dead.

✳✳✳

Me and Christian, roysh, there was no way we were going to carry on working in the steamhouse after Fionn and Oisinn left, so we jacked it in, roysh, and basically ended up getting jobs in Ascelpis Healthcare, this, like, pharmaceutical factory, roysh, we're talking, like, twenty bills an hour for doing basically fock-all, just letting them use us as sort of, like, guinea pigs to test out all these vaccines they're developing for malaria and shit. The goys said we were off our whacks, but they were bulling because they know we're going to be earning serious sponds. There's really fock-all to worry about, although we did have to sign this, like, waiver, basically saying that if we suddenly grow, I don't know, horns and a focking beak, we've no comeback against the company. But it's only, like, malaria tablets, so me and Christian are there, 'Twenty bucks an hour? Where do we sign?'

We spotted the ad in the *Ocean City Advertiser*. It was like:

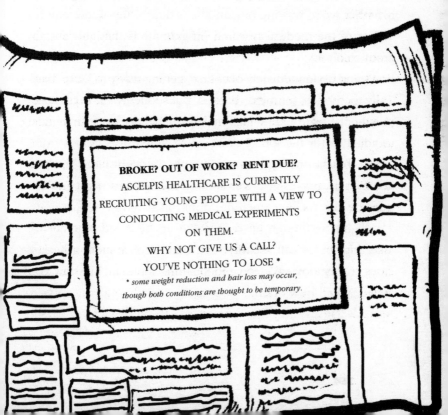

BROKE? OUT OF WORK? RENT DUE?
ASCELPIS HEALTHCARE IS CURRENTLY
RECRUITING YOUNG PEOPLE WITH A VIEW TO
CONDUCTING MEDICAL EXPERIMENTS
ON THEM.
WHY NOT GIVE US A CALL?
YOU'VE NOTHING TO LOSE *

* *some weight reduction and hair loss may occur, though both conditions are thought to be temporary.*

Fionn's giving it the usual routine, calling us Frankenstein's monsters, trying to get up my nose. But fock him, we phone the freephone number anyway and the next thing we know, roysh, the two of us are sitting in this goy's office, we're talking the Head of Research. The first thing he asks us is, 'Do you guys drink?' and of course me and Christian look at each other and we're thinking, Happy Days, and Christian goes, 'Pint of Ken, if it's going.' And the goy, something McPhee his name was, big fat bastard with a red face and Bobby Charlton combover, he looks a bit embarrassed, roysh, and he's like, 'Em, I'm just taking your personal details. I'm not asking whether you want ... Look, I'll level with you guys and you can decide right now whether we're wasting one another's time. One of the requirements of the medical research programme is that you abstain from alcohol.'

I stand up immediately of course, getting ready to leave, basically too honest for my own good, but suddenly Christian goes, 'Neither of us drinks. Which makes me believe that we're ideal candidates for the job.' I don't know where this comes from, roysh, but he manages to say it with a straight face. The goy looks at us, roysh – we were out on the lash last night and I'm sure he can focking smell the drink off us – but he just goes, 'Alriiiight,' as though he can't make up his mind whether to, like, hire us or call security, but then all of a sudden he just goes, 'Okay, boys. Welcome to the firm. Come on, I'll show you where you'll be working.'

So there we are, roysh, wandering down all these corridors and he's telling us all this shite about how long the company has been established, the products they make, blah blah blah, and I turn around and go, 'Give us the lowdown on these malaria pills we're going to be checking out for you,' and the goy suddenly stops walking, roysh, and he goes, 'Excuse me?' I'm like, 'We were told on the phone that it was malaria pills?' And the goy goes, 'It is. But we don't talk about products that haven't yet been passed by the FDA. That's ground rule number one. It's best that you know nothing about these pills. In fact, it'd be better all round if you forgot my name. And what I look like.'

He brings us into this, like, lounge area and Christian pulls me to one side and goes, 'Suddenly, I have a baaaad feeling about this.' I go, 'So do I, Christian, but we need the shekels.' He goes, 'There must be another way.' This goy McPhee, roysh, he hears us whispering and he goes, 'Problem?' and I'm like, 'Just give us a minute to talk,' and he sort of, like, makes himself scarce.

I turn around to Christian and I'm like, 'What did you have for dinner yesterday?' and he looks away from me and goes, 'You know what I had for dinner yesterday.' I'm there, 'Just *focking* tell me. What did you have?' and he's like, 'A bowl of Cinnamon Grahams. The same as the night before.' I'm like, 'And the night before that. Well tonight, Christian, you're having a change. There's no milk left. So it's Cinnamon Grahams with water. That's until the Cinnamon Grahams run out. And then ...'

He just nods his head, like he's resigned to it. I go, 'Look, we'll get this fat focker to sub us a hundred bucks each out of our wages. Think what that'll mean. A hot meal tonight. Think about it. We won't have to hide under the stairs again when Peasey comes around for the rent. We can sort out that misunderstanding with AT&T. Make outgoing calls again. Just think of it. You could maybe ring that Lauren bird back home.' He goes, 'I haven't stopped thinking about her for the last week. Do you think I could?' and I'm there, 'Of course. Although she might not want to know you when she sees you've storted growing hair on the palms of your hands.' We both crack our holes laughing.

The bossman comes back. He's like, 'All sorted out, boys?' and we're like, 'Yeah,' and he brings us into this other room, roysh, this, like, adult playroom, with a big fock-off television and DVD player, computer games, the whole lot. And food. Tables and tables of nosebag. I'm like, 'This is where we're going to be, like, *working?*' and the goy goes, 'Sure. There's nothing to the job, like I told you. You take a couple of pills in the morning. We hook you up to a heart monitor and you spend the rest of the day in here, watching the television, playing computer games, whatever you want. End of the day, we take a blood and urine test from you and then you go home. Look, I'll leave you guys to get acquainted with the place.'

He focks off, roysh, and me and Christian just look at each other and break our holes laughing. I go, 'A hundred and sixty bucks a day to watch 'Jenny Jones' and play *Grand Theft Auto II*. We've struck gold, dude.

And about half-an-hour later, roysh, this McPhee dude comes back into the room and he goes, 'I have your waivers here for you to sign. Oh and tuck into the food. Eat as much as you can. I didn't mention it before, but we pay an extra forty bucks for any stool samples you can give us.'

Christian goes, 'And we shall provide. We SHALL provide.'

✳✳✳

MTV's on, roysh, but no one's really watching it, we're all just spacing, focked after the weekend, when all of a sudden Peasey comes in and asks what happened to the bag of green shit that was in the attic. He goes, 'You guys snort that stuff?' looking me and Fionn up and down, like he's looking for side-effects or some shit. I'm like, 'We never touched it,' and I'm giving Oisinn daggers, roysh, basically telling him to make up something fast because it was him who took it. But then, all of a sudden, roysh, I notice that the front door's off its hinges – another keg porty at the weekend, don't ask – and quick as a flash I go, 'The place was, em … raided. The Feds.'

Peasey throws his hands up, roysh, and he's like, 'Hooooly shit,' and I'm like, 'You probably noticed the door on your way in.' He doesn't seem to mind about the door, just goes, 'You tell 'em anything?' and I'm there, 'No.' He goes, 'You mention my name?' I don't even know the mad bastard's name. I'm like, 'Course I didn't.' He goes, 'And they took the shit with them?' Fionn goes, 'They didn't charge us or anything. They just said they had to take the stuff away for analysis,' and he pushes his glasses up on his nose, like the nerd that he is.

Peasey sort of, like, nods, roysh, really slowly, as though he's trying to, like, take this in. Then he goes, 'Don't worry, guys. You're safe. Ain't no scientist even heard of that shit yet.' Then he's like, 'They, em, mention anything about that robbery on Hudson and Atlantic? Jewellery store?'

My blood just runs cold. I look at Fionn. He was the one who said the photo-fit on 'America's Most Wanted' last night was him. Fionn goes, 'No ... em ... they don't seem to be on to you,' and Peasey's like, 'Let's keep it that way. Now I'm going down the beach. Fly my kite. Still got these goddamn headaches. Could be meningitis. But that doesn't explain the goddamn voices.'

On his way out, he bumps into Christian, roysh, and he puts on this, like, leprechaun voice and he goes, 'Top o' da morning, to ya,' even though it's, like, midnight.

✹✹✹

Me and the goys are in Hooters, roysh, two o'clock on a Saturday afternoon, slowly getting shit-faced, watching the ice hockey on the television in the corner of the bor, when I hear this laugh that, like, sends a serious shiver down my spine. It couldn't possibly be ... No, it couldn't, so I carry on chatting to the goys. Christian says that another of his toenails has fallen out, which makes four, and I go, 'There's no proof that it's the drugs,' and Fionn goes, 'It'll be a beak and webbed feet next,' the shit-stirring focker.

Then I hear the laugh again. It can't be. *It focking is!* Sat over the far side of the bor, cigar clamped between his teeth, a bird either side of him, hookers by the looks of them, is ... Hennessy. Oisinn cops him at the same time as me. He goes, 'Isn't that your old man's solicitor?' and I'm there, 'Unless he's got a focking double.' He hasn't. He twigs me and goes, 'Hey, young Ross. How the hell are you?' I'm like, 'What the *fock* are you doing here? My old man sent you to spy on me, didn't he?'

He staggers over to the other side of the bor where we're sitting, totally off his tits he is, and he goes, 'Ssshhh! Ssshhh! My name's Edward. Edward Horlock. And I'm in real estate. Got it?' I'm there, 'What are you focking talking about, orsehole?' and he offers to buy us all a drink. Wanker or not, none of us is gonna turn that down. He goes, 'Skipped out of Ireland a week ago, chaps. Suppose you could call me a fugitive.' I'm there, 'Why?' He goes, 'They're trying to put me in prison for something I didn't do.' Fionn goes, 'Yeah, pay your taxes. My old man told me, it was on 'Primetime'.'

Hennessy goes, 'Oh, let's not worry about the what-nots and the who-nots. Let's – what is it you young people say? – party on,' and he shouts over to the birds, 'Ladies, come and meet the chaps. A splendid bunch.' The birds come around. None of your gap-toothed, Bulgarian lap-dancers these two, roysh, these are, like, high-class prossies, probably five hundred bucks a night and *way* out of our league. One of them – a blondey one, real innocent-looking in a, like, Britney Spears kind of way – she turns around to me and goes, 'So, how do you know Edward?' and for a second I'm totally thrown and then I remember she's talking about Hennessy and I go, 'He used to be my dealer,' totally ripping the piss. She goes, 'Coke?' and I'm like, '*Every*thing,' and suddenly, roysh, she obviously gets the smell of serious money off the dude because she storts, like, rubbing the back of his neck and playing with the little bit of hair he has left over his ears.

The bird behind the bor goes, 'You boys want more drinks?' and Hennessy goes, 'Oh good Lord, yes. Same again. Keep them coming. Tonight's on me.' The other hooker, roysh, a black one, not *that* unlike Beyoncé Knowles, she says why don't her and the first hooker – Sugar, she said her name was – go and score some coke, 'like last night,' and Hennessy goes, 'Okay, but don't let me get up on that balcony again,' and he peels about four hundred dollars off a wad of bills, hands it to them and slaps both of their orses on the way out. He lorries another brandy into him, then goes, 'Decided to go to America to lie low for a bit. I remembered your father telling me you were in a place called Ocean City, so I thought, why not? Place sounds as good as any.'

Free drink or not, roysh, the goys are getting pretty focking bored with the twat at this stage and we're about to, like, make our excuses and leave when all of a sudden he goes, 'You know what those fools think I'm worth?' I drain off the last of my pint and I'm there, 'Who?' He's like, 'The cops back in Ireland. They've put a reward out for me. Ten measly grand. Surely I'm worth more than that. I mean, who'd turn me in for that kind of money?' I look at the goys in the mirror behind the bor and I'm thinking, Well, there's four of us here would.

Oisinn's first up off his seat. He goes, 'Must go to the toilet.' I'm there, 'Yeah, I've got to go get cigarettes.' Hennessy's like, 'I didn't know you smoked, Ross.' Christian goes, 'I need some … em, air.' Fionn doesn't even bother his orse trying to think of something. The four of us are out of there and straight across the road where there's this, like, bank of payphones. We all get there at the same time, bang in 911 and then it's a matter of who's the lucky bastard who gets an answer first.

✳✳✳

I get home from work and there's, like, post for me and it's, like, a cord from Sorcha that the old pair have sent on. I stare at the front of it for ages, roysh. It's, like, the Sydney Opera House, I can see that, and loads of other, like, skyscrapers and shit and on the front it says, *City Skyline from Kirribilli*, and I head into my room and lie on the bed and read the back ten, maybe twenty times. She says she's basically having the time of her life, even though it's pretty cold over there because it's, like, winter at the moment. She's working in, like, *Golden Pages*, roysh, or whatever the equivalent of it is over there, basically taking ads over the phone. She's only going to be able to work there for, like, three months, roysh, unless they offer to sponsor her, which they probably won't, but she doesn't care because she so wants to travel and see a bit of Australia, especially Cairns and the Gold Coast, which are supposed to be amazing, and Uluru and Darwin.

She says she might be doing the bridge climb next weekend, even though she's, like, really scared of heights and she says she wouldn't mind getting four or five bottles of Smirnoff Ice into her first, but they actually breathalyse you before they let you do it, and she says that Dorling Harbour is amazing, especially at night, but she was really disappointed with Bondi Beach, which is basically a dump and a bit of an Irish ghetto and that's the reason she's pretty much staying away from it.

I notice that she hasn't mentioned that penis she went with once and at the end, roysh, she says she really misses me and after her name she's put, like, three kisses. I hear the rest of the goys coming in from work, roysh, so I slip the cord into my back pocket. Oisinn says he's got something he thinks I should see, but I tell him I've got to go to Foodrite because we need, like, beers and shit.

Instead I head down to Cindy's, this diner down the road from our gaff, and I order coffee and sit there, in one of the, like, booths, reading the cord over and over again, then taking it line by line, trying to pick up, like, hidden meanings that may or may not have been there, then just studying her handwriting, trying to imagine what was going through her head when she said that she missed me, whether she put that on everyone's cord, or whether she really meant it in my case, and what she was thinking when she put those, like, three kisses on it.

I stort thinking about going home, which I'm dreading, for loads of different reasons. And, of course, for one in particular. Christian's old dear basically throws herself at me and I'm going to be the one who ends up taking the heat for her and Christian's old man breaking up. I focking know it. Explain that one to me. I'm wondering whether anyone at home knows. Christian's bound to find out, I know that. He can't stay not talking to his old man forever and his old man's not going to let his old dear be the one who comes out of this looking like the innocent porty. He'll definitely tell him.

But she basically threw herself at me. If Christian doesn't understand that, then he's no kind of best mate.

But I know that things would be so much simpler if I never went home. Maybe I could stay in Ocean City. Keep taking the tablets, although I've been really badly constipated the last couple of weeks and it's storting to worry me. I could stay here for a few more months, save up enough money to go to Australia myself and see how serious things are between Sorcha and this Cillian tosspot.

I take off my baseball cap and scratch my head and a huge clump of hair comes off in my hand. Might not be the tablets. Might be allergic to, I don't know, coffee. I just, like, drop it onto the floor under the table and read the cord again, and suddenly I hear Cindy, the owner, going, 'Stare at that any lawnga and the print's gonna come awf. You want more cawfee?'

I tell her no, roysh, best be going and I head back to the gaff. Oisinn, Christian and Fionn are sitting around the table in the kitchen, staring at this piece of paper. Oisinn goes, 'Ross, you *really* need to take a look at this.'

Straight away, of course, I'm thinking, It's a letter from Christian's old man, spelling the whole thing out, blow by blow, so I end up going, 'One thing you have to understand, Christian. I tried to fight her off, but she was gagging for me.'

He looks at me like I've got ten heads and he goes, 'Those drugs are *really* focking up your head, Padwan. I mean, I've lost some hair and I haven't had a shit in a week, but nothing as bad as you.'

I'm thinking, *Fock*, it must be something else. Oisinn goes, 'Have you been thinking much about Sorcha lately?' I'm like, 'Sorcha? No, she's made her bed.' Fionn goes, 'And someone else is in it,' and he straightens his glasses, which are going to be shoved up his orse in ten seconds flat. Oisinn goes, 'Come on, Ross, what's the *scéal*. It's confession time. For the last week I've had this unbelievable urge to ring Emma Halvey. And Christian says he's thinking about this Lauren bird again ...' Christian nods. I'm there, 'I wondered why we were getting through so much bog roll,' but no one laughs. Oisinn goes, 'Fionn was on the Internet at lunchtime,' – focking geek – 'and he found this. It was in *The Irish Times* last week.' He hands me the sheet of paper. Fionn goes, 'Do you want me to read it out for you?' but I ignore the focker.

> 'Two members of a local sub-aqua club have recovered a stolen statue from the sea in Dún Laoghaire. Gardaí have confirmed that the statue of *Eros*, the God of Love in Greek Mythology, was stolen from the Classics Department in UCD some time ago. Gardaí kept news of the

robbery and a subsequent ransom demand
quiet in an attempt to flush the
thieves out. The statue was found on
the seabed, close to the West Pier, on
Saturday morning. Gardaí admit they
have no leads as yet, but have ruled out
paramilitary involvement. Eros was the
son of Aphrodite and was represented as
beautiful but irresponsible in his in-
fliction of passion.

'It's an absolute miracle to get the
statue back,' said Francis Hird, Head
of the Classics Department. 'We don't
know how, but they do say that love always finds a way.'

Fionn goes, 'Very good, Ross. You managed to read it without putting your finger under each word,' and I'm like, 'Shut up,
you geek.' Oisinn goes, 'Answer my question, Ross. Have you
been thinking about Sorcha?'

***

There's another message from Orsewipe on the answering-
machine when I get home. It's like, 'Pick up if you're in, Ross.
It's a disaster. Pick up if you're in, Ross. Pick up if you're in. It's
your mother's car, Ross. The Micra. It's *failed* the NCT. Again,
stay where you are. There's nothing you could do even if you
were to come home. She's heartbroken, though, Ross.
Heartbroken. Capital H and everything.

'I told her of course that I'd buy her a new one, but no, if she couldn't have her Micra, she didn't want anything. Took to the bed for a few days. Now I'm not what you would call, inverted commas, anti the environment, Ross, you know that, but this whole car-test business is nothing more than a money-making scam by the government. Force people to buy new cars. Dress it up as an environmental concern, fuel emissions and so forth, and nobody dares to complain.

'Oh, I phoned up the so-called Department of the Environment on Monday morning, gave them a right earful. Asked to speak to the Minister, but ended up getting some bloody minion. As if the Government doesn't get enough money out of me already, I said. I employ over two hundred people. "It's the law," he said. *"But you made the bloody law,"* I told him. Hung up on me, he did.

'Such a pity Hennessy's out of commission. Not sure if you heard, but he's been arrested. In America, of all places, and not a million miles from you. They're talking about extraditing him back. Go on, Hennessy, give the bastards hell. A witch hunt, that's all this nonsense has ever been about.

'But ... oh yes ... the car test. Oh the day of the test was painful, Ross. Like a funeral. And it was in bloody Deansgrange as well, appropriately enough. An 8.30am appointment, quote-unquote. I won't bore you with the details, but we drove into the industrial estate, parked the car outside and this chap in green overalls came out, asked your mother for the keys. Of course getting them out of her hand was a job in itself, but eventually, using a few stern words, not to mention the car-jack, we managed to loosen her grip on them and then the chap drove the car into this garage affair and I helped your mother into the office, where they asked for our details and the logbook.

"When will you know?" your mother asked the lady behind the desk. "Forty-five minutes," the lady said. It was an hour at least. Your mother spent the whole time pacing up and down the floor, asking me every five minutes what I thought was keeping them. "They have a lot of checks to make," I told her. "Sit down. Read a magazine. Look, *VIP* have done an eighteen-page feature on 'At Home with IFA farm leader Tom Parlon."

'Well, the bad news was that the chap returned after what seemed like an eternity, all full of himself with his clipboard, and delivered the verdict. Wheel alignment, front axle – FAIL. Wheel alignment, rear axle – FAIL. Shock absorber, front axle – FAIL. Shock absorber, rear axle – FAIL. Brake test, front and rear axle – FAIL. Service brake performance – 40% and FAIL. Parking brake performance – 10% and FAIL. Exhaust emissions – FAIL. Right indicator, steering lock, tyre pressure, windscreen wipers – all defective, FAIL. Dip beam, full beam, fog lights – FAIL, FAIL, FAIL.

'It was too much for your mother, of course. She collapsed. And while the staff tried to resuscitate her, I got on the phone, called the bloody gangster we bought the car from in the first place. "Good morning," he says, without a care in the world. "I haven't got time for good-mornings," I told him. "I think you know why I'm phoning."

"Who is this?" he said, just out with it like that. I told him I'd a complaint to make about a car he sold me. "What's the matter with it?" he said. What's the matter with it, ladies and gentlemen. Well, I gave it to him. "Pretty much everything except the radio, according to the NCT people. And even that chewed one of my Phil Coulter cassettes."

"When did you buy the car?" he asked. "It was 1993," I said. "Sorry," he says, "did you say 1993?" "That is what I said, yes." "Well," he says, "it'd be out of warranty by now." I said, "Don't give me blasted warranty. You told me the car had one previous owner. An elderly lady, you said. Used it to go to the shops and back." He says, "Yes." I said, "Where were these bloody shops? *Kabul?*"

'Had to hang up on him in the end, Kicker. Could see I was getting nowhere, and anyway your mother was starting to come around at that point. I offered the car-test chap a couple of hundred pounds to, well, basically pass the car, but he got all offended, told me that was called bribery and that he was going to report me. Bloody tribunal culture has a lot to answer for. Are you listening to me Mister G Kerrigan Esquire, Middle Abbey Street, Dublin 1?'

I actually nod off for a few seconds, roysh, but then when I hear the next bit, I'm suddenly sitting up straight in the chair and my whole body goes cold.

He goes, 'There's also something your, em, mother wanted me to put to you, Ross. Em, it's delicate. Bit embarrassing. But there's a certain rumour going around about, well, Christian's mother and father, or, well, Christian's mother mostly. Oh, it's nothing of course, just rumours, I told her, I'm sure there's nothing in it. It's just that people are, em, people are saying that the reason they broke up, or one of the reasons they broke up – it's never really one thing that breaks up a marriage – the reason was that, well, you might have something to do with it, shall we say. You know the way people like to gossip, Ross. Especially at those coffee mornings your mother goes to. But maybe give her a call. Put her mind at rest.'

✳✳✳

I'm in the jacks in work, roysh, sitting in Trap Two having a shit, basically trying to get a few bills together for the weekend, when all of a sudden I hear the door open and then Christian's voice going, 'What are you doing, Luke, ones or twos?' He goes into Trap One and I hear him, like, undoing his belt and his trousers and sitting down. I presume he's talking to me. I go, 'Em, twos.' He goes, 'Panning for gold, huh?' and I'm there, 'Think I'm constipated again. Looks like I'm staying in this weekend.'

I can hear him opening a newspaper. After a couple of minutes of rustling, he goes, 'When he said they pay for stool samples, do they pay for each one, or is it based on, like, tonnage?' I'm there, 'He didn't say,' and he's like 'You'd think he would have, wouldn't you? Could save an embarrassing court case some way down the line.'

Christian goes back to reading his paper and I go back to reading the graffiti on the wall. There must have been, like, loads of Irish students working here before us because there's a couple of names I think I recognise and the rest is, like, bands, the usual shit, Therapy?, Marilyn Manson, U2, AC/DC, all that stuff, and then a couple of old jokes that I've seen loads of times before, Dyslexia rules KO, shit like that.

I think being away from home has really, like, helped the dude. I mean, yeah he's still a spacer, roysh, but he just seems a lot happier. I've been able to, like, *reach* him, if that doesn't sound too gay.

I still can't shit.

Christian goes, 'Home next week. You looking forward to it?' and I think about our friendship and how it's about to come to an end and I go, 'No. Wish I could make time stand still.'

But then I think to myself, *fock it*, I am SO not taking a hit for this one. His old dear, roysh, she threw herself at me. She was *gagging* for it. I can't help it if I've got the looks. What am I supposed to do – sit at home all day in a focking darkened room? She wanted me. And she had to have me. Couldn't control herself. I just took what was going. Like any goy would. Fed my needs. Use and abuse is the name of the game. If Christian doesn't understand that, then fock him. He can get himself a new best friend.

I go, 'You finished with the sports section?' and the next thing it comes flying over the wall between the two traps. I flick through it. It's full of focking American sport, which I hate.

I hear the door into the jacks opening again, roysh, and someone coming in. I hear footsteps and then they stop. I can see a shadow under the door. Whoever it is knocks on the door of Trap One. Christian goes, 'This one's taken. And I may be some time.'

Then I hear, 'Christian, we need to talk,' and I'd recognise that voice anywhere. And this, like, shiver runs up my spine. *Holy fock*! Not here. Not now.

Christian goes, '*Dad?*'

His old man's there, 'I had to come, Christian. Couldn't leave it a day longer.' Christian's like, 'What the *fock* are you doing here?' and the old man goes, 'There's things I have to say to you.' Christian's there, 'I told you already. I have nothing to say to you.' But his old man goes, 'I know you're upset at what's happened between your mother and me, but there's things you need to know.' I close my eyes and get ready for the worst. He goes, 'There's things you need to know. And some of them you're not going to like …'

And suddenly, I'm not constipated anymore.